What was happening to him?

Justin couldn't remember the last time he'd felt so out of control with a woman.

"What's going on back at the resort that you'd rather go there than spend time with me?" He tried sounding playful but even to his own ears he sounded defensive.

Lilah's gaze sobered. "What happens if one of us gets more attached than the other? Someone is going to get hurt."

Someone must have hurt her in the past. "I would never hurt you, gorgeous. I swear it."

"I know that. I was talking about you."

Justin stared. She was afraid he was going to be hurt? That he was going to get too attached? Ha. But as a quick denial bubbled to the surface, he realized, hot damn, she could see right through him.

Dear Reader,

Nowadays, it seems everyone can relate to a family member suffering from the effects of Alzheimer's or dementia. It is an intolerable cruelty to watch a loved one who is hale in form and body slowly succumb to the indignities of their deteriorating brain function. This Family in Paradise series has been particularly meaningful to me as my own paternal grandmother has been affected by this very affliction and although my heart is shattered at losing the woman I knew as strong, shrewd, smart and kind, I know I'm not alone as many have endured this pain.

As the final story in the series, I hope you have come to love the Bell family as much as I have. Throughout these books, you've been witness to their struggles, their triumphs and most important, their ability to persevere through the strength of their love for one another.

Lilah's story has a very deep arc as she finds her true self through a journey of self-love and finally, the love of a good man. I hope you enjoy this story as much as I enjoyed writing it.

Hearing from readers is a joy. If you'd like to send me a snail mail letter, send to: P.O. BOX 2210, Oakdale, CA 95361. If you'd like to send me an email, send to: author@kimberlyvanmeter.com.

And for updates about upcoming releases and other cool stuff, check out my website at www.kimberlyvanmeter.com.

Kimberly Van Meter

Something to Believe In

KIMBERLY VAN METER

entertain, enrich, inspire™

Recycling programs
for this product may
not exist in your area.

ISBN-13: 978-0-373-71826-9

SOMETHING TO BELIEVE IN

Copyright © 2013 by Kimberly Sheetz

www.Harlequin.com

Printed in U.S.A.

ABOUT THE AUTHOR

Kimberly Van Meter wrote her first book at sixteen and finally achieved publication in December 2006. She writes for the Harlequin Superromance and Harlequin Romantic Suspense lines. She and her husband of seventeen years have three children, three cats and always a houseful of friends, family and fun.

Books by Kimberly Van Meter

Other titles by this author available in ebook format.

To anyone who has watched a loved one slowly succumb to Alzheimer's or dementia and cried tears of grief at the ambiguous loss...I'm right there with you. The deepest sorrow is looking into the eyes of your loved one and realizing they are no longer there.

To my paternal grandmother...in my heart you will always remain the smart, shrewd, kind, generous, crafty woman you ever were. You taught me so much. My life was blessed to have you in it. I miss our chats, your laughter, the smell of your kitchen and your wealth of knowledge. All I have now are my memories.

CHAPTER ONE

JUSTIN CALES FEARED his father was going to have a coronary event as he crumpled the gossip rag in his hand until it was a tight, ink-smeared ball of newsprint before throwing it in the wastebasket with far more force than required.

"Calm down before you hurt yourself, old man," Justin muttered, failing to see what his father was losing his temper over. "It's no big deal. You can barely make out my face anyway and it was a joke. Benny thought it would be funny if—"

At that Senator Vernon Cales growled, "Am I laughing? I fail to see what's laughable about the fact that your fool head is stuck between Starr's giant melon breasts."

Justin chuckled at the memory but sobered immediately when he saw his father was really about to lose it. "It was Benny's idea to go to that strip club but we were only there for maybe a half hour before this happened. It was a total joke but—"

"But a photographer managed to catch the shot because he sure as hell knew who you were and who you were connected to. Damn it all to hell, Justin! What are you trying to do to this family?"

A familiar resentment rose in his chest that threatened his earlier decision to ride out the storm of his father's anger with a humble attitude. Screw that. The old man could kiss his ass. He hadn't done anything wrong—per se. It's not as if he was out whoring and visiting strip clubs all the time. For God's sake, it was one time and they'd been clowning around. "It's always about the *family*. Let's get real, Dad. It's about your image, not mine."

"I've built a solid political foundation on morals and family values and I'm not about to let you tear it all down with your irresponsible ways. Everyone is toeing the line, but you."

Justin exhaled a short breath, quickly losing interest in the You're-a-Screwup show his father loved to roll out. He'd seen this show before and he didn't much care for the way it ended. "Is this what this meeting is about? If so, I'm going to bounce. I don't need this. It was a bit of harmless fun. There were half a dozen guys doing the same exact thing as me."

"But you're my son." Vernon's tone lowered with finality and there was something in his eyes Justin had never seen before. Hell, maybe the old man was serious this time around. Vernon drew a deep breath as if needing calm to proceed, then returned to his highback leather chair. "Things are going to change," he announced, sliding paperwork to the forefront and steepling his hands over it. A sense of foreboding followed as Vernon continued. "You're thirty-two years old. It's time to start acting your age and take your responsibilities serious."

Justin rolled his eyes in ill-disguised irritation. This again? "I have a college degree, even a master's degree in business. I think I've fulfilled my debt to your expectations. You need to back off and let me live my life."

His father ignored him and continued undeterred. "When I was your age I was already working my way up the political ladder. It's time you start making your mark, too."

"I'm not interested in politics," Justin said flatly. He hated politics and his father knew it.

"I've decided not to run for my seat in the Senate," Vernon said, shocking Justin and sending a trickle of unease into his gut. He didn't like the general direction of the conversation. Vernon met his stare squarely. "I want you to run in my stead. I want you to be the next Cales New York senator."

"No." Justin sat straighter. "Dad…no. What are you doing? You can't be serious." As far as bad jokes went, this one sucked pretty hard. Justin excelled in doing nothing, being highly educated for zero purpose—and he liked it that way. He liked hanging out with his over-privileged friends who had trust accounts with more money than some small countries. He fully embraced his bacchanal lifestyle and a career in politics would definitely put an end to those types of shenanigans. He swallowed the spurt of raw panic but before he could launch a suitable protest, his father had begun again.

"I am serious. I've let you dick around too long and *that*—" he pointed to the ball of incriminating evidence in his wastebasket "—is proof. Your mother and I have come to a decision regarding your future. You're going to take a monthlong vacation, someplace warm and sunny, where you can appropriately say goodbye to your wild ways. At the end of that month, you will return home where you will immediately clean up your act and start the campaign trail for my seat. Of course, you'll have our full support and resources behind you. I've been assured your candidacy would be looked upon favorably."

"How is that even possible?" he asked, sweat beading his upper lip. "It's not as if I've been the model son, as you've enjoyed pointing out. Who the hell would put their resources behind me as a candidate?"

His father shot him a quelling glance. "Yes, who would? Well, let's just say it helps to have friends in high places. Most times your antics never made it to the press if it could be helped. This time was unfortunate," he said, referencing the stripper episode. "But with some creative handling, we should be able to maneuver around it. However, once your candidacy is announced it's important to avoid any more of these types of incidents. Am I clear?"

Clear? Was his father joking? Not hardly. "I'm not doing this," he said, shaking his head.

"You will." It was the certainty of his father's voice that deepened the chill chasing his spine. Justin felt the walls closing in on him, squeezing out the oxygen in the room.

"No!" Justin jumped from his chair. "I've never harbored any desire to follow you into politics or expressed any interest in current events or world issues. You know this, Dad. Why are you doing this to me?"

"Because it's time you stop thinking about just yourself. The Cales name has been associated with strong politics for generations. I'm not about to let my only son ruin that legacy without a fight."

Suddenly logic calmed his panic. His father couldn't make him do anything. He drew a deep breath and shook his head. "Sorry, Dad. I know I'm letting you down but I'm not about to jump through your hoops just to satisfy some ego stroke for you. I'm not that guy and if you thought I was, you obviously don't know me at all." He turned to leave, finished with the conversation, but his father's voice at his back pulled him around.

"I know who you are and who you can be. Today you're a lazy, spoiled playboy who spends more than he makes and depends on his trust fund to survive. You haven't held a serious job since graduating college and you have a penchant for fine things and expensive pastimes. Oh, son…I know quite well who you are *right now*. But I'm not interested in that person. I'm interested in finding who you *can be*. And I have a feeling that person is going to be someone worth knowing. So here's the deal… You will go on your vacation, leaving tomorrow. Mourn your playboy days and then when you return, you will devote your considerable energy on securing your campaign funds for your candidacy."

"And if I don't?"

Vernon's gaze hardened and Justin knew he wasn't bluffing. "You will be cut off. Permanently."

Justin balked, not quite comprehending what his father was saying. It seemed unbelievable in this day and age, something so medieval as familial extortion would become part of his father's arsenal but as he stared, meeting his father's steady and unflinching gaze, he realized the senator was as serious as a heart attack. "This is bullshit," he finally murmured in a shaky voice, unable to hide his shock. "And beneath you."

"You brought us to this end."

"A little archaic don't you think?" he bit out.

His father shrugged. "Some methods haven't lost their effectiveness no matter their age."

Justin felt betrayed by his own blood. He'd always

known his hard-nosed father was a bit of a ruthless bastard when it came to getting what he wanted but he never thought he'd get caught in those deadly crosshairs. "Mom in on this, too?"

"She is agreed."

Swell. There went his only ally. Could he handle life on his own? Away from the safety net of his parents' influence and resources? He liked to think he could but he'd become accustomed to the privileges wealth provided and the idea made him shift uncomfortably. Before this moment, getting a job, having a career had been a back burner priority. Now it seemed paramount if he wanted to survive. He didn't like that feeling. Not at all.

He hated the idea of yielding to his father even more. *Pushy, overbearing jackass.* He shoved his hands in his pockets to hide the hard clench of his fists. He needed time to think his way out of this. A month ought to be long enough. So, he'd take a vacation in a tropical paradise on his father's dime all the while figuring out his exit strategy. Sounded doable. He relaxed his fists, drawing air through his tight chest and forced a cool smirk. "A vacation it is, then. But here are my terms if I'm going to give up my life, I want top shelf, five-star accommodations. I want a credit card without a limit and I want you and Mom to leave me alone for the month that I'm *mourning*—as you put it—my playboy ways. No calls, no nagging emails or texts... family-free. Got it?"

His father nodded, accepting Justin's terms. He picked up the paperwork on his desk and held it out for Justin to grab. "I anticipated your answer—as well as your demands—here are your travel documents, plane ticket and whatnot. You leave at 8:00 a.m. for St. John. Enjoy your vacation, son. I look forward to your return."

Justin accepted the documents, his lips pressed tight. *Go to hell, Dad.*

LILAH BELL RELIEVED Celly, Larimar's one real employee, for her lunch break and took her spot behind the front desk of the airy resort she'd known as home since she was old enough to remember. Her grandparents had bought the resort shortly after they'd married and they'd planned to live their lives out among the surf and sand. Well, Grams had accomplished that goal having died from breast cancer ten years ago but Pops was still kicking, even if his mind was quickly losing its sharpness.

Lilah loved Larimar, and the fact that it was in trouble caused a flutter of real panic to steal her breath. No, it was going to work out, she told herself fiercely. Her oldest sister, Lora, had come home—and fallen in love with her former arch nemesis, Heath Cannon—and Lindy, Lilah's twin, made frequent visits home with her new fiancé, Gabe Weston, and for the first time in a long time, Lilah wasn't suffocating under a blanket of depression.

All in all, things were looking up.

Now, if only everyone would stop treating her as if she were going to break.

Apparently, one suicide attempt was enough to put you on permanent mental health watch.

She smiled in spite of the topic, noticing Maho, her adopted cat, winding his way between her legs, meowing for her attention. She picked him up and cradled the cat like a baby.

"Lilah, what did I tell you about that cat?" Lora said, entering from the private section of the resort, wearing a frown. "I know it's a lost cause to ask that you find a different home for him, but at the very least, please don't keep him at the front desk. What if our guests come in with allergies?"

Lilah shrugged. She used to worry about her sisters' approval or disapproval, as it were, but not anymore. She knew there were bigger issues to worry about on any given day and potential dander allergens for guests was not one of them. "When is Lindy flying in?" she asked, pressing a quick kiss on the top of the cat's head before gently setting him on the floor.

"She had to reschedule her flight," Lora said. "Something about Carys's school and not being able to get her independent study approved. Sorry, Li, but she said she'll be on a plane as soon as possible."

"It's okay," Lilah said, smiling to hide her disappointment and her mild irritation that everyone felt the need to tiptoe around her feelings. It wasn't as if she were going to fling herself into the sea with every drop of bad news. She twisted a hank of her long hair and secured it to the top of her head in a messy knot, then busied herself with straightening the desk. "It isn't that big of a deal."

"I know, but you miss her so much when she's gone. I wish I could understand that twin thing but…well, it's a mystery to me."

Lilah's smile widened at her sister. To look at Lora today was to see a woman transformed by the power of love. Corny as it sounded, it was true. Lora had once been a royal bitch to put it lightly. Now, she was still Type A—which rubbed against Lilah's naturally creative and flighty Type B personality—but at least now she didn't make small children cry with a look from those witchy blue eyes. "It's okay. Besides, now that she's engaged to the CEO of a multimillion dollar company, her visits aren't so few and far between."

"Gabe has been good for Lindy," Lora agreed. "And not just because of his frequent-flier miles."

Lilah chuckled. "Yes. He's been pretty good. I wish I could've seen her first play. I'm sure she was amazing."

Since moving from Los Angeles to San Francisco, Lindy had hooked up with a theater group that actually appreciated her acting talents and not just her pretty face and body. For that, Lilah was inordinately grateful. She'd always been uncomfortable with the lifestyle Lindy had been immersed in while living in L.A.

"Are you thinking of going out tonight?" Lora asked, switching gears.

Her tone was innocent enough but the concern beneath the innocuous query smacked of trepidation. Lilah withheld her annoyance, knowing her sister's concern was coming from an honest place but it raked against her raw nerves all the same.

"I'm just wondering… Thought maybe I'd go with you," Lora added, trying to offer a plausible excuse.

Lilah gave her sister a knowing look. "You haven't been interested in going out in years but suddenly you want to spend a night out on the town?"

"That's not true," Lora protested, going so far as to seem wounded. "I didn't have time to go out before… now I do."

Lilah sighed. It was pointless to argue. Lora wasn't going to admit she was being overprotective. "I was thinking of going to the Rush Tide. There's going to be a live band tonight. Reggae."

Lora tried not to wrinkle her nose but Lilah knew her sister hated reggae almost as much as she hated jazz. Finally, Lora gave up on the false smile she had frozen in place and broke down to admit, "No, you know I hate reggae. Gives me a headache."

Lilah smiled and glanced away, privately relieved. It wasn't that she didn't love her sister, but since the whole embarrassing incident happened a few months ago, she'd been trying to get her head on straight and so far, she was succeeding. But when her sisters handled her with kid gloves, it made her want to do something recklessly stupid. And Lilah knew that wasn't a healthy impulse.

"All right, Celly is taking the night shift then?" Lora asked, and Lilah nodded. "Okay. Well…have fun and be safe. Are you meeting friends at least? I hate the idea of you going out alone. I know you don't worry about this, but there are freaks out there. It's not the same island we grew up on."

"You worry too much," Lilah said, but the dark, pained look Lora flashed gave away her guilt. Somehow Lora thought she was responsible for what Lilah had done. It didn't matter how many times Lilah assured her nothing she'd said or done had been part of her thought process the day she'd walked into the ocean and tried to drown herself, but it didn't matter. Lora shouldered that guilt nonetheless. Lilah sighed, hating how everything had changed. She almost wished Lora would just snap at her and stop acting like a neutered dog.

"Yeah, I'm meeting Stacy at the bar for hot wings before the show," Lilah lied for Lora's sake. Maybe if she thought she was meeting up with friends she'd lose that perpetually worried frown line creasing her forehead whenever they talked.

"Oh, good," Lora said, openly relieved and breathing easier. "I'm glad to hear it. Okay, well, have fun and be safe out there."

Lilah nodded. Watching as Lora walked away, she wondered if there'd ever come a day when everything would be normal again.

Likely not.

Her family was suffering from a psychic scar that she created and she didn't know how to fix that. Dr. Veronica said time would help but Lilah was afraid she'd broken something intangible and there would be no going back to what once was.

And a part of her was okay with that because to go back to what it was like before would be to return to those dark days of endless insomnia and the suffocating cloak of sadness that dragged on her shoulders each day.

A delicate shudder followed the thought. No, she thought fiercely, anything was better than that, even if it meant fielding her sisters' overprotective questions and putting up with their worried expressions each time she sneezed or wasn't smiling.

She took a sip of her iced tea just as a tall, lean but well-built man walked into the lobby. His expensive Teva sandals and equally expensive sunglasses gave him the air of someone accustomed to fine things, even on vacation. While Lilah would ordinarily steer clear of such a self-important ninny, a smile warmed her mouth as if she was helpless to prevent it. For the first time in months, Lilah felt the faint tingle of attraction. It'd been so long since she'd felt anything remotely resembling attraction that at first she didn't recognize the feeling.

The man walked to the desk with a lazy gait, alternately taking in the surroundings and Lilah in turn. It appeared by his widening smile that he appreciated both.

"Welcome to Larimar," Lilah said brightly. "Do you have a reservation?"

"Not yet," he said, his New York–accented voice sending goose bumps rioting up and down her forearm. He removed his sunglasses and leaned into the counter, his brown eyes gazing at her with such impish playfulness that Lilah immediately smiled in return as he said, "Here's the deal, seems my hotel double booked my reservation and I need a place to crash for a few days. I asked around and the locals said Larimar was a pretty nice place. I can see they weren't lying," he added, openly flirting with her. "What's your name, gorgeous?"

"Lilah," she answered. "And yours?"

"Justin—" there was the slightest of pauses "—Cales."

Nice name. It rolled off the tongue like a fine wine. "Well, Mr. Cales, you're in luck. We happen to have a bungalow open. It's the prettiest one, too," she confided. "It even has an open-air shower big enough for two." She met his stare boldly, not caring that she was flirting shamelessly. Lindy would've been so proud.

His grin deepened, revealing the cutest dimple she'd ever seen. He was gorgeous, no doubt about it and she wouldn't mind getting to know him better. Those dimples alone should be against the law. It'd been a while since she'd had anyone to cuddle with. She didn't care for the term *boyfriend*. She much preferred to consider her love interests as friends, though not *friends with benefits* because that just sounded wrong. Besides, life was too short for labels anyway. Lora's voice in her head reminded her of one of the rules: no fooling around with the resort guests, and Lilah's mood dampened slightly. Although, Lindy broke that rule and it seemed to have worked out fairly well for her.

Technically, this guy would only be their guest for two days.

After that, he was fair game.

"I don't think I can resist the temptation of an open-air shower big enough for two," Justin said with mock seriousness as he handed her a platinum credit card. "Does it come with room service?"

She offered a throaty laugh, unable to stop flirting. There was something about him that drew her and she had no interest in fighting it. Dr. Veronica said she needed to start interacting with people outside of her comfort zone. Well, now seemed like the time to give that a try.

"Your room key, Mr. Cales," she said. "Enjoy your stay."

He accepted the key and grinned as he shouldered his bag. "Something tells me I will."

And something told her, she was going to make sure of it.

CHAPTER TWO

JUSTIN FOUND THE BUNGALOW and let himself in. It smelled of coconut and lavender and he half wondered if the cute receptionist smelled nearly as good. He had definitely caught the vibe from the slender blonde that she was game for a little fun if he was interested. And he was definitely interested. She'd been just the right kind of woman for his tastes, willowy with bee-stings for breasts, and doll-like blue eyes that a man could get lost in for hours. Oh, yes…just his kind of woman.

He did a quick wander around the bungalow and found it more than adequate for his needs while he waited for a room at the Worchester. There was a bohemian charm to the place even though it wasn't like one of those eco-friendly hotels he'd seen on Discovery Channel where everything was made from hemp. He made a beeline for the open-air shower and, just as Lilah had promised, it was certainly big enough for two, especially for him and a certain blonde.

He jumped onto the bed and tested the springs, noting with satisfaction that they were silent as the grave, which would certainly be appreciated when he put those springs to use.

He pulled his shirt over his head and tossed it to the floor with a mild groan. The balmy air of St. John felt like a moist blanket wrapped around his lungs and it was taking a bit to get used to. The moment he'd stepped from the plane in St. Thomas he'd been gobsmacked by the humidity. As a native New Yorker, he knew a bit about humid weather but this was taking things to a new level. A clap of thunder surprised him and he popped to his feet to peer out the wide window. Dark clouds boiled on the horizon, looking ominous and foreboding. Damn, that storm rolled in quick. A flash in the sky followed the noise and he frowned. So much for going to the beach to cool off. He'd done a little checking before arriving and it was supposed to be the drier season, but apparently he'd brought the rain.

He fished his phone from his shorts pocket and dialed his best friend, Keenan Lincoln. It was about three in the afternoon in New York, which meant Keenan was probably still lounging in his pajamas, nursing a nasty hangover.

"Hey, man, how's paradise?" Keenan asked in a sleepy tone when he picked up. Justin could almost picture Keenan kicked back in his favorite chair, trying to shake off the previous night's drinking binge, as he slowly returned to the land of the living.

"Hot and humid," Justin answered, frowning as rain started to hit the flagstones. "And wet."

"Wet? Isn't it supposed to be the dry season?"

"I'm not sure there is a dry season in the tropics. But yeah, it's supposed to be less rainy. I guess." Since he didn't call to chat about the weather, Justin got to the point. "I want you to come down here and help me tear up this quaint little place. We'll put a New York stamp on every hot chick from here to St. Croix. What do you say?"

"Sounds fun," Keenan said, though there was a definite catch to his tone that puzzled Justin. If anyone was down for some wild debauchery it was Keenan Lincoln. The man had partying down to an art form. "Listen, man, I gotta be honest with you… Your old man doesn't want me following you to St. John."

"Excuse me?" Justin said.

Keenan sounded uncomfortable as he said, "He said something about you needing some alone time to think things through and I don't know what that means but he was real serious about you not having your friends with you. He was pretty clear on that score." Keenan paused, then said, "Your old man was real mad about that tabloid story, huh?"

"You could say that," Justin grumbled. "What did he say to you?"

"He… Well, you know your dad… He's got some serious connections and I sure as hell don't want to end up in his crosshairs. My old man would shit a brick if he found out I'd done something to piss off Senator Cales. That's just plain stupid, you know?"

Yeah, he knew, Justin thought bitterly. In other words, his father had strong-armed his friends into staying away. That son of a bitch.

"Screw him," he said recklessly, anger clouding his thinking. "What's he going to do? Ruin your career? You don't have one. You're just like me, highly educated for zero purpose and you like it that way. Who cares what some self-important politician told you to do or not do."

"Yeah, easy for you to say. And eventually, I'm going to have to get a job. My old man is getting tired of my antics and he's making some serious rumblings about me growing up and taking care of my affairs. And frankly, if that's the case, I don't want to shoot myself in the foot over this. It's not worth it, man."

What was the world coming to when Keenan passed up the opportunity to thumb his nose at an authority figure? Hell, that had to be a sign of the Apocalypse.

Keenan tried to smooth Justin's ruffled feathers. "Hey, so you're being forced to party alone. That never stopped Justin Cales, right? You can find a good time at a funeral, my brother," he joked, but Justin wasn't in the mood to laugh. He was too pissed. He'd figured if he was going to vacation, he wanted his usual crew to vacation with him. He'd been looking forward to tearing it up Caribbean-style with some New York flair. But no...his father had known that'd be exactly what he'd do and had taken steps to suck the fun out of his plan.

He had half a mind to call up the obnoxious prick and tell him to stick his vacation up his tight ass but self-preservation won out.

"I'm sorry, man," Keenan said, sounding as if he felt wretched about bailing on him like a puss. "I hope you understand."

"Yeah, no worries," Justin said, but there was a definite edge to his tone that he couldn't hide. "Take it easy, man."

"C'mon, don't be like that," Keenan said. "I feel bad enough as it is that we got snapped by the paparazzi. Maybe if that damn picture hadn't run, we wouldn't be in this mess."

"Maybe," Justin agreed, but in his heart he knew it was bullshit. His dad had been quietly fuming about his lifestyle for months. The tabloid picture had simply been an accelerant for his father's plans. Anger percolated deep inside at being forced to dance to *Senator*

Cales's tune. "I'll send you some Caribbean rum, so you know what you're missing."

"Sounds good," Keenan said, but Justin could tell Keenan still felt like a rat for leaving him high and dry. Selfishly, Justin was glad. Whatever happened to fraternity brother loyalty? Apparently, it had its limits.

"Hey...try to have fun. I mean, how bad can it be? You're on a tropical island, right?"

"Yeah," Justin said. "It'll be fine. It's just nice to have a wingman, you know?"

"You, my brother, have never needed a wingman. Go tear it up. I expect to hear wild tales of total debauchery when you return. Do something that'll really piss off your dad. Kinda like one last hurrah!"

Justin smiled, warming to that idea. "That's a thought with merit."

"All right." Keenan yawned. "I'm about two cups short of my usual coffee infusion... Catch you later, Cales."

"Later, Lincoln," Justin said, and clicked off. He tossed his phone to the bed and stripped. If he wasn't heading to the beach just yet, he could at least rinse off the travel grime. He stepped into the open-air shower and started the water. Before he could step into the spray, the heavens opened up and the rain poured down.

He hoped this wasn't an omen for his life now that the senator was in control.

He had one month left of life as he knew it.

He wasn't about to waste it.

CHAPTER THREE

LILAH LIFTED HER FACE to the clean, sweet night air as she walked into the Rush Tide bar and restaurant and smiled as the faint breeze caressed her cheek. The waves lapped at the beach a mere fifteen feet away as she took a seat at the bar.

Donna, a longtime waitress at the Tide, came over with a smile. "What can I get you tonight?" she asked.

"My usual," Lilah answered. "Who's playing tonight?"

"Local band, Shiver Me Timbers. You heard of them?" Donna asked as she slid a virgin mojito Lilah's way.

Lilah shook her head. "No, but I'm sure they're good, if you booked them."

Donna nodded, leaning across the bar to share information with Lilah. "They play a number of places in St. Thomas. Got a pretty good fan base, actually. They've got a rockabilly funk sound. I think you'll like them."

"Cool," Lilah said as she sipped her drink, feeling only slightly guilty for lying to Lora about the band playing reggae but she could only take so much of her family's babying at this point. Out of habit, she took a pen from her purse and started idly doodling on a napkin.

Donna sighed as she cocked her head, watching Lilah

do a quick sketch of an iguana sunning itself on a palm tree. "You make that look so easy when I know it's not. I wish I had your talent, girl."

Lilah smiled briefly. "Well, napkin drawing is hardly what I'd call a talent," she said. "Besides, slinging drinks is a far more marketable skill. It's not like I can put this stuff on my résumé."

Donna shook her head, plainly disagreeing with Lilah's assessment. "You have a gift. I know good stuff when I see it, even if I can't do it myself. Trust me."

Lilah accepted the compliment but otherwise let it drop. She hated talking about her art. It was one of those private things that she preferred to keep in the background of her life because although she lived and breathed art, her supposed talent hadn't gotten her very far.

"So what's new?" Lilah asked, making general conversation until she realized Donna's attention was riveted elsewhere. She swiveled on her stool and found Larimar's newest guest sauntering into the Tide, looking sharp, edgy and completely take-your-breath-away hot.

"Who is that?" Donna asked, her eyes lighting up with obvious interest. "He is definitely not local."

"His name is Justin Cales," Lilah answered, toying with her straw, watching him. "He's staying at Larimar."

"Very nice. If only all the tourists were as hot as him."

Lilah chuckled and swiveled back around. Lora would jump all over her if she started flirting with a guest. No matter how cute he was, it wasn't worth the hassle.

"Don't look now but you've been spotted," Donna whispered before pulling back with a wide grin.

Lilah turned to see Justin heading straight for her. Her cheeks heated and an inexplicable moment of panic colored her thoughts, almost prompting her to make a hasty exit. But she wasn't fast enough and within seconds, he was sliding into the seat beside her just as she crumpled the napkin in her hand and surreptitiously dropped it into her purse.

"Welcome to Rush Tide," Donna said. "What can I get you?"

He glanced at Lilah with a playful grin. "Any recommendations?"

"Anything with the local rum," Lilah answered, smiling as she leaned in to add, "It's kind of our thing. You can't leave the island without having something with rum in it."

"Sounds serious," Justin said.

Lilah nodded with mock gravity. "Oh, it is. Donna, can you please set our new guest up with the house special?"

"One, one-horned butt fish, coming right up."

Justin mouthed the drink special with a dubious expression. "Am I going to regret this?"

"Depends on how many you drink and what actions qualify as regretful."

His grin widened. "I think I'm going to have fun here." He gestured at her drink. "What's your poison?"

She hesitated but then shrugged and answered. "Virgin mojito."

His raised brow said it all but she didn't feel the need to explain that alcohol messed with her meds. She certainly didn't feel like sharing all her dirty secrets in one sitting. A girl had to hold on to a little mystery, right?

"So, let me get this straight, you're pushing rum concoctions my way, yet you're drinking slushies? Are you trying to take advantage of me?" he asked playfully.

His grin did funny things to her stomach. He was either very dangerous or just what she needed—and it was too early to tell which it was going to be. "Something tells me the idea doesn't bother you too much," she countered with a sly smile.

"Guilty. I'm a sucker for a beautiful woman. Take advantage all you want."

"Duly noted." She sipped her drink, smiling as his gaze fastened on her lips with interest. The sparks kindling between them were difficult to ignore, and even so, she couldn't think of a single reason why she would want to.

She imagined taking him home, stripping his clothes and climbing him like a tree; a thought that nearly took her breath away at the reckless abandon. She wasn't generally a spontaneous person—that was Lindy's department. But there was no denying the fact that Justin made her feel alive for the first time in a year.

"What brings you to St. John?" she asked.

"Ahh, small talk. I should warn you, I excel at small talk. Practically majored in it in college."

"You have the look of an educated man," she agreed, regarding him speculatively. "Probably some expensive Ivy League school, if my intuition is correct."

He waited to answer until he'd taken an exploratory sip of the rum drink, then said, "If I tell you that I went to Yale for my undergraduate degree, then went on to Harvard Business School would that make me completely pretentious and untenable to be around? I mean, I don't want to be *that guy,* you know, the one who throws around his education like it means more than it does. An education is an education, right?"

She shrugged. "I wouldn't know. I never went to college."

"No? Why not?"

Lilah held her smile in place but inside she froze. She should've known this line of questioning would end up in bad territory. She'd planned to go to art school in Florida, but she hadn't been accepted. The blow to her ego and her fragile sense of talent had been fatal. College after that had seemed pointless. "Just not my thing," she answered blithely. "So…Mr. Highly Educated…business or pleasure?"

"Definitely pleasure," he answered with a mischievous look. "I have a month to do what I want and I plan to make the most of it."

"Why one month? You have a deadline for the end of your fun?"

His smile remained, but there was something about his expression that seemed hard as he said, "Life can't always be about fun and games, or so I'm told. But a man can do a lot in a month, right? So, what do locals do around here for fun?"

She lifted her drink. "You're looking at it." At his laughter, she added with a chuckle, "Well, that, and sail, scuba dive, snorkel, parasail… Oh, and if you have your passport you can take a charter to St. Croix and Jost van Dyke."

"I'll put them all on my to-do list."

Could you put me on your to-do list? The thought jumped in her brain before she could stop it but she didn't mind. He was only staying for a month. Plus, he wasn't from around here so he didn't know anything about her. She could be anyone—such as a girl who hadn't tried to kill herself a few months ago. The freedom to start fresh created a brighter smile for Lilah. Yes…Justin Cales could be just what she needed.

In all sorts of ways.

IT COULD'VE BEEN THE RUM, but Justin found Lilah irresistibly sexy. Her long blond hair drifted down her back in a waterfall of gold that made him want to twine his fingers in the soft strands, and her sweet, playful smiles made his gut tighten with the need to know more about her.

Oh, and did he mention she was sexy? Her white shorts hugged her pert rear end like a second skin and her loose gauzy shirt covered a bikini top over those perfect palm-sized breasts that he was dying to get to know better.

He was torn between spending more time with her or just staking his claim and then moving on. The island was probably filled with Caribbean cuties. Why should he get locked in with only one?

Besides, he wasn't looking for a relationship—good God, no—but then again, it didn't seem that Lilah was in the market for a boyfriend, either. Maybe she was game for a little fun.

"So…attached?" he asked courteously, though it wouldn't have mattered. If she had a boyfriend, he certainly wasn't around, so she was fair game in his mind.

"No attachments," she answered in a husky voice that sent shivers of awareness down his spine. "You?"

"I wouldn't be imagining all the things I'd like to do

to you if I were," he said in an equally low and seductive tone. He wasn't lying—when he was attached, he didn't stray, which was why he made it a point not to get attached. He liked variety in his carnal diet.

"Oh, really?" Her brow raised slightly. "Such as?"

He moved closer and whispered in her ear, "Come back to my room and I'll show you. All. Night. Long."

Her light laughter warmed him as if a ray of sunshine had just bathed his insides, and he suddenly hoped his cheesy pick-up line would work.

"Does that line work where you're from?" she asked.

Damn. He should've known Lilah wouldn't fall for something so crass. "Well, not always, but sometimes... and I'm an opportunist. Can't fault a guy for trying, right?"

She laughed again and sipped her drink, her eyes dancing. "Well, keep trying. I think you're closer to success than you know."

"Is that so?" he asked, surprised and delighted. His forced vacation was off to a great start. His dad would be so pissed. No doubt, the senator had hoped with out his friends he'd spend an entire month moping and moldering on this humid speck of land. *Well, sorry to disappoint you, Dad. I'm hooking up with the hottest chick on the island.*

An almost coy smile played on Lilah's lips and he was irresistibly drawn to her soft, sweet mouth. His palms moistened and he blamed the humidity, but as he locked stares with the enigmatic woman, he felt something shift inside him. He'd never been accused of being a romantic at heart, but for a wild second he wondered if this was what it was like to fall in love at first sight. If Keenan had heard him say something so girly, he'd keel over laughing and between gasps ask him if his subscription to the Lifetime Movie channel had expired. But how else was he supposed to explain how his heart rate had sped up at the thought of taking her to his room? He pulled back, putting some distance between them by reaching for his drink. God, he was overthinking things. She was hot. He was available. End of story.

"You want to get out of here?" she asked.

"Where?" he asked.

"How about the beach?"

A vision of the infamous scene in *From Here to Eternity* flashed in his mind and he hopped from his stool with a ready grin. "Show me the way and I'll follow wherever you go."

Lilah's small hand slipped into his and he instinctively squeezed, liking the feel of her hand in his. He imagined he was going to like the feel of Lilah—period.

CHAPTER FOUR

LILAH TOOK HIM TO A BEATUP Jeep and they climbed in. "This yours?" he asked, buckling up.

"It belongs to Larimar, but Pops and Grams always said we could use the resort vehicles to get around as long as we didn't do anything too stupid. They were pretty laid-back about certain things."

Justin thought of his father and how he wasn't laid-back about anything. Even though he'd bought Justin a BMW Roadster for his sixteenth birthday, the man had dictated where and when he drove it. Limits were fine—hell, he'd been a spoiled rich kid up to no good most times— but the senator had taken it to extremes. It'd gotten to the point where Justin had just said screw it and found alternate transportation. In the end, he'd been happier, if not as stylish. To this day, that Roadster sat in the garage, collecting dust.

Lilah drove like a native, taking the sharp curves with ease, as the Jeep rumbled past the resort and up a steep incline.

"So where we going?" he asked, reaching up to hold on as she shifted the Jeep into a lower gear to climb the hill.

"My favorite beach," she answered with a smile. "Hawksnest."

"Sounds exotic." He grinned. "You're not taking me

up here to have your wicked way with me are you? I'm not that kind of boy, you know." Her light laughter teased a wider grin from him. "Not buying that, huh? Which part?"

"We're almost there," she said by way of answer, and he chuckled, happy to be there with her.

Justin leaned his head against the headrest and breathed deep the lush scent of the tropical foliage that flanked either side of the road as they drove out of town. It smelled fertile and ripe, almost sweet.

"Smells good, doesn't it?" she asked.

He nodded, his eyes still closed. "Yeah…it does. Better than New York on a hot summer day that's for sure."

"That where you're from?"

"You mean my accent didn't give it away?"

"Well, it did but I didn't want to assume."

"No worries. I'm a proud New Yorker. I'm a moderately fanatical Yankees fan, my favorite food is a dirty water dog, and I knew my way around the subway before I was ten. So yeah, New York, baby, all the way. Greatest city on earth. Have you ever been?"

She shook her head, almost shyly, and he nearly offered to take her sometime. Thankfully, he reined in that errant thought before it popped from his mouth and ruined an otherwise fabulous night with promises he didn't intend to keep. "So, tell me what it's like to grow up in paradise?" he asked.

"See for yourself." Lilah chuckled and pulled off the main road. The beach was only ten to twenty feet from the road. The soft lapping of waves against the sand combined with sounds in the sweet, redolent night air that he'd never be able to identify and he found himself struck by the sense of peace that followed.

Bright moonlight bathed the darkness with milky light, giving the water a silvery sheen, and he momentarily worried about the things in the water they wouldn't be able to see. But his worry was soon eclipsed by the realization that Lilah wasn't waiting for him as she grabbed a large beach bag stuffed in the back of the Jeep and then struck off toward the beach.

She pulled a large blanket from the bag and spread it out, and then she shocked him when she simply stripped, shimmying out of her white shorts and gauzy top. His eyes bugged at the tiny bikini clinging to her lean curves but she didn't stop there. She cast him a sweetly provocative smile before untying her bikini top and letting it drop to the sand.

All he could do was stare. Words dried up in his mouth and she took his shocked silence as proof that he liked what he saw. Then, she wiggled out of her bottoms and walked into the ocean. Her perfect, heart-shaped ass was the last thing he saw before she dove into the dark water.

Holy hell! Was she some island goddess? Was he awake or dreaming? He struggled out of his shorts and nearly tripped and fell on his face in his haste to join her. *Get a hold of yourself,* he chastised himself as he splashed into the water. This wasn't his first rodeo with a gorgeous naked woman, but one would never know it from the fumbling awkwardness he was displaying.

The warm water closed over his head and he was grateful for the split second to compose himself. When he reemerged, she was floating not far from him, pleased that he'd joined her so readily.

"If you are trying to have your way with me, you're off to a good start," he warned playfully. He reached for her and she glided just out of reach. "Where you going?" he asked, grinning. "Because I'll follow wherever you go. Now that I've seen the goods…you'll never be rid of me."

It was a playful statement but there was a chord of truth that clanged inside him that gave him a second's pause. But his libido quickly pushed away anything that even remotely resembled serious thought.

She responded with a small giggle. "You'll have to catch me first," she said, and dove under the water.

LILAH DARTED AWAY FROM Justin, kicking with quick, strong strokes but the New Yorker must've put in some serious time on the swim team because she nearly swallowed a lungful of water when his arms wrapped around her waist. He'd caught her easily and pulled her into his chest. Her arms wound automatically around his neck and her legs around his torso. He swam until his feet could touch the bottom and then they simply drifted together. Lilah sighed as the tepid water swirled around them like a liquid blanket of security and warmth, almost drunk with her own abandon.

"You're unlike any woman I've ever met," he murmured against the shell of her ear. She shivered at the spike of arousal that followed. "If I didn't know that sirens were mythical, I'd say I'd caught one."

"You don't catch sirens…they catch you," Lilah said, tightening her hold around his neck, pressing her breasts against him. She felt the nudge of his erection prodding at the cleft in her backside and she smiled against his shoulder. It'd been months since she felt even a flicker of desire, but here with Justin, every feeling that'd been languishing beneath the weight of her depression came kicking to life. She was nearly delirious from the intoxicating wash of desire and recklessness and she wanted to saturate herself within the feelings of happiness. She didn't want the night to end if it meant the light of day would diminish what she was experiencing right now. Propelled by her newfound abandon, she found his mouth quickly, surprising him with an ardent and insistent kiss that left nothing to the imagination. She wanted him desperately—and he felt the same.

They melted into one another, feeling as one, as their tongues danced and dueled, and the water caressed them with soft waves against their naked bodies.

She clung to him as their kisses turned into a storm of need and want, buffeting her against the knowledge that what they were doing was neither responsible nor prudent given her situation but she didn't care.

Before she realized it, they were out of the water and tumbling to the blanket. She squeezed her eyes shut, moaning as her body came alive beneath Justin's expert touch. There was no fumbling awkwardness inherent to the first time with a stranger, but rather a complimentary give-and-take that worked like a fine-tuned machine. His mouth and tongue delivered sensations that alternatively seemed foreign and familiar and she gasped with the need for more.

His firm, lean muscles strained with delicious precision as he entered her. She moaned, holding back nothing as he pushed himself deeper. He rocked her pelvis, grinding against her pubic mound with enough pressure to make her cry out and cling to him, needing more. "Yesss," she sobbed, unable to stop the rushing tide of sensation swamping her body. She wasn't alone. Within moments of her shuddering completion, Justin followed, crying out with a hoarse, throaty groan that echoed in the still night.

"Oh, God, woman," he breathed, rolling off her to his back, his chest heaving. For a long moment, neither spoke. The cacophony of night sounds filled the air with beautiful music and Lilah couldn't help the sudden rush of tears. Alarmed, Justin rolled to his side and wiped the tears away. "What's wrong? Are you okay? I thought you wanted this?" he asked, distressed.

She offered a watery chuckle at his concern but didn't know how to explain without oversharing. "I've been under a lot of stress," she finally said. And it wasn't a lie, per se. Trying to kill yourself, getting committed, all the while trying to save your family's resort was stressful. She forced a smile. "I'm sorry. I ruined the moment."

His relieved expression was worth the small lie. "For a second there I was worried I'd misread the signs."

"I'm not sure how you can misread a naked woman with her tongue down your throat."

"Well, I did feel pretty secure that I was heading in the right direction until just now." He smiled ruefully and she giggled. "So, stress, huh? What's happening that's got you all stressed out?"

She shook her head. "Let's not ruin the night with reality—it'll come soon enough. Let's just enjoy ourselves."

"Oh, crap. You're married, aren't you?"

Lilah laughed out loud. "No, of course not," she assured him. "Things are just…complicated and I don't want to think about all that stuff right now." She popped to her hands and knees and then straddled Justin, positioning her moist, hot heat right over his rapidly stirring penis. "What do you say we jump in the water, rinse and repeat?"

Justin smoothed the hair from her eyes as it hung down and tickled his chest with the damp strands, and she was struck anew how handsome—borderline adorable—he was. Likely, he was the one with a wife. But that wasn't her concern. Not tonight. He rose up to meet her mouth, capturing it with firm, possessive pressure, pushing her down until she was on her back again. She thrilled at the way his stare devoured her body and came back for more. "I say that's a stellar idea," he agreed with an openly lustful gaze. "Because by the time we leave this beach, I want to know every inch of your perfect body."

"Is that so?" she asked, drowning in the darkness of his eyes.

"Yes."

She licked her lips, fastening her gaze on his delectable mouth. "Then what are you waiting for?"

"Saucy wench," he growled before capturing her mouth and pinning her to the blanket.

Lilah gasped and realized as his mouth traveled to her breast…they weren't going to make it back to the water.

Not yet, anyway.

CHAPTER FIVE

AFTER SEX, JUSTIN ALWAYS felt good. All those endorphins rushing through his body, that nice, satiated feeling permeating his bones—hell, sex was just what the doctor ordered most times.

And so yes, Justin felt good.

But there was something else...something he couldn't rightly put his finger on, that was tugging at him.

Maybe it was because, even as they were packing up to return to Larimar, he still didn't want the night to end.

That in itself was troubling.

He wouldn't call himself the wham-bam variety of man, but he wasn't a cuddler, either. Most times, it just felt awkward and weird and he spent ninety percent of that cuddling time wondering when it would be acceptable to get up and leave.

But Lilah wasn't clinging to him or pestering him for his number or acting like most random hook-ups, and while he should've found that refreshing...he found himself wondering why.

"So...what's your schedule look like tomorrow?" he asked as they walked back to the Jeep.

"I have to work," she answered, tucking the giant beach bag into the tiny space behind the backseats before climbing into the front seat.

"What time do you get off?" he asked, hating how needy he sounded. "I mean, if you're not busy maybe we could get a bite or something?"

She graced him with a sweet smile but didn't commit, saying, "Maybe. We'll see."

Wait a minute... Did she just give him the polite brush-off? Yes, he was fairly certain she had, because he recognized the signs from his own playbook. "It's cool, I just thought, you know, if you weren't busy or anything. I'm probably going to drive around the island, thought it'd be nice to have my own personal tour guide."

Way to go, Romeo. I only want you around to work for me. Nice. He tried clarifying to salvage his statement, but he knew there was little hope. "No worries. Maybe I'll charter a boat or something."

"Call Billy Janks. He's a personal friend. He has good rates and he won't rip you off if you tell him I sent you," Lilah said, seemingly oblivious to his growing irritation at himself and the situation. "You have to be careful, some of the charter companies are major criminals. They charge a ridiculous amount of money if they think you'll pay it."

"I'm not worried about money," he said. Let the old man choke on the Visa bill when it came. "Is it a nice boat?"

"It won't sink," Lilah answered with a hint of cheek.

"Important quality in a boat," he noted, lifting his face to the breeze as they rumbled down the mountainside. "So...I had a great time tonight," he said, fishing for some kind of confirmation that he wasn't alone in his feelings.

"Me, too," she said without hesitation, even smiling brightly. He relaxed just a little, but still found his ego bruised by her attitude. They drove into Larimar's driveway and she parked in the private parking lot. She grabbed her bag and then faced him with a cheery smile. "It was so fun tonight. I hope you enjoy St. John. It's a wonderful place and I'm sure you'll take home plenty of fantastic memories." She turned to walk away, leaving him flabbergasted, then stopped and added, "Oh, there's a continental breakfast available in the formal dining room if you like. Lots of fresh fruit and sometimes banana pancakes if Celly is feeling up to it. Good night!"

"Wait," he called after her, unable to believe she was leaving without so much as a *hey, the sex was amazing, let's get together again soon,* but instead she left him with a breakfast reminder! "Okay, clearly I'm not speaking your language… I want to see you again but you haven't picked up on any of my signals."

"Oh, I caught them," she said, surprising him and further wounding his pride when she added, "I just chose to ignore them."

"Why?" he asked, suddenly indignant. "I thought you said you had a good time."

"I had a great time," she agreed with a vigorous nod. "It's just that I don't have room in my life for attachments, even short-term ones. When I said my life was complicated, I wasn't exaggerating. If I were to tell you everything, you'd thank me for giving you a graceful out. I had the *most* amazing time, truly. But…you and me…it just doesn't gel for anything beyond the superficial."

"How do you know? You haven't even given me a chance to ruin your opinion of me," he said.

At that she grinned and his heart did a funny flop at the way her face lit up when she smiled. She reached up on her tiptoes and brushed a sweet kiss across his lips. "Good night, Justin. Sleep well."

And then she was gone, leaving Justin to wonder how she managed to make him feel as if he could fly in one minute and then leave him to feel as if he'd just belly flopped onto concrete the next.

His dignity demanded that he shrug off her polite rejection and find a less complicated woman to spend time with, but even as his angry steps punctuated his growing irritation, he had a hard time even pretending that he was going to do that.

Back in New York he had to whack women off with a stick to keep them from getting their claws into his skin. But here? Well, the one woman who intrigued him had just said *thanks, Bud, but I think I'll pass on a rematch.*

Was he a bad lover? Had he totally misjudged his skills with the horizontal mambo? A moment of insecurity badgered him until he was half tempted to bang on her door and let him have a second chance but that was ludicrous and he knew it.

Oh, God. He was turning into a woman. Why was he stressing about something so completely out of his wheelhouse? Of course he was a good lover. Never had any complaints in that department.

Never stuck around long enough to listen, a small, crafty voice whispered in his head.

Yes, it was official.

He had estrogen running through his veins.

On the wings of that depressing thought, Justin found his bed and tried to find sleep.

LILAH LAY IN HER BED, staring at the ceiling. Sleep should've been easy. Her bones felt soft beneath her skin and her body hummed with satisfaction.

And yet, her eyes refused to close.

If she were a different person with a different set of circumstances she could've easily seen herself spending more time with Justin. He was funny, charming and had a body that didn't quit.

But when she traveled down that road for just a moment—testing out the possibilities—she hit a mental roadblock.

She wasn't ready to share her recent past with anyone aside from family. For that matter, she didn't really want to share it with them, either, but she didn't have a choice. But if there were some way to erase from their memory what she'd done, she'd jump at the chance.

Of course, that wasn't a possibility so she dealt with the consequences; the thought of sharing that burden with even one more person...it made her shudder with shame.

Dr. Veronica often had to remind her that she was a different person today than she was several months ago when she walked into the ocean ready to die.

But sometimes she worried her unwell mirror image was just beyond the thin film separation and one wrong move could send her tripping past the barrier into oblivion.

Her heart kicked up a beat and she closed her eyes and visualized the ocean because it soothed her most. She breathed through the mild panic attack and rolled onto her side, determined to fall asleep.

She realized she knew very little about Justin aside

from the surface stuff, which was how she'd deliberately framed her relationship with him.

But her mind wanted to know more. There was something behind those smiling eyes that begged for a little digging. She knew something about being a still pool of water running deep. People underestimated her all the time because she wasn't loud and in your face with her opinions or actions, but it didn't mean she wasn't a person interested in having her thoughts and feelings known.

Dr. Veronica was helping her find her voice but old habits died hard.

If things were different...

She couldn't imagine a better person to spend a little time with than Justin.

CHAPTER SIX

THE DAY BROKE MUGGY and overcast but Lilah didn't mind as she sat chatting with Celly, their one remaining full-time employee, at the front desk.

Celly, an older Crucian woman with a thick accent and an allergy to nonsense, had taken a shine to Lilah from the start, though she still bristled around Lora. Lilah suspected it was because Lora had made the mistake of talking down to her when they first met. Or it could be that Lora still hadn't given up the notion that they ought to let Celly go.

Lilah wasn't worried on that score. For one, Pops loved Celly for her island ways, and honestly, if he wasn't still in love with his dead wife, he might've actually taken a shine to the Carib woman. And two, as much as Lora and Celly rubbed each other the wrong way and groused and griped about one another, they each served an important role at Larimar.

So basically, no one was going anywhere for the time being.

"Yah smile wit a light, chile," Celly remarked slyly, clucking her tongue knowingly. "Yah meet a mon when yah out and about last night?"

Lilah laughed, only slightly unnerved by how accurate Celly's intuition was at times, and said, "You're seeing things. I smile all the time now. Dr. Veronica says it's good practice."

"Yah can't fool dis ol' woman. There's only one way a woman gets dat kind of glow. Either yah pregnant or yah seeing someone that lights yah up from de inside. Come tell Celly who put dat glow on yah face?"

"Celly," Lilah said, blushing with mild exasperation. "There isn't anyone. I just had a great time last night and it's been a while since I could just enjoy myself, so I'm soaking in it."

Celly shook her head with a smile. "Yah be lying, chile, but that's okay. A woman has her secrets, be fine wit me."

Lilah sighed happily, unable to contain the sound. Her stare drifted to the open window and gazed out at the ocean view. Even shrouded in clouds the color of dirty snow, the island was a beautiful place. She inhaled the sweet scent of tropical flowers wafting from the large vase in the foyer and her good mood was dimmed only slightly by the realization that Larimar wasn't in the clear.

She and her sisters had been trying to devise a plan to save their beloved family resort but thus far had only managed to meet their payment arrangements agreed upon by the IRS. Lindy's fiancé, Gabe Weston, who happened to be the CEO of Weston Enterprises, had offered to kick in some cash to help with the resources but Lora had staunchly disagreed, saying it would muddy the waters between family members. Lilah wasn't sure, especially when saving the resort, however they could, was the primary goal. But, in the end, they all agreed that they wouldn't lean on Gabe unless it was absolutely dire. That seemed to be an agreement that everyone was on board with but it hardly seemed fair that they'd have to battle not only the government who was pressuring them for payment, but also Pops and his rapidly deteriorating mental state. Frankly, Lilah had wished they'd simply accepted Gabe's help to get at least one monkey off their back while they focused on another.

As if sensing the train of her thoughts, Celly said, "Yah know, Jack heart-sick. Dis what happens when the soul cries for its mate. Your Pops, he good mon, but there come a time when there's not much else can be done that nature won't take care of itself."

"What do you mean?"

"Yah know," Celly answered cryptically, and left it at that.

Lilah looked away, not ready to go there. Eventually Pops would become a danger to himself. He'd already given them plenty of scares when he'd wandered off, fallen, or ranted and raved about something that happened decades prior. Once, he'd even taken the ferry to St. Thomas. That'd been a frightening ordeal—for everyone. They hadn't found him until the following morning.

Lilah suppressed a shudder. She hated the feeling that her time with Pops was coming to an end. Even though it'd been ten years, she still hadn't come to grips with the loss of her Grams.

"Celly, we have to find a way to save Larimar," Lilah said quietly. "It's the glue that holds this family together. What will happen if we lose Pops and Larimar? It's too awful to even contemplate."

Celly patted Lilah's hand with her careworn and roughened one and said, "Yah be surprised what one family can handle when they made to. Yah worry too much. Everything will happen as it should." A smile creased her mouth as her gaze canted sidewise. "Don't look now but there's a beautiful mon walking dis way. Yah call dibs?" Lilah gasped at the island woman's bold suggestion and swatted at her. "What? A woman has needs, yah know."

Lilah swallowed her laughter when she realized it was Justin walking their way. He walked into a room like a playboy just looking for a good time, but there was something that pulsed just beneath the surface of that easygoing exterior that spoke of deep strength. Since going through everything, Lilah had gained something of a sixth sense about people. Celly insisted that it was because she'd straddled both worlds with one foot on the earth and the other in the heavens until modern science had yanked her back to her body. Of course, when Lora had heard that theory, she'd snorted in derision and muttered under her breath something unflattering about "that superstitious Crucian woman" and had rolled her eyes so hard, she nearly tipped over. Lilah didn't know what to believe. She just seemed sensitive to people now. And there was something about Justin that drew her—which was exactly why she needed to avoid him.

"Are all the island women as beautiful as you?" he asked, staring at Lilah, then deliberately switching his gaze to Celly as if the question had been directed at her all along. Lilah blushed and looked away. He extended a hand to Celly. "Justin Cales. Larimar guest. And you are…?"

"Yah be smooth as the underside of a conch shell yah be and just as pretty." She chuckled. "What can we do yah for?"

"Actually, I was hoping maybe you could help me to convince Miss Lilah, here, to show me the sights around your lovely island. Obviously, I'm not from around here. I stick out like a sore thumb. The locals will see me coming a mile away and I'm sure I'll pay way too much for even a taxi. Can you help a poor guy out? I promise I'm not a pervert or ax murderer…just a mildly adorable tourist who has a soft spot for pretty tour guides."

Lilah smothered the grin that found her lips anyway. He made her insides feel like warm chocolate melting in the humid heat. Damn, he was charming. And those eyes ought to be illegal.

"Sorry, I have to work," Lilah declined sweetly.

"Foolish girl," Celly said, shooing her away from behind the counter. "When a good-looking man come knockin' yah don't show him de door until yah've had some fun. Now go, chile. Nothing here I can't handle for de day."

"But Lora—"

"Bah, Lora is in love wit de sound of her own voice. Things get done, that's all dat matters. Show this young mon the island the real way."

Justin grinned, placing his hand over his heart in a show of utter gratitude. "Bless you for helping a poor guy out. Karma will surely smile on you."

"Go on wit your pretty mouth," Celly said, waving him away, but a smile flirted with her mouth. She waved a finger at him though, saying, "Don' mess wit my favorite Bell or I send a *jumbie* after yah."

Lilah laughed at Justin's quizzical frown. "A ghost," she explained, moving from behind the counter against her better judgment. "But don't worry, as far as I know *jumbies* are out of season right now." She cast Celly a playfully exasperated look and then followed Justin outside. "What are you doing? I told you I wasn't interested in anything serious."

"Who said anything about serious? I just need a tour guide I can trust," Justin said innocently. "I mean, just because we knocked boots doesn't make us married, right?"

Her cheeks heated just a little and she lifted her chin with a small laugh. "Right. Okay. I guess I got the wrong impression last night. I thought you were interested in something more…"

"Let's not get ahead of ourselves. We had a great time. Where's the harm in spending a few more hours together?"

She weighed his logic and when she couldn't find an obvious flaw she grudgingly agreed. What was a day or two? It wasn't as if they were going to fall helplessly in love in the space of a few hours. She smiled. "All right. You got yourself a tour guide. But the minute I feel things are getting…attached between us…"

"Sounds perfect to me. If you knew me better, you'd know I'm the last person who's looking for deep and meaningful. I promise."

"That's a dubious way of reassuring me."

"But does it work?"

"Knowing that you have commitment issues and are likely a major player?" She took a moment to consider, then answered, "Yes, actually it does."

"Great." He grinned. "Now that we have that out of the way…refresh my memory on the sex part? Is that part of the tour guide special?"

She gasped and climbed into the Jeep but a secret

smile lit up her insides. "Get in or you're going to end up walking into town."

"Yes, ma'am," Justin said, chuckling as he climbed into the Jeep beside her. Then he cast her a glance as he said, "So...just to be clear, would it be terribly inappropriate if I told you how sexy you look this morning?"

"Yes." But she loved it. "Try to keep that kind of talk to a minimum."

"Where's the fun in that?" She leveled a serious look his way and he lifted his hands in mock surrender. "Can't blame a guy for trying. But I should warn you—"

"Warn me about what?"

He leaned forward and she saw it coming but couldn't seem to pull away because as much as she was putting up fences, she was secretly delighted when he pushed them down. "I'm terrible at following rules that don't suit me," he murmured right before brushing his lips against hers.

Oh. Damn.

JUSTIN KNEW HE SHOULDN'T but he really, honestly couldn't help himself. It sounded corny—and if any of his friends could see him right now, they'd laugh their asses off—but Lilah was a drug he wasn't quite ready to quit. Maybe it was because she sweetly but plainly told him that she wasn't interested in anything serious, which was a 180 from the women that usually pursued him. In his current circles, it was as if he had Most Eligible Bachelor stamped on his forehead in neon letters, because they simply flocked to him, draping themselves over him and availing him to their generous assets without reservation. But he could spot a socialite on the marriage prowl within seconds of meeting a woman. His buddies called it a gift, a calling to help prevent untimely snaring, so he definitely knew Lilah wasn't simply being coy.

But he didn't care. She was unlike any woman he'd ever met and he wanted more—any way he could get it.

He pulled away and her eyelids remained fluttered shut; her dark brown lashes rested on her cheeks as a tiny smile flirted with her mouth. "You are impossible," she said, slowly opening her eyes.

"I like to think of myself as an opportunist," he clarified.

"And you felt I'd left you a wide-open opportunity to kiss me?" she asked.

"Can I help it that you are just irresistible? Really, I think that's more on you, than me. I'm defenseless against your beauty and charm."

LILAH ROLLED HER EYES and gave him a gentle shove as she started the Jeep. "Don't push your luck. Now, do you want to see St. John or not?"

He grinned, not the least bit sorry for stealing that kiss. *As long as it's with you, darling...I'd visit the moon.* And in fact, he was going to steal as many kisses as she'd let him. "I'm all yours, sweetheart," he said, sliding his sunglasses into place.

Lilah chuckled and put the Jeep into Reverse, muttering with a headshake, "Tourists."

CHAPTER SEVEN

LORA CAUGHT A GLIMPSE of Lilah leaving in the Jeep with someone she didn't recognize and she immediately went to find answers. She withheld an audible sigh when she saw the only person who might have those answers was Celly.

"Where is Lilah going?" Lora asked, getting straight to the point.

Celly shrugged. "I'm not her keeper. She no baby."

"I know that but why are you working her shift? Is she coming back in a few minutes or something?"

Celly sighed and cast Lora a short look. "Yah treat her like a chile when she a woman grown. Mind yah business, leave her be."

Lora held her temper in check by the thinnest of margins. Why did this woman insist on pushing her buttons? Didn't she realize that Lora was her boss? "One, she's my sister, and two, she's supposed to be working, and three, she's been through a rough ordeal. I don't think she needs to invite complications by starting a relationship."

"Who say she startin' anything?" Celly waved Lora's concerns away with an irritated flick of her wrist. "I say I will take her shift. She's young. She doesn't need to be cooped up like a bird in a cage. She needs to stretch her wings if she going to fly."

Lora narrowed her gaze at Celly. "Need I remind you that Lilah nearly drowned a few months ago? We all thought it best to give her some space but look how that turned out." Celly looked away, finished with the conversation but Lora wasn't. The steam building under her collar was beginning to redden her ears. "Celly, I know you feel a certain amount of protection because my grandfather has a soft spot for you but you are not irreplaceable. You need to show me a bit more respect."

"And why is dat? Yah threaten to fire me the minute yah walk on de sand and yah expect me to grovel at yah feet wit gratitude? Yah crazy, girl. Yah *earn* respect not demand it."

Lora felt distinctly chastised, which only served to anger her more. She sputtered, all manner of hotheaded, ill-conceived words threatening to fall from her mouth, but Pops wandered in and Lora was forced to stuff them down with a dark glower promising a return to the topic later. "Pops, what's wrong?" she asked, when his typical easygoing smile was replaced with a confused frown.

"I can't find your Grams... She's not anywhere. I—I don't remember when I saw her last. Do you?" He turned frightened, somewhat glazed eyes to Lora and she smothered a flutter of panic. She wasn't very good at pretending, even for Pops. It wasn't natural for her to lie, even if the lie was for the greater good. She glanced around, looking anxiously for Heath. He was so much better at this than her. But Heath was nowhere to be seen. Pops's lip quivered and he scratched at his head, his voice wobbling with uncertainty. "I got bad things in my head, sugar bird. Was she sick? No, that can't be right. Is she at the doctor, maybe?"

Celly moved in, smooth as whipped cream, and

gently led Pops out of the foyer, saying, "Mr. Jack, she went to town on an errand, said she'd be back latah. But she told me to make some fresh banana bread for yah and I think it's just about ready to eat. Let's go take a look."

Pops relaxed and wiped a dot of sweat from his brow. "That Lana…always shopping. She's going to bleed me dry one of these days but she knows my weaknesses, that's for sure. Banana bread, you say?"

"Fresh from de oven," Celly said with a proud nod. "With just a touch of coconut to make it island bread."

Lora watched as Celly expertly maneuvered Pops out of the foyer and into the private residence of the resort. The tightness in her chest loosened but it was replaced with a different sort of frustration. As much as she and Celly seemed to butt heads at every turn, the Crucian woman was adept at handling Pops. Of course, now there was no one to man the front desk. Sighing, she slipped behind the counter and resigned herself to a little reception work but was soon distracted by the total chaos on the desk. There were paper clips mixed with loose staples and sticky notes all over the place with various reminders and important dates, which she noted with irritation, should've been transferred to the calendar so everyone could, at a glance, know what was needed or happening. *Damn it, people.* They needed to adhere to some kind of organizational structure if they were going to save Larimar. Everyone running around doing their own thing with their own little quirks and touches was part of the problem.

She was knee-deep in organizing the chaos when Heath entered the lobby. Even as irritated as she was, the sight of Heath momentarily took her breath away.

He was the most handsome man she'd ever known. And she wasn't just saying that because she slept next to him every night. He still walked with a mild limp from his fall off the roof but she hardly noticed anything but his dazzling smile because when he looked at her, the world disappeared.

Briefly.

"Celly is going to kill you for messing with her system," Heath joked, reminding Lora of the ugly business earlier.

She stiffened and returned to her task. "Well, Celly needs a new system. One that isn't grounded in chaos theory. This is a mess."

"Well, I'm just saying, she has a system and it seems to work fairly well and since she works the front desk the majority of the time, I'd leave her to it. I know I'd have a fit if someone came into my shop and started rearranging my tools."

Lora paused, struck by the uncomfortable reasoning. Heath was right. But Lora struggled with admitting that simple fact, not because of Heath but because of Celly. She glowered at Heath for making his point. "I didn't mean to start changing everything… It's just that she had staples mingling with paper clips," she said as if her reasoning ought to be self-explanatory.

"A crime, I'm sure," Heath said, smiling and not the least bit offended by her scowl. "Now stop rearranging someone else's workstation before they cut you off from the boiled bananas."

Celly made boiled bananas better than The Wild Donkey, which was saying something considering the ramshackle eatery had been serving the local fare since the 1930s.

And it just happened to be Lora's favorite.

She groaned. "Why does she hate me?" she asked, trying to return the desk to the way it was but in the end she gave up and resigned herself to another tongue-lashing, or worse, sullen silence.

"She doesn't hate you," Heath assured Lora. "But you do have a way of talking down to her that probably doesn't help your case."

"I do not," Lora retorted indignantly. "I state my mind and I don't mince words, that's all. I'd think she'd respect that seeing as she's the same damn way."

Heath's look said he didn't buy it. "Lora, you got off on the wrong foot is all but that can be fixed. She's a great woman if you give yourself a chance to know her. Grams would've loved her. In a way—"

"Don't say it," Lora warned with a growl. There is no way that hard-bitten woman with the bad attitude was anything like her Grams. Not in a million years. Not even if Grams had been a long-haul trucker who chewed cigars and spit chewing tobacco. She shuddered at the thought. "Grams was sweet and loving and just a bit quirky—" *and she loved me* "—whereas Celly—"

"Celly what?" The strident query followed as Celly returned to the front desk. Lora didn't have the chance to answer for Celly's gaze lit on the desk and her frown darkened to a deep, angry scowl. "What is *this?* My desk has been ruined." Her accusatory gaze swung to Lora with knowing ire. "Yah did this?"

Lora lifted her chin. "I did."

Heath sensed the tension ballooning in the air and tried to intervene with his signature good humor but Celly silenced him with a wave as she addressed Lora. "Yah made dis mess…yah clean it. Yah seem to know what's best for everybody even if yah don't know what's best for yahself," she said darkly. "Until yah keep your nose out of what's working…I'm going home."

"What?" Lora said, dumbfounded. "What do you mean you're going home? Who will man the front desk?"

Celly grabbed her purse and slung it over her shoulder. "That's yah problem. Not mine."

"Now, wait a minute," Lora protested, following Celly and imploring with Heath to help her. "You can't just leave in the middle of the day like that. You told Lilah you would cover her shift…"

Celly stopped and skewed her gaze at Lora. "I did. But yah out of control. Learn some manners and I return."

Manners? Lora stared after the woman as she walked out the door. "What just happened?" she asked Heath. "Did she just quit?" Then hearing the plaintive tone in her voice, she straightened and said, "Well, then fine. She can be replaced. This is good, actually. I'll just go through the applications and find someone more suitable for our needs."

Heath frowned, unhappy with her solution. "That's not going to work. Celly is like family. Just go apologize for messing up her desk and she'll come back. Her feathers are just ruffled."

"Apologize?" Lora repeated, her ire returning. "Why should I apologize to a staff member for trying to keep a workstation tidy? That doesn't even make sense."

"She's more than an employee, Lora. That's your problem right there. She's family to everyone here, except you. You need to make this right or there's going to be hell to pay. Lilah is very close to Celly and so is Pops. She does a lot to keep Larimar running smoothly."

"I'm not going to apologize," Lora said stiffly. She didn't care how much Celly coddled Pops. Seemed ever since Lora moved back to St. John everyone and their uncle had been telling her to apologize for one thing or another. Well, she was finished apologizing.

Heath saw the set of her jaw and shook his head in disappointment. "You're making a huge mistake."

"Says you." She sent a hard stare at Heath, irritated and hurt that he wasn't immediately on her side. Wasn't that part of the deal when you loved someone? They had to be on your side. She was pretty sure that was an un-written rule. "Well, I have phone calls to make so that puts you on reception duty. Perhaps you could persuade Celly to come back. In the meantime, I'm going to go through applications."

"So where are we going?" Justin asked with a smugly triumphant smile that should've been a put-off but ad-mittedly he wore it well enough for her to forgive him.

"Well, I thought we'd take a drive to Coral Bay. It's a scenic drive and there's some cool history along the way."

"A history lesson? Is it boring?"

"Would you like to walk?" she asked sweetly.

He chuckled. "I'm all ears as long as there isn't a test later," he said on a yawn. "Sorry, I didn't sleep very well last night."

"Something wrong with the room?" Lilah asked, concerned.

"No, the room is perfect. My mind wouldn't let go of a certain someone…"

She blushed but kept her eyes on the road as she said airily, "I slept like a baby. More relaxed than I've been in a long time." She cast him a mildly coy look as she added, "Thank you for that."

"That's me," Justin said. "Helping women find a good night's rest since 2001."

Lilah laughed and smiled into the sun streaming into the Jeep, loving the warm kiss on her cheeks. She caught Justin staring and she became self-conscious. "Something wrong?"

"Nope," he answered. "Just wondering how I got so lucky."

"You mean you were wondering if you were going to get lucky again," Lilah teased.

A grin broke out on his lips. "Well, there is that."

"You're impossible." Laughter bubbled up inside her. It felt uncommonly good to joke and smile and tease with someone who knew nothing about her past. The freedom was intoxicating. "Okay, first part of the history lesson starts now. You see that broken masonry that's crumbling to dust." She pointed off road. "That's what's left of a sugar plantation. Back in the 1700s St. John was known for its sugar production. Slaves were taken to St. Thomas where plantation owners would purchase them for their plantation workforce."

"So I take it that when slavery was abolished it really took a bite out of the local economy," Justin remarked wryly to which she nodded. "It's hard to say that sucks because slavery is wrong but I imagine a lot of people lost their livelihoods when they couldn't farm the sugarcane any longer."

"Yeah, actually St. John has quite a bloody history. At one time the slaves outnumbered the freemen and a brutal revolt 'turned the waters red' as the old-timers say."

"Every place inhabited by humans has its dirty secrets," he said with a grim smile. "Even places as beautiful as St. John I suppose."

She nodded in agreement. "With such a brutal past, it's easy to see why the Caribbean people are so superstitious. The island is overrun with stories of vengeful or sad *jumbie* floating around."

"Tell me a *jumbie* story," he prompted with a big grin. "I love spooky stories."

She laughed. "I don't have any good ones. Heath said he saw the ghost of Maunie Dalmida on the Reef Bay Trail but I've never actually seen any ghosts."

"And who is Maunie Dalmida?"

"A young boy who was killed in a sugar mill accident. The stories are that Maunie roams the trail."

"Creepy."

"Yeah, but like I said, I've been all over this island and never seen anything like that. I wish I had. I used to hope that something otherworldly would happen to me but it never did." Well, except dying, she thought but kept that little tidbit to herself. "Anyway, anything like that happen to you in New York?"

He paused to think for a minute, the dappled sunlight playing with the lighter brown strands in his dark hair, and then said, "Well, the boarding school I attended was pretty old and there were rumors that the ghost of a young girl haunted the cafeteria. I never saw anything but my best buddy, Keenan, swore to all that was holy he saw her standing over the mashed potato tray one afternoon. No one but Keenan saw her but he looked pretty freaked out. I believed him. He also never ate the mashed potatoes again."

"I don't think Heath has ever hiked the Reef Bay Trail again, either," she said, laughing. They settled into an easy silence as she drove, but then she remembered a small snippet of shared information and decided to comment on it. "Boarding school, huh? So…something tells me you weren't ever a free lunch recipient at school?"

Justin shifted just a little as if caught and said, "My childhood was comfortable," he admitted. "I guess you could say privileged. You're not going to hold that against me are you?"

"Of course not," she said. "I never hold someone's past against them, particularly their childhood. I choose to judge people on their actions."

"Good to know," he said, looking as if he were vastly relieved, which made her wonder what other little truths he didn't want to be judged on. She'd meant what she said. She was the last person to pass judgment on someone else but, unfortunately, she found herself itching to know more details about him. *Not only a bad idea but hypocritical,* she chastised herself. *Focus on the road, not the distracting cuteness.*

Which, she could tell, was going to be impossible.

It'd be a miracle if they didn't end up in a ravine.

CHAPTER EIGHT

JUSTIN INHALED THE SWEET scent of green things and enjoyed his stroke of luck. He was spending the day with Lilah on an island paradise. Things couldn't have worked out better if he'd planned them.

He couldn't quite put his finger on why he was so taken with Lilah but he didn't need to dissect his feelings to simply enjoy them. She made him feel alive, as if someone had flicked a switch inside his brain and suddenly everything was illuminated for the first time. He chuckled privately at how ridiculous he was being but he was smiling from the inside out and that was a fact. He didn't mind that they seemed to be driving to the moon with enough switchbacks to make a person sick to their stomach. He didn't even mind the history lesson. If Keenan could see him right now, he'd assume there'd been some sort of head injury to make him act like this. Almost lovesick if there was a thing. But hey, whatever it was, it was fun and that's what Justin was all about with this trip.

Just the mere brush of reality threatened to sour his mood so he ruthlessly kicked it away. He'd almost blown it by admitting he'd attended a boarding school—who aside from rich kids attended boarding school?—but she'd been cool about it. She hadn't even pestered him for details, for which he'd been grateful but mildly disappointed. Most women already knew everything about him, but wanted to know more. Lilah knew nothing about him and seemed content with surface details yet he wanted to tell her things that he ought to keep private. Such as the fact that his prick of a father was strong-arming him into a political career he didn't want. Yeah, great conversation starter. Talk about a surefire way to kill a mood.

Soon, however, they drove into a sleepy little cove town that he assumed was Coral Bay and he was astounded by the number of donkeys milling about, both on the side of the road and on the road. One mangy-looking beast eyed him with zero fear and remained stationed dead center in the middle of road as if he owned it. Lilah honked the horn but the donkey merely flicked one long ear at the intrusive sound and continued to stare balefully, as if they were in the wrong spot instead of him.

"One of the main annoyances of Coral Bay," Lilah admitted. "The wild donkeys."

"Boy, he thinks he owns the road, doesn't he?"

"Yeah, they all do," Lilah agreed, honking the horn again. "All right, you stubborn ass. I guess I'll have to go around."

Justin laughed as Lilah eased the Jeep around the donkey and they continued on their way.

"So this is Coral Bay?" Justin observed, wondering if he was missing something as he took in the rustic environment and almost forgotten ambiance. "Is this the place time forgot? Seems lost in the '60s."

An old gas station, rusted and crumbling into orange-flecked dust, was near an equally old corner store. He wasn't sure if anyone actually lived here aside from the donkeys.

"Well, it used to be a thriving town for artisans and a few still call this place home but it's true there's not much to draw the tourists anymore."

"Seems a good place for a serial killer to hang out. You know they make movies in towns like this," he joked, although there was a grain of truth to his ribbing. It probably had its charm for some people, but it was a little too…earthy for his tastes. He glanced at Lilah. "Does this conclude the tour? Or is there more?"

"You don't like it?" She pulled off onto a secluded side street, though there was zero traffic and even fewer humans milling about, the sound of the Jeep idling seemed unnaturally loud against the drowsy quiet of the town.

"It's… Yeah, I'm not going to lie…not my cup of tea. Let me guess, you love this place."

Lilah smiled. "Well, I love all of St. John. It's easy to love Cruz Bay—it's where the cool shops and restaurants are, which is why it fares well with tourists, but it takes someone who truly loves the island to appreciate the value of Coral. You're right, it's not flashy and pretty. There are donkeys everywhere and there's only two good places to eat, but there's a beauty beyond the surface stuff here. I like the quiet rhythm of life here. It's soothing. Sometimes when I'm overwhelmed I take a drive here and by the time I'm done, I don't feel suffocated by whatever was bothering me."

Justin quieted at her frank admission. Lilah radiated love and acceptance as her gaze roamed the jungle depths and the cove dotted with boats. In that moment he saw through her eyes what was so special about something seemingly ordinary; the diamond in the rough. He thought of New York and how he'd stopped seeing the beauty of the city a long time ago and simply roamed the streets with blinders to the wonder and patriotic heritage of one of the States' proudest cities. He'd love to see New York through Lilah's eyes, watch her discover all the things about the city that made it great, like "dirty water dogs" from a street vendor in Times Square or walking Central Park in the spring, not to mention the museums and art galleries. Damn, he'd stopped noticing all those things so long ago.

"Thanks for bringing me here," he said with a slow smile. "It's beautiful."

Her eyes warmed with sweet joy and she blushed just a little. "No problem," she said. "I'm glad I could show you."

She looked so soft and lovely, almost ethereal as the sunlight slanted through the open top of the Jeep, bathing her in a golden glow, that he didn't stop to think, he just leaned forward and gently took her mouth. Her soft lips yielded to him without reservation and their tongues met in a gentle yet sensual dance. His heartbeat kicked up as heat and lust kindled between them like a dangerous spark in a banked fire pit that drifted on a warm breeze in search of something to burn. Lilah's moan pushed him deeper into the void where only their bodies and the need to touch existed. His hand gripped the back of her head, slanting his mouth over hers in a raw need to possess this unique creature who captivated him in a way that astounded his rational mind. But there was nothing rational about the way they both tore at their clothes, eager to feel skin on skin. The Jeep was small but Lilah fit perfectly in his lap as she straddled his thighs and closed her delicate hand around the straining, desperate length of him.

He felt fevered, perilously close to losing control and embarrassing himself. "You're the most amazing woman I've ever known," he said, tipping his head back on a groan as Lilah's hot core enveloped him in liquid pleasure. "Oh, God, Lilah…"

Her answering moan as she braced herself and rocked her pelvis against his erection buried deep inside her, touched off another wave of insane pleasure as sweat beaded their bodies and the sound of their harsh breathing filled the cab and drifted into the quiet jungle. "Anyone can see us." He bit off a warning growl but truly, he didn't much care at that moment if they had a popcorn-munching audience. He was losing himself in Lilah's heat and gladly burning alive. She clamped her muscles around him and his eyes rolled back in his head as she panted with her own pleasure. "Lilah," he gasped, gripping her hips and helping her ride him as he pumped against her, grinding against her until she squealed and moaned and shuddered as she found her release.

He had two seconds to be relieved that he'd lasted long enough before his own release shot out of him, clenching every muscle in a powerful spasm that he felt deep within his body, hurtling jets of fluid from him and into her. "God, Lilah! Ahhh!" he groaned, his fingers curling into the soft flesh of her lean hips as he filled her. He could feel her body spasming around him still, milking every last wave and shudder, and then she leaned forward and rested her head on his shoulder as she caught her breath.

"Oh, God…that was…magnificent," she admitted

with a shaky laugh and he couldn't agree more. She pulled forward and bit her lip in a vulnerable manner as she started to lift herself off but he tightened his grip on her hips. "Where you going?" he asked. He liked the feel of her hot body on his, even as his spent manhood slipped from her sheath.

She laughed, the sound soft and playful. "I can't stay here like this all day."

"And why not?"

She blushed. "Because I need to clean up."

He supposed that was a valid reason, but privately he liked the idea of his seed on her. It was primal and entirely caveman mentality but the need to possess her in some way was frighteningly strong. Geesh, he thought shakily, as he helped her return to her seat and find her bikini bottoms. What was happening to him? He couldn't remember the last time he'd felt so out of control with a woman. A thought occurred to him, albeit a bit late, and he asked with desperate hope in his voice, "Are you...protected?"

She laughed. "Of course. I'm on the Pill, silly. Although, we probably should've worn a condom, right?"

"Yeah," he agreed, but he rushed to assure her, saying, "I'm totally clean. I get checked every three months. You can never be too careful, you know?"

She laughed. "Excellent. Well, glad that conversation's been covered. Are you hungry?" she asked, settling into her seat and adjusting her top. "There's a little place just around the corner that has pretty good food."

"I could eat," Justin agreed, suddenly ravenous. "Hey, what are your plans tonight?"

"I don't know, probably stay in. Why?"

His hope dimmed when she didn't immediately offer

to spend time with him but he didn't let it show. "I thought we could check out what band is playing at the Rush Tide and hang out."

"Sorry, I can't tonight," she said, twisting her hair up in a messy bun before putting the Jeep in gear and rumbling back onto the deserted and pocked roadway. "But you should go. Rush Tide always has great bands. And the best drinks. Definitely. Have fun."

"Why don't you want to go together? What's happening back at the resort that you'd rather do than spend time with me?" he tried sounding playful but even to his own ears he sounded defensive, which was fair seeing as he was deeply disappointed and feeling a bit like a leper. He was good enough to sleep with but not spend any real time with? Good God, he truly was turning into a woman. "I mean, yeah, it's cool. I just like hanging out with you. I think the feeling's mutual, right?" he asked, fishing just a little. Maybe he was way off base here. Maybe… Ah hell, he hated this guessing game.

She smiled as she made a quick turn into a tiny eatery, so tiny in fact, Justin would've missed it because it looked like someone's house, not a restaurant. "Justin, I thought we went over this. Of course I like spending time with you." She lowered her gaze and blushed just a little. "I mean, I don't have casual sex with just anyone. I like you a lot, but that's sort of the problem. My life—"

"Is complicated and there's no room for a *plus one,* I get it," Justin finished for her, a bit irritated that he couldn't just let it go. "Trust me, there's no room in my life, either. But, we're pretty good together. We definitely click sexually, why not see where this could go? Just for fun?"

Lilah's gaze sobered. "And what happens if one gets

more attached than the other? Someone is going to get hurt."

Ah, he thought with sudden understanding. She was afraid of getting hurt. Someone must've hurt her in the past. He'd show her that he wasn't that guy. He softly knuckled her cheek and said, "I would never hurt you, gorgeous. I swear it."

She surprised him with a low chuckle. "I know that. I was talking about you."

Justin stared. She was afraid he was going to be hurt? That he was going to get too attached? Ha. But as a quick denial bubbled to the surface, he realized, hot damn, she could see right through him. If he didn't know better he'd say he was falling for Lilah in record time. Even if he was blind, she obviously was not. He pulled away and chuckled darkly. "Right. Okay. It's all good." A sigh rattled out of his chest and a scowl threatened even though he tried his best to smother it under a flippant smile. "I just thought it'd be cool to get to know each other. But I'm good with just screwing around if that's your thing. Trust me, I'm more than good with that."

And he was lying through his ever-loving teeth.

Hopefully, she couldn't tell that, too.

"So, where's that place to eat? I'm starved."

LILAH FELT THE MOOD CHANGE as if it were a physical thing and guilt nagged at her. Wasn't it better to be honest? *Well, you're not exactly being totally honest, now are you?* A snarky voice countered to her exasperated self. No, she supposed she wasn't. But she'd rather preserve the illusion that she was pushing him away for superficial reasons rather than because she was reluctant to share her dirty little secret. She could only imagine how that adoring light in his eyes would dim if she were to tell him what she'd done only a few short months ago. She heard Dr. Veronica's voice in her head, advising her to abstain from any deep romantic attachments while still healing emotionally and her resolve strengthened by a grim notch. This was better...no attachments. He would leave St. John with great memories and she'd go on with her life, healing and growing.

It was the sensible, responsible thing to do. Dr. Veronica would approve.

So, why did Lilah feel a lead weight in her chest?

Did she feel this way organically? Or was it a product of her depression? She worried her lip without thought but Justin caught the telling motion.

"Why are you pushing me away? Something's wrong. I can feel it. I know we haven't known each other long but...whatever it is, you can tell me. You can trust me."

Trust me.

The words hung heavy and obtrusive between them, an elephant in a crowded room.

I'm not supposed to date.

I tried to kill myself.

She opened her mouth but the words died in her throat. She couldn't tell him that. He was a stranger and as a stranger wasn't burdened by the knowledge of her recent past. To him, she was simply a normal, perhaps slightly enigmatic, girl.

And she wanted to keep it that way.

Lilah sent a blinding smile his way, concealing the odd pang in her heart at shutting him out, and said, "You see things that aren't there. And this conversation is way too serious for such a wonderful day. Let's keep it light, okay?" She didn't wait for him to agree and simply popped from the Jeep toward the restaurant. "You coming? Best johnnycakes around St. John. I promise you'll love it. Come on, slowpoke." She cast one last look Justin's way and saw him exiting the car, a perplexed expression lingering behind the easy smile she was beginning to suspect was his defense, just as walking away was hers.

CHAPTER NINE

BY THE TIME LILAH AND JUSTIN had suffered through a painfully awkward and tense lunch and a quiet drive back to Larimar, Lilah was more than ready to escape to her room, but as Justin left her with a flip goodbye Lora waylaid her in the foyer.

Lilah tried not to let her gaze follow Justin as he disappeared from the main lobby but it was as if her eyes were locked on target and wouldn't let go until he was out of sight. When she reluctantly dragged her stare back to Lora, it was then she realized Lora was hardly ever behind the reception desk. "What are you doing? Where's Celly?" she asked.

Lora's jaw tensed in a subtle manner as she answered. "Celly has quit, which is probably for the best. She wasn't a very good fit here at Larimar and I've been trying to find someone to replace her for quite a while."

Lilah's eyes bugged and she shook her head as if Lora's statement didn't make sense, because frankly, it didn't. "Celly wouldn't quit," she stated flatly. "What did you do? Did you fire her?"

"Of course not," Lora shot back. "Don't put this one on me. She quit of her own accord. Just ask Heath."

"I will," Lilah said, her ears becoming hot as something close to anger and panic coalesced into a toxic mess inside her. "What happened?"

Lora didn't look as if she were interested in answering questions and thus, simply shrugged. "I tidied her desk and she overreacted. Now—" she drew a deep breath and squared her shoulders "—we need to talk about other things. Such as who were you with? You know how I feel about dating the patrons. It sets a bad example. I know it worked out for Lindy but let's not make a habit of using Larimar's guests for a dating pool. Okay?"

Lilah stared at her sister, freshly irritated that she could so easily sweep under the rug that she'd somehow gotten rid of Celly and then chastise her for going out with a patron. Of the two, in Lilah's mind, Lora had committed the bigger sin. "Celly cannot be replaced," Lilah said in a low voice, nearly trembling with anger. "And I don't need you telling me who I can and can't date."

"Lilah, I'm not trying to be bossy," Lora said. "I'm just trying to look out for everyone's best interests. And as far as Celly goes…she made her choice."

"You did something to make her leave," Lilah said. "I need to talk to her."

At that Lora slammed the papers she'd been shuffling onto the desk with more force than necessary. "Why does everyone assume I'm the bad guy in this? Celly was an employee. Not a member of this family. I don't know why everyone feels the need to rush to her defense but I get thrown under the bus."

"Because she *is* family!" Lilah practically shouted, shocking Lora. "She helps take care of Pops, she cooks all our favorite meals, and she helps Larimar run smoothly when it should be falling down around our damn ears! How is it that *you're* the only one who doesn't see how everyone loves her!" Lora blinked and the corners of her mouth turned down but she otherwise remained silent, the stubborn woman. Lilah threw her hands up and did an about-face. "I need to talk to Celly. Maybe salvage this mess before it's too late and we lose someone else in this family."

Lilah climbed back into the Jeep and wiped away the tears that had begun to leak down her face. *Damn you, Lora.*

And damn you, too, Justin.

Perhaps it wasn't fair to throw Justin into the blame category but it felt good to vent her anger over how their afternoon had ended. She'd been on a glorious high until he'd started pushing, wanting more than she was offering.

And now Celly was gone? The world had tipped upside down in a space of five hours.

Since when did guys want to get all lovey-dovey? What guy wouldn't love the chance to simply let things remain superficial? Sure, she was stereotyping but the reason stereotypes existed was because there was a certain amount of truth to them.

Maybe she should've just accepted his offer to go to Rush Tide. Where was the harm? It wasn't as if she was afraid of falling in love with him. She knew it was a vacation thing for him and that was okay with her. So why'd she shut him down so quickly?

Was she afraid of becoming attached?

Don't be silly and start focusing on what's truly important—getting Celly back. A transient patron who just so happens to make her stomach do strange things was not the priority.

Besides, as much as she hated to admit it, Lora was

right. Dating the patrons was probably a bad idea, even if it had worked out really well for Lindy.

Speaking of... Lilah put the Jeep in gear and pulled out onto the road. She couldn't wait for Lindy to get here. She needed some twin time in the worst way.

LILAH CHECKED THE ADDRESS and pulled into the overgrown driveway to park in front of a tiny house that appeared as though a stiff wind might tear it down. Lilah blinked at the poor conditions and her ire at Lora bloomed fresh. "Celly?" she called out, exiting the Jeep and walking toward the front door. The jungle foliage crept and intruded on the small yard until it was difficult to discern where the yard started and stopped. She frowned, wondering why Celly didn't ask Heath to do some clearing for her. He'd gladly do it if he knew Celly needed it. Lilah made a mental note to ask him herself.

She knocked on the weathered front door and waited. It was several minutes before the door opened a crack and Celly peered out from behind the door. Her eyes registered surprise until a frown quickly formed. "What are yah doing here?" she queried.

"Celly, I just found out about what happened at Larimar. Or, actually, I don't really know what happened but whatever it was, I hope we can make it better because we need you."

"Bah, yah don't need an old woman like me. Lora made that perfectly clear," Celly said.

"Can I come in for a minute?" Lilah asked, perplexed by the way Celly was acting. Celly hesitated but finally relented. "All yah Bells de same. Stubborn and nosy," she muttered, opening the door and walking away.

Lilah followed Celly into the musty house, her nose

tingling at the mildly damp smell, and wondered how Celly lived in these conditions but she kept any comment to herself for fear of offending the older woman.

Lilah took a seat on an aged sofa while Celly settled herself into an equally old and threadbare chair. "What happened?" Lilah asked, getting right to the point. When Celly remained stubbornly silent, Lilah pressed gently. "Listen, I know Lora can be as prickly as a sea urchin sometimes but she's just under a lot of pressure. I'm sure she didn't mean whatever she said to offend you."

Celly harrumphed and looked away. "Dat woman is worse than sea urchin."

Lilah sighed. "Celly, I'm sorry that she's difficult to get to know but she's trying to make everything work and sometimes she gets so focused on the problems, she forgets about the people. But her intentions are good. You know that, right?"

Celly shrugged but Lilah sensed she was gaining some ground. "Please come back. I'm sure Lora is sorry."

Celly pinned Lilah with a sharp look. "If she so sorry, why are yah here saying it instead of her?"

Lilah squirmed a little. Good point. "Deep down Lora is sorry, but she's stubborn…like you. Give her time. She'll come around."

"No."

"Celly," Lilah implored, unable to believe how obstinate the older woman was being. "Come on…please?"

At that Celly's hard gaze softened a little and she said, "Lilah girl, yah good soul. Yah spend yah time and energy caring for everyone but yahself. It's time for yah to worry about yah own pretty skin. Lora is a

big girl. If she so sorry…she can find me. Until then…
I stay here."

Lilah couldn't help but cast a dubious glance around
the dilapidated home and Celly stiffened. "Keep yah
eyes in yah head. Nothing wrong with my home. I've
lived here since I was a chile and my parents lived here
before dat."

"Oh, gosh, I'm sorry, Celly," Lilah said, immediately
chastised for being so transparently appalled at her living conditions. "I didn't mean to offend you. I'm sure
it's a great place, but it seems that it's fallen…apart."
She bit her lip. "I'm sorry. Why haven't you asked Heath
to come and help you out with some of these repairs?
You know he would."

Celly lifted her birdlike chin. "I don't need charity.
I work for whatever goes into my pocket."

"Of course, Celly. It's not charity when you help out
family." She reached over and grasped Celly's hand.
"And you are family. Just as much as Heath is, you
know that, right?"

Celly blinked away the sudden shine in her eyes and
murmured, "Yah a sweet chile, girl. But not everyone
feels as yah do. That's just the way of tings as dey are."

Lilah stifled a sigh. Celly needed to hear the words
from Lora, not her. And likely, Lora would rather
eat a Japanese pufferfish than apologize. Lilah rose.
"Celly, your job is waiting for you. I promise. Come
back when you're ready." She walked to the door, then
turned. "Also, I'm sending Heath over to do some repairs. And don't even think about saying no because I
won't listen." She sent a quick look around the small

house, then muttered, "And neither will Heath so don't waste your breath."

"Stubborn Bell," Celly called out after her, and Lilah smiled. Yeah, she supposed that was accurate.

CHAPTER TEN

LORA DRAGGED HERSELF TO BED, her head throbbing. The day had been a trying one to say the least. She changed out of her clothes, slipped into something that flowed loosely around her body and slid into the bed beside Heath, grateful for the day's end.

She and Heath were still at odds but he reached over and started rubbing her shoulders when he saw the tension in her body. "Everything all right?" he asked.

"No," she admitted wearily. "Pops kept asking for Celly and when he couldn't understand why she wasn't around, he became more confused. It was awful."

Heath's sigh said volumes. She looked at him sharply. "She quit. I didn't fire her," she said defensively.

Heath's mouth tightened but he remained silent and continued to rub her shoulders. His touch soothed the knotted muscles but did nothing for the turmoil in her head. Celly was the one who had overreacted. Not her. So she'd tidied her desk a little…was that really cause to freak out and quit? A small, nagging voice reminded her that she hadn't been welcoming to Celly from the minute they'd met. But surely, they'd gotten over that small bump since then? "Everyone treats me the same as before even though I've changed. Why doesn't anyone see that?"

"Sometimes you're stubborn, that's all. What you

need to do is go to Celly and simply apologize. That's all she wants."

Lora frowned, irritated. "Why should I apologize? I didn't do anything worth apologizing for."

"How about going to her and clearing the air? You know, I think you felt threatened by Celly, like somehow she was going to replace Grams, but you know that's not true. She's a part of Larimar and we need her. And, honestly, she needs us, too. She doesn't have any family left on the island, and she's embraced the Bells in her own way. What more could you want in a loyal employee other than someone who truly cares about the place and people they work for?"

Damn, she hated when Heath was right and she was wrong. She sighed and turned to him, wrapping her arms around his solid torso and burying her nose against his skin. "I know she's not going to replace Grams. But I get prickly when I'm around her. I don't know why."

"It's because you hate change," Heath said, a smile in his voice. "But change isn't all bad."

"Says who?" she groused, internally processing his point. He was right; she hated change. But to be fair, change in her life had rarely come without painful consequences. She preferred order and stability to the chaos of new adventures or new people. "The damage is done. I doubt she'll come back even if I begged, which I won't do, anyway. It's a moot point. I just need to find someone to fill her spot."

"Lora…" Heath's disappointment weighed heavy in his voice and she lifted to meet his gaze. "You're making it ten times worse than it needs to be. You two need to sit down and have a heart-to-heart. That's all.

And then things will improve between you. I can almost guarantee it."

She scowled. "You don't know that and I don't feel like sacrificing my dignity to beg someone to work for me."

"How about begging someone who cares about this family to return because we all miss her?"

Lora groaned and pulled away from Heath. "I'm tired and my head is ready to explode," she said, turning on her side and communicating that she didn't want to talk about it any longer. She hated being on the opposite side of *everyone,* but it particularly hurt when Heath wasn't on her side. Tears tingled behind her eyes and she squeezed them shut to block the moisture from escaping.

Why did the hard decisions always fall in her lap?

JUSTIN WOKE IN A FOUL MOOD, still unsettled by the way things had ended between him and Lilah yesterday, but he was determined to get her out of his mind. If she didn't want to hang with him, fine. There were plenty of beautiful women just waiting to spend a little quality time at his side.

Well, at least there were in New York.

Here on an island paradise he shouldn't have a problem finding someone to waste a few hours with.

He spent a long time under the cool spray of the outdoor shower and then dressed quickly.

Whistling to himself, he passed by the open dining room and saw Lilah fixing breakfast. He should've kept walking, barely taking notice of the petite, lithe woman, but just the sight of her tugged at him and made him feel as if the humidity in the air had suddenly worsened. He sucked air through his lungs but his heart was kicking up a rapid staccato.

Her hair was tucked into a messy bun on top of her head and plenty of tendrils were drifting along her cheekbones, gently swaying on the subtle breeze coming through the wide-open portal. She wore a light gauzy skirt that dusted her ankles and a tank top that wrapped tightly around her middle, baring a tiny expanse of golden skin that he distinctly remembered tasting just yesterday.

Damn it. He shook off the desire to join her for breakfast as if all was forgotten and forgiven and instead purposefully strode away. Justin Cales did not moon over any chick. No matter how adorable she looked in her hippie-chic outfits or how his breathing still hadn't returned to normal.

And definitely no matter how miserable he felt at the prospect of simply roaming around St. John without her gorgeous behind right beside him.

He muttered an expletive and climbed into the rental Suzuki Tracker that looked as if a donkey had used it for target practice, determined to have a good time without her.

LILAH SAW JUSTIN IN her peripheral vision but pretended otherwise. She held her breath, wondering if he was going to casually stroll in and grab a banana as if things hadn't ended so awkwardly between them or if he was going to ignore her.

A part of her hoped he kept walking. An angry Justin would likely move on more quickly, but she actually hated the idea of Justin being angry with her even more than she disliked the fact that he'd walked right past her as if she hadn't existed.

Oh, geesh. Pick a side, she told herself crossly. *You can't be so wishy-washy.* She wanted to discourage any attachments and so, her method had worked. If only she didn't feel unsettled inside, almost carsick at the thought of what he must be thinking about her at this very moment.

She took a bite of banana and slowly chewed, frowning as she processed the mess in her head. Pops interrupted her mental turmoil by adding his own. He'd been having some bad days, which had only worsened when Celly left.

"Morning, Pops," Lilah said, forcing a smile as if it were the most natural thing in the world to see her Pops looking as lost as a baby sea turtle far from the shore. "Are you hungry?" Pops turned hazy eyes toward her, his mouth working subtly, as a confused frown marred his beloved face. Lilah swallowed and the butterflies in her stomach worsened. "Pops? What's wrong?"

"Well, it's just sad news. Just sad, sad news."

"What sad news?"

"She's gone. Our Lisa…she's gone. Lana she's holding it together but… Well, her heart is broken."

Lilah sucked in a tight breath at the mention of her mother and realized Pops was talking about when her mother died. She exhaled softly and nodded, not sure what to say. "It's very sad, Pops," she agreed. "But she's in a better place now."

God, how she hated that saying but she didn't know what else to offer.

"We always wanted more babies," he admitted, wiping at his eyes. "But all we had was Lisa. She was our island treasure. Ahhh, Lisa…and she's left behind three babies. It's hard to know what to tell them, they're so young. Especially the twins."

Tears sprang to Lilah's eyes and she choked back a well of grief that bubbled from a hidden spot of pain buried deep inside her. "It's okay, Pops," she managed, grinding the tears from her eyes. "It's okay. They have you and Grams. They're so lucky."

He seemed lost in a memory, shaking his head with raw sorrow that was tinged with confusion, and Lilah wanted to run away from the evidence that Pops was rapidly deteriorating. She dropped her banana to the counter and wrapped herself tightly around her grandfather. "I love you, Pops," she whispered. "You and Grams were always there for us. Don't be sad. Please don't be sad."

Pops patted her back and she inhaled the soft scent of coconut that lingered on his skin from the sunscreen he wore and she wished she could go back in time to when life was simple and straightforward.

"What are we going to do without her?" he murmured in a cracked voice that splintered her heart. She wasn't sure if he was talking about Lana or her mother. Perhaps he didn't know, either.

"I'm here for you, Pops. We're all here. Your sugar birds," she said.

"Sugar birds…sweet, sugar birds," he repeated as if saying the words gave him strength. "Yes…we always have our sugar birds."

"Always, Pops," she said. "Always."

Standing in the dining room, hugging her beloved grandfather, Lilah wondered how they'd manage to get through everything they were facing without losing their sanity. Was it any wonder she'd walked into the ocean? The threat of losing everything they'd ever cared about was almost too much to bear. But she'd never take such a cowardly step again. Her Pops needed her.

Her family needed her. Even though she was scared to death of failing, she'd give everything she had to Larimar.

She owed it to Pops and Grams.

Which left little room for pining over men who had no permanent place in her life.

She drew a shaky breath and pulled away from Pops. "Want to share some papaya on the patio with me? You can tell me stories of how you wooed Grams with your irrepressible charm," she teased through a sheen of silent tears.

At the mention of his past with his soul mate, he brightened. "Papaya is my favorite, you know."

"Of course I know that," she said, smiling as she grabbed a papaya and the necessary tools to cut and serve. "And I also know that you love to tell stories. So let's go, I can't wait to hear a few."

And it struck her as they walked to the patio that there would come a day when Pops wouldn't be around to share his stories—whether they were made up or true, the girls were never quite sure—so she was going to savor every moment she had left with him.

CHAPTER ELEVEN

THE NEXT FEW DAYS PASSED by in a blur as everyone pulled double shifts to keep Larimar flowing on an even keel, which was no small feat given how many bad days Pops had been having. Lilah knew it was because Celly's disappearance had thrown off his routine but Lora stubbornly refused to simply set things right with a much needed sit-down with the older woman. Lilah checked on Celly each day to make sure she was doing okay, but also to try and persuade her to return, but Celly was as stubborn as Lora and both refused to budge.

The only upside to an otherwise irritatingly frustrating few days was that Lindy was flying in that afternoon.

In fact, Lindy and her newly adopted gang were all coming. It would be good to see Carys, Lindy's eleven-year-old soon-to-be stepdaughter who was a Bell in sheep's clothing. Lilah had never met a child so similar to Lindy in spirit and attitude than that towheaded precocious girl and Lilah loved every sassy bit of her.

As excited as she was to have her twin home for a few weeks, Lilah was not looking forward to the family meeting on the schedule.

They'd been putting their collective heads together to think of a way to make Larimar more profitable in a short time frame and they'd been hitting brick walls.

Sure, they'd made the IRS payments—by the skin of their teeth—but that wasn't a way to sustain the resort in the long-term.

Which was exactly why Lora always had dark circles under her eyes; she worried enough for them all.

Yet, they still didn't know how to save Larimar.

And that scared them spitless.

The very idea of losing their foundation was enough to make them *all* lose their marbles.

"What time is Lindy's flight?" Lora asked, checking her phone for the daily schedule.

"Noon," Lilah answered. "I'm picking her up at the ferry at one-thirty."

"Good. Hopefully she won't be too jet-lagged to have the meeting tonight."

"I'm sure she'll soldier through," Lilah said wryly. If Lora had changed since falling in love, Lindy had, as well. In fact, before Lindy had met and fallen in love with Gabe, Lindy had been a bit of a… Well, *flirt* is a mild term. Lilah loved her twin to death but Lindy had always been a wild child. Now she was settled and more mature with a kid no less and she was loving her new role as if she'd been born to it. Which was downright *Twilight Zone*-ish.

But if changes were to be made, Lilah supposed these were the good kind to make.

She wondered wistfully what kind of changes love would make to her. Immediately—and unwelcome— Justin's adorable mug jumped to mind and she frowned. Fall in love with Justin Cales? An admitted playboy who was here today and gone tomorrow? Not bloody likely. Her gaze drifted to the pile of paperwork that needed filing from the previous day's checkouts and she sighed. Who had time to fall in love? Not this chick, that was for sure.

So why did her gaze inadvertently search out glimpses of Justin around the resort? Admittedly, her heart did a little happy dance when she saw him now and then as he went about his business. She tried not to notice that he didn't smile or wave when he went by. She tried not to take offense when he plainly seemed amenable to her suggestion that they remain casual.

But she'd be a liar if she didn't admit that she wished he'd ignored her refusal and simply pursued her anyway.

Well, it was a woman's prerogative to be fickle, right?

Another deep sigh escaped and she fought to shake off the melancholy she felt creeping toward her like an unwelcome shadow. A yawn surprised her and she rubbed at her eyes. She hadn't slept well last night. Too many worries, too many thoughts crowding her brain. At first she feared the insomnia was returning but after yoga on the beach, she felt far more centered and balanced and the worry dissipated.

But the yearning for someone she couldn't have simply wouldn't abate no matter how many times she drew deep calming breaths and stretched her muscles until she was as loose as a fatigued rubber band.

So when Justin happened to pass by, wearing board shorts that accentuated his lean, narrow waist and showed off way too much golden skin, she couldn't help the hello that popped from her mouth.

Which was mistake number one.

JUSTIN WAS DOING A BANG-UP job ignoring Lilah's presence every day, purposefully striding past her without so much as glancing her way as he went about his day exploring the island and enjoying his forced vacation, but the minute he heard his name on her lips, his feet took over and he spun around with a silly jump in his heart.

"Yeah?" he queried, knowing he should've pretended not to hear her and kept walking. Damn, did she always have to look so beautiful? It was like staring at an angel who had fallen to earth or something. He didn't even have the right words to describe how she took his breath away, only that he went to sleep thinking of her, spent the evenings dreaming about her, and spent way too much time trying to find new and inventive ways to avoid being around her. And yet, when he had the opportunity to move to the Worchester, he'd canceled his reservation.

Smooth move.

But there was something about Larimar that spoke to him, and it didn't have everything to do with Lilah. There was an energy in the resort that resonated within him, made him feel right at home in spite of having never been there before.

He wasn't normally a woo-woo type of guy but there was a real sense of family at Larimar that he knew he wouldn't find at the Worchester.

Maybe it was because his dad was being such a royal prick that he found comfort in someone else's family, if even peripherally, but he liked the vibe at Larimar and he wasn't leaving until his vacation was over.

All he had to do was, somehow, stop hoping for a little attention from the cute blonde who was tipping his world upside down.

"So what's on your agenda today?" she asked.

He shrugged. "Beach, water, rum. In no particular order, of course."

"Of course," she said, smiling. "Did you have a chance to check out The Wild Donkey?"

"To eat boiled bananas? I confess, not really high on my desirable list, but I did get a fresh fruit smoothie from that guy in the plaza. You're right, it's pretty damn divine. Who knew fruit could be so good, right?" He should've grinned and waved goodbye, keeping it as casual as she said she wanted it, but now that he was talking to her again, he couldn't bring himself to walk away. The natural light in the foyer picked up the sun-kissed highlights in her blond hair, giving a halo effect that only made her look more ethereal than she already did in his mind. "Got a lot on your plate today?" he asked.

She nodded, excited. "My twin sister and her family are flying in today. I'm picking them up at the ferry."

"You're a twin," he said, surprised and a little intrigued. "Identical?"

"No, fraternal. And we couldn't be more different."

He wasn't sure the world could handle more than one Lilah running around anyway. How pathetic was it that he wanted to fish for an invitation to go with her to pick up her sister? Very. And because of that, he kept his mouth tightly sealed. A guy had his dignity.

"I noticed you're still with us," she said brightly, switching directions. "I would've thought you might've moved to the Worchester by now."

"I like it here," he said with a shrug. "Besides, I think I'm in love with the outdoor shower. If I didn't run the risk of freezing my balls off, I'd have one installed at my place in upstate New York."

"You have a place in upstate New York?" she murmured, then remembered, "Ah, that's right. Private school kid."

"Says the girl living on a tropical island at a five-star resort," he teased.

Her cheeks colored a bit as she laughed ruefully. "It's not quite the same but I get your point. However, looks can be deceiving. We're not rich by any means."

Justin cast a speculative look around the surroundings, then said, "Well, it looks like you're doing all right just the same."

"We are," she agreed. "So…have fun at the beach. Lift a glass for me while you're out and about."

He took that as a sign it was time to make his exit gracefully but he was enjoying himself too much to listen to the voice in his head. Besides, it'd been days— almost a damn week, actually— since he'd been with Lilah and he was jonesing for a fix from his island girl. The question was, how to convince her she needed the same…

But logic told him that with her twin sister flying in, Lilah's attentions would swing toward her family. He was an only child so he didn't have those kinds of attachments. Sometimes he wished he'd had a brother so his father would've split his single-minded focus between two targets. Alas, Justin was the bearer of all those good intentions as his mother would say.

Good intentions, my ass. More like fulfilling an ego stroke.

He dodged the direction of his suddenly dark thoughts and moved away from the counter. "Have fun with your sister," he said, smiling.

She returned the smile and nodded. Justin turned and walked away, his step decidedly lighter as he realized with a triumphant grin that he'd seen disappointment lurking in his beautiful islander's eyes. His grin deepened as he formulated a plan to destroy her resistance. By this Friday, he'd have her in his arms again.

Now that was a goal worth shooting for.

CHAPTER TWELVE

LINDY BELL, SOON-TO-BE Lindy Weston, had butterflies in her stomach, which had begun fluttering around her midsection somewhere over Florida. By the time their plane had landed in St. Thomas, Lindy was fairly certain she might need to throw up.

She missed her sisters and the island so much that it was always like this when she came to visit but this time felt worse than usual.

"You okay?" Gabe asked, reaching over to gently rub her hand. "Do you need some ginger ale or seltzer water?"

"I'm fine. I'm just excited to see my family and eat Colly's cooking."

"I do miss those boiled bananas," Gabe agreed, settling back in his seat.

They flew first-class so there was plenty of legroom for the long flight, which was nice, but there was no getting around the fact that the flight always felt as if it took years from her life. Carys, her future stepdaughter, was accustomed to the long flight, having made this trip with Lindy several times, and was entertaining herself with a plethora of electronic gadgets.

Lindy had long since lost interest in the magazines she'd brought and was anxiously awaiting their landing. It's funny, before Lilah's momentary lapse of sanity, she'd go months without seeing her twin because she'd been living in Los Angeles doing the actress thing and couldn't always afford hopping a plane to return home.

But now, it seemed that spending time with her family was the most important priority.

Maybe because sometimes at night, she relived that moment when Lilah sank beneath the waves and in her nightmares, Lilah's fine silk blond hair slipped through her fingers and she drowned. Her chest tightened as the breath seemed caught in her lungs and Gabe's reassuring touch brought her back to the here and now. "Are you sure you're okay? You seem on edge," he remarked, concerned.

"I am a little," she admitted. "I just feel as if something big is in the air and it makes me nervous. I mean, that's how it'd felt right before..."

None of them liked to talk about Lilah's suicide attempt. The words always seemed like poison in their mouths. But the fact was plain and stark. Lilah had tried to drown herself. If it hadn't been for Lindy...

"Hey," Gabe said softly, snagging her chin gently. "Everything is going to be fine. Lilah is fine. The last time you talked she was doing great. There's no need to borrow trouble where there isn't any, right?"

She allowed a reluctant smile. "You're right. She's fine. I'm just...I don't know...feeling weird. I'll be fine as soon as we get to Larimar."

Gabe smiled and settled back again to close his eyes for a bit. God, she loved that man. How she ever got so lucky was beyond her but she wasn't about to second-guess fate's benevolence. She followed Gabe's lead and closed her eyes. With any luck, she'd catch some z's and before she knew it, they'd be in St. Thomas.

LILAH SQUEALED WITH OPEN JOY as soon as she caught sight of Lindy and her gang disembarking from the ferry in Cruz Bay. She didn't waste time and simply ran to her twin sister and hugged her tightly.

Gabe wore a grin as he waited a safe distance while the sisters squealed and danced and hopped up and down in each other's arms, because he'd been witness to this scene many times since becoming a part of the Bell household.

Not to be left out however, Carys ran and wiggled her way between Lindy and Lilah, her high-pitched squeals only adding to the decibel level.

Lilah pressed a kiss to Carys's forehead when they were finished hugging. "Have you grown again?" she exclaimed, knowing Carys loved it when Lilah fussed over her. "I'm fairly certain you are a few inches taller since I saw you last."

"It's possible, she's always insisting on new clothes," Lindy teased. "A trip to the mall is always an expensive one."

"Hey, I *am* growing," Carys insisted, looking to Lilah. "You just said I looked taller, right?"

"Absolutely," Lilah agreed wholeheartedly, giving Carys's chin a gentle shake to emphasis the point. Carys rewarded her with a blinding smile, which Lilah returned. She loved this kid. "How was the flight?" she asked as they started walking to the Jeep.

"Long but uneventful. Last trip, the turbulence over Florida freaked me out. I thought we were going to land in the Everglades and get eaten by crocodiles," Lindy answered with a shudder. "Glad to be home, though. What's new? I haven't heard from you in a few weeks. Anything up?"

Lilah heard the faint fear in her sister's tone even though she tried to mask it with a lighthearted smile and it hurt that she'd caused that worry. If she hadn't tried to kill herself, Lindy wouldn't have thought twice about a few absent phone calls. She gave Lindy a knowing smile. "Everything is fine. More than fine, actually," she said, immediately thinking of Justin. "I've just been busy that's all."

Gabe nudged Lindy. "See? I told you. No need for worry." To Lilah he said, "I thought your sister was about to drop out of her play she was so anxious to return to Larimar. Somehow I convinced her not to, but the plane ride was not only long, I think she bit her nails clean off."

At that Lindy hid her fingernails behind her back with a sheepish smile. "It's a twin thing, I guess. I was on edge for some reason. Are you sure there's nothing going on?"

Lilah weighed the possibility of sharing her feelings about Justin but as she glanced at the trio, she realized it was a private conversation if she were going to have it at all. She trusted Lindy but she worried that Lindy would side with Lora and start warning her off from dating. And frankly, Lilah didn't want to hear it parroted at her from all angles. "Will you stop worrying?" she said, allowing a hint of exasperation to leak into her tone. "I'm fine. What's wrong with you? What happened to my devil-may-care twin sister?"

"That's my fault," Gabe said. "I made her all civilized and responsible when I asked her to be my wife."

"And my mom," Carys chimed in. "She even makes me eat vegetables."

Lindy laughed. "It's true. I've turned into a suburban

housewife and the ceremony hasn't even taken place yet."

Lilah grinned, then whispered to Carys, "Lindy never ate her vegetables unless they were slathered in cheese. Grams said with as much cheese as she ate, she'd never be able to go to the bathroom again."

Carys giggled and Lindy glared at Lilah for sharing secrets but it was all in fun and it felt so good to joke around like they used to in the old days.

But Lilah had forgotten to mention one crucial detail, one that was immediately noticed the minute they walked into the lobby of Larimar.

"Where's Celly?"

Carys's question seemed to echo off the travertine tile floor and Lilah turned to Lora who was manning the front desk.

Lora's mouth pinched with irritation and perhaps guilt as she sent Lilah a dark look for not preparing them before they arrived. "She quit," Lora said brusquely but forced a smile for everyone. "But we're all still here. Welcome home!"

But it didn't feel like home and Lilah knew by the crestfallen expression on Carys's face and the shocked expression on Lindy's face that this issue was not over no matter how Lora hoped it would be.

No…now that Lindy was home…Lora was going to get a fresh earful.

And Lilah couldn't say that Lora didn't deserve it.

HEATH HUGGED LINDY AND CARYS and shook Gabe's hand, but even as it was a happy moment, the undercurrent of tension was palpable between the sisters. He withheld a sigh. He supposed some things would never change.

"How about I man the desk while you girls catch up?" He tossed keys to Gabe. "Bungalow number two is ready for you."

Gabe, sensing the undercurrent as well, took the hint. "C'mon, Carys, let's get settled in and maybe rinse off some of the travel dirt."

"That's what the beach is for, Dad," Carys said, but followed her dad just the same.

Gabe had just cleared the lobby when Lindy started peppering Lora with questions.

"What do you mean Celly quit? How could this happen? She loved it here. We were her family."

Lora ground her teeth and actually snapped. "Well, apparently she was just an employee because she didn't have a problem walking out on us when we needed her most."

"That's not true, Lora," Lilah chimed in, scowling hard. "You can't tell a half-truth. You have been treating her like an outsider since the day you returned and then you went and rearranged her space when she had a system that was working quite well."

"A system," Lora scoffed. "It was chaos. Who knows how many clients we've lost due to that mess."

"No clients were lost. She had a system that worked and you came along and pushed your nose where it didn't belong and instead of apologizing like you should, you've stubbornly refused."

"Lora—" Lindy started but Lora cut her off.

"I am not going to stand here and let you two gang up on me for making a hard decision. And for the record, I didn't start this, she did. I am her boss—"

"That's the problem right there," Lindy's voice rose over Lora's. "She was more than an employee."

"Says who?"

"Says us!" both Lindy and Lilah said with exasperation.

Lora stared and tears actually welled in her eyes but before they could make amends, she turned on her heel and walked stiffly away. "Fine," she called over her shoulder. "You obviously love her more than your actual sister. Please, by all means, do what you feel is right. I sure as hell don't have a clue, it would appear."

Heath muttered an expletive. "Did you have to tag team her?"

"We didn't mean to," Lilah said.

"But she's plainly not listening to reason," Lindy added. "How hard is it to go see an old woman and say 'I'm sorry'?"

"Out of the entire English language, you know those two words are the hardest for your sister to say," Heath said. "Cut her some slack. She's under a lot of pressure."

"We all are, Heath," Lilah reminded him. "Which is why we shouldn't be cutting off our nose to spite our face. We need Celly. Pops is a wreck without her. She provided some semblance of routine for him and now, it's all out of whack and he's deteriorating quickly."

"How bad?" Lindy asked, her expression worried. "Worse than the last time I was here?"

"Much worse," Lilah answered sadly. "I think we're losing him much more quickly than we anticipated."

"What does the doctor say?" Lindy asked.

"The doctor said structure is important, keeping a routine, which is why it was so devastating when Celly left. We didn't realize all the things she would do for Pops because we were off doing our own thing but Celly really kept things moving smoothly."

Heath didn't want to side with the sisters but there was a certain level of truth to Lilah's statement that he couldn't deny. "We need to get Celly back without making Lora out to be the bad guy." When both sisters simply stared at him, he threw his hands up and said, "Look, there's gotta be a way. They're both being stubborn. End of story. I went out to her place and tried to talk to her but she's being as rigid as Lora so there are two sides to this story."

Lilah sighed. "Well, he's right about that. I went out there, too. She's being a pill even though she wants to come back. I can tell."

"Maybe a visit from Carys will change her mind. She dotes on the kid," Lindy offered.

"True," Lilah said, nodding. "That might be the ticket, actually. How about tomorrow?"

"Sounds good to me."

Heath breathed an audible sound of relief. "I'll be happy to work on Lora if you guys can work on Celly. This feud has to stop. We have enough on our plates. We don't need to add this to the mix."

Lindy stretched, relief in her expression. "Okay, now that's settled, I think I'm going to go change and hit the beach with the new fam if that's okay with you guys. We have that business meeting tonight after dinner, right?" Heath nodded and Lindy sighed. "Then I definitely want some beach time before that happens. Something tells me it's not going to be pretty."

Heath couldn't agree more. Larimar's fate seemed to be resting precariously on too many what-if ledges.

To Lilah, he said, "I'll take the desk if you want to hit the beach with Lindy."

"Thanks, Heath," Lilah said, smiling. "I'll take you up on that offer."

Heath watched as Lilah and Lindy walked in opposite directions to their respective rooms and he wondered if Larimar was going to survive everyone's good intentions.

Hell, even he was guilty of grand plans and crappy follow-through.

His gaze wandered to the gift shop that he'd hoped would be Larimar's salvation with his fused glass creations and was swamped by regret and guilt.

The fused glass wasn't selling badly, but it wasn't moving as readily as he'd hoped. After much discussion, they'd all agreed it was time to return some tourist-friendly merchandise to the shelves to give the patrons more options.

Talk about hopes and dreams crashing and burning.

Yeah, tonight's meeting was likely to be as pleasant as a sugarcane-flogging on wet skin.

But it couldn't be helped.

Something had to be done.

CHAPTER THIRTEEN

JUSTIN TOOK A SEAT at the bar at Rush Tide and smiled at the bartender, a woman he recognized as the waitress Lilah had been talking to that first night. A gold necklace with the name Donna was strung around her neck, which matched her gold hoop earrings.

"Hey there, handsome," Donna said with an appreciative grin. "What can I do you for?"

"Whatever you recommend."

"Sex on the beach is always popular."

Justin laughed. "I bet," he said, glancing around at the packed open-air establishment. There was no shortage of laughter, bikini tops and board shorts but he didn't see a woman who held a candle to Lilah. A small part of him wished another woman would turn his head. It would simplify this baffling and, at times, frightening change of behavior he was experiencing. But it wasn't happening. No one had that certain "it factor" that Lilah had, and therefore every other woman seemed bland and unappealing.

Which meant he was sticking to his plan.

"So, Donna…tell me about Lilah Bell," he said, dazzling Donna with another signature grin. He'd often been accused of using that charm for less-than-honorable purposes and he couldn't deny the charge, but right now he just wanted to find out more about the elusive island girl so he could find a way past that wall she'd put between them.

Donna slid a fruity drink toward him and smiled knowingly. "I called it when I saw you two."

His brow climbed. "Oh? And what did you see?"

"A good match."

He chuckled ruefully and took a sip, glad to play the jilted lover if it got him information. "Well, someone ought to tell Lilah that… She's been a bit difficult to get to know beyond the superficial. How well do you know the Bells?"

"It's a small island. Everyone knows everyone and their business. Usually that's a pain in the ass but sometimes it's a cool thing. I've known the Bells for about five years now. They're very good people. So you've taken a shine to Lilah?"

"Yeah, you could say that. She's unlike anyone I've ever met and that's saying something because honestly, I'd become a bit of a cynic when it came to people."

"So worldly," Donna said, rolling her eyes. "Let me tell you something. When you're a bartender you meet all kinds of people and I'm always surprised by the types of people who find their way to my bar."

"That's a good way to be," Justin said. "I like it better than the jaded me I was before I got here."

"Well, it's the island air. Does good things to a person."

"So…what can you tell me about Lilah?"

She cracked a laugh. "Sorry, bud. If you can't get the information on your own, you're out of luck. If Lilah wants you to know more about her, she'll share. If not, that's your bad luck."

"Awww c'mon, help a guy out," he pleaded. "I really

like her but I'm out of my element here. I just want to show her that I'm not the guy she thinks I am."

"Which is?"

"Just some guy looking for a good time. That I really like her for more than just her looks."

"Then your actions will tell the story, not your lips."

"She won't let me show her. I can hardly get any time with her." He sensed Donna was wavering and pushed his advantage. "Listen, this is the craziest thing I've ever said to another person and I have to trust that you're not going to screw me over, but here's the thing—I think I'm falling for her. I mean, seriously, head over heels, falling for her. Does that sound like someone just trying to have a good time?"

Donna sighed. "I'm a sucker for a romantic. But I can't give you what you can't find yourself. However, I will say this…Lilah is an amazing artist. I mean, talented enough to be in one of those fancy galleries. And that's all I'm going to say. The rest is on you."

Justin grinned. "Donna, you just gave me the keys to the castle."

"Uh-huh… We'll see…"

Justin took another swallow of his drink, tossed enough cash to pay his bill and leave a hefty tip, and then left to gather supplies.

THAT NIGHT, THE ENTIRE GANG was settled into the office with the exception of Pops and Heath. Heath took Pops to St. Thomas for a doctor's appointment and then dinner as an excuse to give the group a chance to meet and discuss the situation.

As usual Lora took point, being a former marketing

executive, talking about strategy and whatnot was in her wheelhouse.

Now that Gabe Weston was part of the family, he also brought some valuable insight as well as contacts to the table.

As for Lindy and Lilah, they were bewildered by business details but willing to pitch in however needed.

"I appreciate everyone coming tonight," Lora began. "I know it's been a rocky road to this point. We've all made sacrifices to help save Larimar and I just want to say thank you. I know it hasn't been easy on any of us. First, I want to share the good news—we've made all the scheduled payments to the IRS and we've managed to clear the back taxes that were due. So, yay for getting caught up," she said, clapping her hands for emphasis. Lilah smiled as polite applause followed. "Now for the bad news. We used up our income to pay the last of the shortfall, which puts us back to square one when taxes come due again for this year. We have no reserve and we need to find a way to create more income in addition to what we're pulling in regularly. As we all know, Heath had hoped that the gift shop would pull in more revenue. That hasn't exactly been the case. His fused glass sells but not enough to sustain the gift shop, which is why we've brought back a smattering of the previous inventory of standard tourist fare. We're at a crucial stage for the gift shop. We might need to rethink the plan all together if we're going to keep the gift shop open."

"The art is original and it sells. I think we need to give it more time," Lilah said.

"Time is something we don't have," Lora said. "I wish we did. I love Heath's creations but we need more income and although the touristy stuff wasn't exciting, it moved units. Let's face it, T-shirts are easy to pack in a suitcase whereas fragile glass art is a nightmare to ship."

"What happened with the idea to market the glass on the website?" Lindy asked.

"We'd have to redesign the entire website from a reservation program to a sales portal and although we queried a few web designers, we just couldn't find one within our price range, which is embarrassingly cheap. And I'm not about to tear down our professionally designed website for one that's substandard. I don't think that will serve our brand at all."

Lilah dishearteningly agreed. "We don't want to go backward that's for sure. What about the charter company idea?"

"Heath talked to Billy Janks about partnering and Billy was leery. I don't blame him. He has a successful operation in his own rights. He doesn't need us and we don't want to start a relationship that's grounded in such inequality. It sets up an unhealthy power balance and between friends, it can be toxic. I'd hate to see Heath and Billy's friendship damaged."

"So what are we going to do?" Lilah asked.

"Well, I've been cultivating a relationship with Sears in the hopes of landing their corporate retreat account but it's not going as smoothly as I'd hoped," Lora admitted.

"I might be able to help in that respect," Gabe chimed in, surprising Lilah.

"How so?" Lora asked.

"I golf with the VP of Foreign Acquisitions and I could nudge him in your direction."

"That would be great," Lora said. "I'll take whatever advantage we can manage. I am without shame at this point."

"No shame in doing whatever you can to save your business," Gabe said, and Lindy leaned over to place a kiss on his cheek with a warm smile. Gabe grinned. "And I get rewards of my own. I'm in."

Lilah smiled at the love flowing so easily between her sister and her fiancé. Someday she hoped to find a man as good as both Heath and Gabe. If only she would be so lucky. She withheld a sigh and returned to the conversation, though her mind kept wandering. What was Justin doing right now? Was he spending the evening with some island girl? She hated that idea and pushed it away with immediate distaste even though she shouldn't care.

"Lilah, have you considered selling a few of your art pieces in the gift shop?" Lora asked, surprising everyone with her suggestion. Lilah froze and sent a panicked look to Lora with a minute shake of her head. Her work certainly wasn't of the caliber worth displaying for sale. But Lora didn't back down. In fact, she stared her down, daring her to defend her work. "Li...you have scores of finished paintings rolled up and gathering dust. Between your art and Heath's, we could make something of the gift shop. Heath and I have already talked about it and he agrees."

"I'm flattered but I think you've overestimated the value of my work. Sorry, Lora."

Lindy seemed intrigued by this idea and jumped in. "Wait a minute, Li. I think Lora's onto something. When we saw your work, your real work, the stuff that you hide away in the broom closet in the atrium, I was astounded by how beautiful and soulful it was. You have real talent. We could have them professionally mounted and have a gallery showing for you."

"No." Lilah hadn't meant to snap but the word jumped free from a place of pain and fear and snarled like a rabid dog in the room. She reined in her initial knee-jerk reaction and tried to smooth things over. "I mean, I'm really flattered but I'd rather not. It's not good enough for one, and two—" she paused, swallowing a lump in her throat "—it's personal stuff that I don't want everyone and their mother to see. It's bad enough that everyone on the island knows what happened to me. I don't need them judging my work, too. It'd be like standing on the pier welcoming the tourists in nothing but my skin. I'm just not interested in being that vulnerable."

Lilah wrestled with the guilt her refusal created that was accentuated by the disappointed expressions reflected in the room but she held firm. Her work wasn't good enough. Anyone with an ounce of true talent could see her obvious technical flaws but beyond that, her art was sacred to her and she didn't want anyone to take that from her.

"You need to stop being so modest," Lora said. "Your work is as good, if not better, than some of the stuff I've seen hanging in galleries in New York. That's the honest to God truth."

Intensely uncomfortable with the direction of the conversation, she shrugged and remained silent. Perhaps if she didn't lend any fuel to the fire it would die out on its own.

Lindy, sensing her distress, piped in. "Well, let's focus on what we know is working and expand on that before we start implementing all kinds of new ideas in a scattershot pattern just to see what sticks to the wall. Lora, you said that reservations were up thanks to the website overhaul?"

Lora nodded. "Yes, we contracted with a company that does online reservations and they've funneled some business our way. We've also contracted with a few travel sites to offer some discount packages to draw more business. So far, it seems to be working. We're taking a hit on the pure profit, but making up for it in volume."

"Sounds like a decent strategy," Lindy agreed, nodding. "Can we find some more travel sites to make the same deal?"

"I'm working on it," Lora answered. "With most people going through travel sites rather than an agent, I figured it would be best to have a presence at the busiest sites."

"Smart," Lindy said. "And I haven't given up on the film industry. I sent pics of Larimar to all the film commissions in California. It's not a quick fix but it's always nice to be on their radar."

The conversation meandered over sales projections and needed repairs and soon Lilah's eyelids were dragging. After months of insomnia, the weight on her lids was always welcome. She knew she'd sleep well, even if her thoughts were a turbulent mess and for that, she was grateful.

"Li? You okay?"

Lilah awoke with a start and realized she'd dozed. She yawned and quickly apologized. "I'm beat." She rubbed her bleary eyes and tried to focus. "What did I miss?"

"Nothing," Lindy assured her. "We're just finishing up. Besides, Heath and Pops will be back soon and we shouldn't be powwowing in his office when he returns. It could set him off."

Another yawn cracked her jaw and she nodded, happy to have an out. "All right. I'm heading to bed, then."

Everyone said their good-nights and Lilah left the office, eager to find her bed.

As her eyelids closed, she sighed when an image of Justin filled her mind as she drifted to sleep.

Drat that beautiful man—there was no escaping his adorable face.

CHAPTER FOURTEEN

THE NEXT MORNING, JUSTIN entered the lobby with a palette and a blank canvas and his backpack slung over his shoulder filled with paint supplies. His mission was simple and to the point: get Lilah to spend time with him. And he wasn't above hitting his target where it would have the most impact.

Lilah was chatting quietly with what he assumed was her twin. Even though they weren't identical, he could see similarities in their mannerisms and the bond between them as they talked. Both women angled their bodies toward one another in an affectionate manner that spoke of their invisible connection as light laughter followed whatever train of conversation they were having. He almost hated to interrupt their girl time—almost.

Lilah looked up and saw him striding toward her, her gaze immediately going to the folded easel in his hand and the backpack slung over his shoulder. Her brow winged upward in question. "Are you an artist?" she asked with open surprise.

"Not exactly," he admitted with a cheeky grin. "But I've always wanted to try. I love art if that counts for anything and I've been told I have a good eye so I thought, what the hell, let's give it a go. I bought a book on watercolors, pastels and oil paints but I haven't a clue as to where to start. I heard through the grapevine that you're a halfway decent artist and thought you might take pity on me and help me out."

Guarded laughter was his answer as she shook her head until her sister piped in, nudging her with her shoulder. "Li, you're a great teacher. And this guy's pretty adorable with those puppy dog eyes. How can you resist?"

Lilah hesitated, her gaze going to her sister with surprise, as if she'd expected her to back her on her polite refusal. "I think if he wants lessons, he ought to pay someone who teaches for a living," she said.

"Teachers get too wrapped up in technique and style. I want someone who can teach me how to tap into that artistic side without clinging to a bunch of rules. My gut says you're just the right person for the job."

If Lindy caught the warmth growing between them, he wouldn't be surprised. Justin was trying hard to seem like a happy-go-lucky tourist, but he couldn't escape the feeling that it was imperative he convince Lilah to say yes. If he were a smart man, he'd count Lilah as a loss and cut ties but he couldn't bring himself to do it. Maybe it was because he wasn't accustomed to losing, or maybe he hated the idea of someone so easily discounting him, but he couldn't walk away.

Not yet.

He'd have to leave in a few weeks anyway. And if he had his way, he'd spend every available moment with Lilah until then.

"You should go," Lindy urged with a grin that bordered on mischievous. "It's a gorgeous day. Perfect for an art lesson."

"I'm supposed to man the desk today," Lilah protested.

"I think I can cover the desk for a few hours. Besides, Gabe and Carys were going to hit the beach for a while anyway. It's perfect. And it helps me to feel as if I'm being helpful when I've been so far away."

Justin grinned and thrust his hand out to Lilah's sister. "You must be Lilah's twin sister, Lindy. Nice to meet you. I'm Justin Cales, a friend of Lilah's."

At the mention of *friend,* Lilah's eyes widened and he choked back a laugh at the private joke between them. Lindy smiled and accepted his handshake with laughter dancing in her eyes. Intuition told Justin that Lilah had shared a little of their involvement with her sister and instead of disapproving, Lindy was wholeheartedly in favor. "I owe you a beer for taking pity on this poor tourist," Justin said, casting Lilah a teasing grin that caused her to blush prettily. Ahh, he liked having Lilah off-kilter. It gave him an advantage that he sorely needed.

"I might take you up on that offer," Lindy said, then gestured to Lilah. "Go on and have fun. Why don't you take him up to Cinammon? There's some gorgeous old growth trees, very wild and untamed that he might like."

"That's not very easy to paint for a beginner," Lilah retorted, slipping from her chair and dusting her behind as she straightened her sarong. She heaved an exasperated sigh and gestured to Justin. "Fine. If you want a lesson, I'll give you one but don't blame me if you don't learn a thing. I'm not cut out to be a teacher."

Justin laughed good-naturedly, not the least bit put off by the subtle snap in Lilah's tone. He got that she was irritated by his open manipulation and he was willing to take a little punishment if it meant he got to spend the day with the woman who was fast becoming his favorite obsession.

He sent Lindy a wink and followed Lilah to the Jeep.

"THAT WAS LOW OF YOU, using my sister to get what you wanted," Lilah said, putting the Jeep into gear and rumbling away from Larimar. "Is that how you do things in New York?"

He didn't even try to offer up a plausible denial. "Pretty much." He grinned and she groaned, hating that his silly smile made her insides light up. He chuckled at her irritation. "What drives you the most crazy? The fact that I don't make apologies for going after what I want, or that you can't seem to say no to me when you claim that you don't want to get involved?"

Damn him. "Why do I have to choose? Both points make me crazy," she groused, downshifting to climb a steep hill. "You are so damn stubborn and single-minded. Why does it matter that I don't want a relationship with you? Why can't you just find some other island girl to spend your time with? What is it about me?"

Her tone voiced complaint but she secretly wanted to know the answer. His pursuit thrilled her to her toes but she hated that she was so affected by it. Lindy had always been the superstar of their family. All the boys had always gravitated toward her blinding charisma and she'd toyed with their devotion without apology, yet they'd always come back running. Lilah had never inspired such rabid interest. Sure, she'd had boyfriends but there'd always been that subtle quality about Lindy that had outshone Lilah every time. So the fact that Justin seemed preoccupied with Lilah for reasons she couldn't fathom, tickled her feminine pride in ways she'd never experienced.

"Lilah, do you really want me spending time with other women?" he asked her pointedly, and she couldn't lie. She shook her head slowly, reluctant to admit such a telling truth. He accepted her answer and smiled with satisfaction. "Good. Because I don't want to hang out with other women. I want you, Lilah. And today, you're going to teach me how to paint."

"Have you ever painted before?"

"Never held a brush in my life," he said without shame. "And I'll probably suck at it, but as long as I'm spending time with you…it's a win."

His words struck a chord deep inside her and she almost had to fight to suck back sudden tears. He made no apologies for what he wanted. She admired his tenacity. She snuck a glance his way and caught his strong profile as the sun shone down on their heads, bathing the Jeep with drowsy, warm light. The wind played with his brown hair and he looked as if he didn't have a care in the world. In that split second, she memorized every line in his face, every subtle nuance of character evident in his profile, and committed it to her private cache of treasures. When he left, she'd remember this day as the one that made her feel special and wanted by a man who was too handsome for his own good and too charming by half.

Oh, to hell with good sense.

She was going to enjoy whatever it was they were doing while it lasted.

LORA WALKED INTO THE LOBBY just as Lindy was finishing a reservation call. Lindy flashed a brief smile, ready to share the good news about booking all the rooms for next month when Lora scowled.

"What's wrong?" Lindy asked, confused. "I just booked the resort for all of next month. A big group is coming in from one of those travel sites you hooked up with. That's good news," she supplied when Lora didn't lose her pinched expression. "What gives?"

"Where's Lilah? She was supposed to work the desk today."

"Yeah, so? I took her shift so she could spend time with that cutie Justin Cales."

"Damn it," Lora muttered, shaking her head. "This is getting ridiculous."

"What are you talking about?" Lindy asked, confused and becoming irritated. Lora's attitude rubbed at Lindy's inborn sense of chaos she used to live by and she had to remind herself that she was not that rebellious kid anymore. "Is there something I should know?"

"Lilah is in a fragile state. She doesn't need to start a fling with someone who isn't going to stick around. Besides, dating shouldn't be her primary concern. Getting well should be," she added unnecessarily, and Lindy couldn't help but bristle for Lilah's sake.

"She's doing very well and you're overreacting. Justin seems like a cool guy and they're just enjoying a little fun together. It's not like they're going to run off and get married."

"Well, it's kinda what you did," Lora reminded Lindy, and she couldn't argue that fact.

"Yeah, well, Lilah isn't going to get married to this guy. She's just having some fun. And for the record,

I'm not married yet," Lindy said, annoyed that Lora was going there. "I honestly don't see what the big deal is."

"I wouldn't expect you to, you're all about living in the moment but that's a dangerous place for Lilah. Surely you realize that if she gets her heart broken, it could send her into a tailspin? Maybe even a regression back into her depression."

Lindy lost some of her irritation and bit her lip. She hadn't thought of that. "We can't put her in a box to protect her from everything, though," Lindy said. "And frankly, she would hate that anyway. She already feels that everyone is walking on eggshells around her and it's driving her a little batty. I think we should follow her lead and support whatever she chooses."

"I just don't want to see her hurt," Lora said.

"I don't, either."

At least in that they agreed but Lindy hadn't considered the potential damage that could happen with Justin. "What do we know about this guy?" Lindy asked.

"Nothing. I mean, he seems like a decent guy but how do we know?"

Lindy toyed with her bottom lip. "We don't. Okay, I'll do some digging and see what I can find. You know, here's something to consider... Lilah is a smart woman and she's changed a lot. Dr. Veronica has worked wonders with her. She doesn't suffer from insomnia any longer and she's happy again. I can see it in her smile and hear it in her voice. Things have changed. Maybe we need to put a little faith in our sister instead of jumping to the worst conclusion."

"I'd love to. I'm just worried and with the luck we've had, I don't want to take any chances. Not with our sister."

Lindy nodded. "Okay. I'll let you know what I find."

Lora sighed in relief. "Thanks. I appreciate it. I don't like being the bad guy all the time when I'm just trying to do what's best for everyone."

"I know," Lindy said. "Sometimes it's easy to fall into patterns…and that goes for me, too."

Lora smiled with gratitude and Lindy felt a pinch of guilt for immediately becoming snarly. She watched as Lora walked from the room, her stride quick and purposeful as always, and smiled with an inborn sigh. Sometimes it didn't matter how much a person changed, at their core lived a bratty teen who believed the world was against her and saw the world in naive shades of black and white.

Had it been only a few short months ago that she'd been that way?

She thought of Carys and how volatile and moody she was at times and chuckled. Yeah…growing up was hard.

Especially when you put it off for so long like Lindy.

Now was the time to be there for her sisters in any way possible.

And that included making sure that cute men with a sweet spot for baby sisters weren't up to no good.

CHAPTER FIFTEEN

"So where are we going?" Justin asked. "Go easy on me, I'm a beginner."

She flashed a grin. "I don't remember that being part of the deal. You wanted to paint something. So I will take you someplace that if you have an artistic bone in your body, will inspire you."

"Intriguing," he said. "Should I be scared or excited?"

"Depends on your sense of adventure," she answered with a shrug that immediately made him laugh.

"Well, I'll have you know I have an overinflated sense of adventure according to my friends. All the best—or worst—escapades we'd ever done were courtesy of yours truly."

"Such as?"

He paused, realizing that he'd have to share some of his real life to answer her question. He wasn't ashamed of who he was, but he'd begun to enjoy the anonymity of being no one. He never needed to worry if Lilah's feelings and opinions were her own or simply what she thought he wanted to hear because of who he was. "What do you want me to say? I was a bad boy," he said, softening his deflection with a smile he knew she'd like. "But I'm a reformed bad boy, I assure you."

"Is such a thing possible?" she teased.

"Put me to the test and I'll prove it."

"And how would I do that?"

"Let me take you to dinner."

She did a double take. "Dinner?"

"Yeah, on a real date."

Lilah's easy smile faltered and he wondered if he'd pushed too hard too soon. The pink tip of her tongue darted out to moisten her lips as she paused to consider his offer. Damn it, he swore in his mind, mentally berating himself for jumping the gun. He opened his mouth to joke his way out of his blunder when she sent him a sweetly coy, but entirely sexy look, and answered with a cryptic, "We'll see how well the painting goes and play it by ear."

He wanted to crow. It wasn't a yes, but it wasn't a no, either. He'd take it.

Justin let out a shaky breath and smiled into the sunlight, eager to spend the day with his mysterious island girl.

LILAH WAS PLAYING a dangerous game but the heady rush was becoming addictive.

She craved time with Justin unlike anything she'd ever experienced. This was normal, she told herself. And if she'd never fallen into a terrible bout of depression, she would have likely ignored her misgivings and enjoyed Justin's company without reservation. The fact that she was operating under an enormous black cloud was becoming an irritant.

"We're going to Annaberg, the remnants of one of the sugar plantations I told you about the other day, in case you're still wondering," she supplied with a grin, pushing the hair from her eyes. "I could take you to the overlook of Trunk Bay, but that's cliché. I mean, it's beautiful, don't get me wrong, but I think there's something melancholy about the ruins that plucks at the heartstrings. At least it does for me."

"Then the ruins it is. I'm eager to see them."

Lilah smiled and pulled off the main road to a smaller road that led to the ruins and before too long they were pulling into the parking lot.

"A regular tourist attraction isn't cliché?" Justin asked, climbing from the Jeep, noting the people milling about. "And here I thought we were going somewhere remote and forgotten."

"You and I can't be trusted with remote and forgotten places," she said. "Our clothes tend to fall off."

"And that's a problem why?"

She gave him a stern look. "Because you're here to learn. Now grab your stuff and we'll head out."

Justin shouldered his pack, grabbed his easel and fell into step behind Lilah. She knew without having to turn around that his attention was centered on her behind so when she heard him curse and stumble on a rock, she couldn't help but giggle. She cast a short glance his way. "Everything okay?"

"Just fine," he answered. "Just gotta keep my eyes on where I'm going, not where I want to be."

Her cheeks flared but her heart skipped a beat. How did she ever hope to keep her distance from this man? At that moment, she was intensely grateful they were surrounded by other people because she had the urge to throw him down beneath the first available sugar apple tree and have her wicked way with him.

"So, Annaberg was once a very prosperous sugar plantation back when slave labor was legal. The life of a sugar plantation slave was no picnic. They worked eighteen- to twenty-hour days, six days a week and even had to farm their own gardens because the plantation owners couldn't afford to feed them."

"Bonus. Art and history lessons," he quipped, and she laughed. "No, don't get me wrong. I love it. If all my teachers had been as hot as you, I'd have been a better student."

Lilah ignored his sneaky compliment and continued, "Well, they also made rum from the sugarcane, so nothing went to waste. It was backbreaking work and the slaves were often starving, diseased and overworked."

"Sounds like they needed to unionize," Justin said.

"Well, they did, 1800s-style. If revolting and overrunning the plantation in a bloody coup can be considered a unionizing tactic."

"Awesome. My kind of history lesson—bloody and violent."

"Yes, I thought you'd find that interesting. Anyway, once slave labor was abolished, the plantations could no longer sustain themselves and sugarcane production in the Virgin Islands fell by the wayside."

"Pretty cool history," he said, adding ruefully, "If not a bit bloody and horrifying on both sides of the coin. I mean, sucked to be a slave but then when the slaves revolted, sucked to be the plantation owner. Hard to believe so much bloodshed happened in a place so beautiful."

She chuckled and shrugged. "Sometimes beauty is a great shield," she said.

"If that's true, you must be hiding all sorts of secrets, because you're the most beautiful woman I've ever met."

If only he knew. She forced a light smile and said wryly, "That was the cheesiest line I've ever heard. Has it ever worked?"

He laughed. "Not even remotely. But I actually mean it this time."

"I feel sorry for all those other girls who thought you meant it the times you said it to them."

Justin clutched at his heart as if she'd shot him clean through and she laughed at his theatrics. "You wound me," he gasped in pretend pain. "You are a cruel woman, Lilah Bell."

"Not cruel, just not naive." She gestured to the top of the hill. "Come on, we're almost there."

They trudged the final distance to the outlook and Justin wiped away the sweat beading his brow as he gently dropped his pack to the ground. They'd pulled away from the throng of people clogging the main artery of the plantation and settled in a spot that had a great view of Tortola.

"Man, you were right. There is a melancholy air to this place," he said, shading his eyes as he scanned the area. "Maybe it's all the souls of those poor slaves who had the misfortune to be brought here."

Lilah nodded and removed her water bottle from her pack. "Makes sense to me."

"You like it here?" he asked, taking in the skeleton of the crumbling plantation and the ruin of the formerly prosperous sugar mill. "It's beautiful but kind of depressing," he observed.

Lilah paused, his casual observance striking a chord. Yes, she supposed it was. Maybe that was why it had always been one of her favorite places. It'd plucked at that dark core of her, singing a melody she could understand but others couldn't quite hear. "Do you believe places can retain an imprint of the people who inhabited them?"

"No."

His blunt answer surprised her. "But what about the stories about the ghost in your boarding school?"

He shrugged. "I never saw her and honestly, I never really knew if my buddy was just messing with me. Keenan is a bit of a prankster so you never know if half of the stories he tells are eighty-percent bullshit." He realized he must've disappointed her with his answer and tried to amend his view. "Listen, I'm open to be amazed, scared or shaken to my core...it just hasn't happened yet so I've had no reason to change my viewpoint."

"Do you believe in God?"

"Whoa. This conversation just got deep. I thought we were going to paint?" he said, half joking. He hated conversations about religion or politics and since he couldn't escape the politics he sure as hell made sure he avoided all topics of religion. He bent to rummage through his pack, drawing out his supplies. "So, Miss Bell, where should we start? Watercolors? Seems less messy than the oils."

She didn't answer, but cocked her head slightly to the side as if listening to an internal voice that bared all his secrets. Of course, that made him nervous. "Why are you really here in St. John?" she asked. "It's not to paint and it certainly must not be all about chasing pretty bikini-clad girls, because you've pretty much focused your attention on me and while that's really flattering, I don't think it's very good game, if you know what I mean."

He laughed and surprised her with a kiss on her

cheek. She startled but a slow smile warmed her lips. "What was that for?"

"Because when I'm around you that's all I want to do."

She laughed, thrilling at his words. His eyes danced with light and the desire that surely mirrored her own. She leaned in, wrapping her arms around his neck. "What a coincidence. That's exactly what I want to do, too," she murmured before descending on his mouth.

Their tongues tangled in a slow, sensual exploration that set her nerve endings on fire and she completely lost sight of the fact that they weren't alone. Frankly, she didn't care. In Justin's embrace she found solace, happiness and the simple pleasure of being with someone who felt the same way and she was greedy for more.

The voice of reason, harping to the point of bitterness, faded to a whimper under the sensual onslaught of Justin's kiss. If there was a better kisser in all of the world, Lilah wouldn't believe it. Her mind emptied and her body cleaved to his, molding to his every curve and solid strength in his sinewy frame. Her hands itched to roam and touch; her core began to heat. "I don't want to teach you to paint," she said, breaking away breathlessly. "I don't want to do anything but feel your naked body against mine."

"Then what the hell are we doing sightseeing?" he asked, equally out of breath, his eyes hot and bright. "Let's blow this popsicle stand."

She didn't want to go to Larimar—her sisters wouldn't leave them alone long enough to get their clothes off—but she did know of a place that was private and most certainly, vacant.

"Grab your stuff," she said, and walked hurriedly to the Jeep. "I know where we can go."

"Hot damn, I'm right behind you," he said, a grin in his voice. "I probably would've sucked at painting anyway."

CHAPTER SIXTEEN

LINDY HATED CONFLICT, which was surprising seeing as she used to cause so much of it back in her wilder days.

But now that she was all *responsible* and *mature* she suddenly understood the appeal of stability and calm situations.

And she knew without a doubt that when Lindy told Lora what she'd found out about Justin Cales, there'd be no hope for any calm and peaceful conflict resolution.

She groaned just as Gabe and Carys entered the bungalow.

"What's wrong?" Gabe asked, taking time to playfully rustle Carys's wet head before she bounded from the room to shower the salt water from her skin. "Hey, don't use all the water, either, Carys. Five minutes, tops!" he called out, both of them knowing the little imp would ignore him.

Lindy exhaled loudly. "I hate being the bearer of bad news and that's exactly the position I'm going to be put in when I tell Lora what I found out about Justin Cales."

"Who is Justin Cales?" Gabe asked, perplexed. "Is he that kid Lilah is hanging out with?"

"He's no kid, he's a grown man," Lindy answered, pushing Gabe away playfully when he leaned in for a kiss. "And he's the son of New York Senator Vernon Cales."

"And this is…bad?" Gabe guessed but remained confused.

"Yeah, because Justin Cales has a bit of a reputation if you know what I mean. I did a Google search and look what I found." She slid the laptop over to Gabe so he could get a good look. It was an online gossip rag with Justin's face nestled squarely between a woman's very large breasts and it didn't look as if he'd been pushed. In fact, it looked as if he was quite content to remain squashed between the woman's ta-tas for the rest of his life. "And that's not all," she said. "This picture prompted me to make a few calls to my east coast friends and they confirmed that Justin Cales is a notorious rich kid bad boy with an endless trust fund and a shortage of morals. He is the last kind of person Lilah needs to be hanging out with when she's in such a fragile state. Damn it," she ended with a mutter, mostly to herself. "Now we have to be the wet blankets and point this out to Lilah and trust me, that's going to go over like a proverbial turd in a punchbowl."

"That's disgusting," Carys yelled from the bathroom.

"Thin walls," Lindy said, sighing. "Sorry!" she called out. "But you shouldn't be eavesdropping."

Carys poked her head out, a towel wrapped around her body. "How else am I supposed to learn what the heck is going on?"

"You have a promising career in espionage, now go get in the shower before you lose out and your dad and I get in."

"Ew." Carys wrinkled her nose and disappeared behind the door.

Lindy chuckled. That kid was a handful but the coolest. Now back to the issue at hand. "How am I supposed to break this news to Lilah?" she said, lowering her voice this time. "I mean, don't you think we have a responsibility to tell her?"

Gabe looked as unhappy about the information as Lindy felt. "Yes, but like you said, the news isn't going to go over well. Here's something, though, and I know I'm going to be the unpopular vote here…Lilah isn't a child. She made choices of her own free will. And even though she wasn't mentally stable at the time, she's different now. Before she got sick, did you ever worry about who she was dating?"

"No. Lilah could handle herself just fine," Lindy answered, mulling over Gabe's point. "But that's just it… she's not the same as she was. And Lora said she's still fragile. I'd hate to blow off Lora's concern and realize she was right. You know? The stakes are just too high."

Gabe pulled her into his arms and she cuddled into him. "You're right. But at some point we have to start putting our faith back into Lilah and trust that she's well enough to handle life. She doesn't want a bunch of babysitters for the rest of her life."

"God, that's an awful thought," Lindy murmured against the solid strength of his chest. She inhaled the sharp, citrus scent of his favorite cologne and for a moment simply enjoyed the feeling of being safe and secure. Her contentment at being snuggled against the man she loved faded as her thoughts turned to the growing problems facing her family. "You know Pops is getting worse by the day. We have to figure out how to keep him safe without compromising the future of Larimar. The other day Heath found him in the shop trying to fire up the welding torch but he'd forgotten how to turn it on—thank God—but that could've been bad." She exhaled deeply and groaned. "I hate dementia. My Pops is disappearing."

Gabe drew a deep breath but otherwise remained silent. She knew there was little he could say that would ease the pain in her heart over Pops but she appreciated his quiet support. She glanced up. "Why are you so amazing?" she asked.

"Because I have to be to be worthy of you."

She smiled and rose on her toes to kiss him soundly on the lips. "Keep making comments like that and I will be forced to drag you to the bedroom."

Gabe shocked her by scooping her into his arms with a devilish grin. "You won't have to drag me. I'll always go willingly."

She blushed and curled her hand around the back of his neck and murmured, "Let's stop wasting time. Carys will be out of the shower in five minutes."

They disappeared behind the bedroom door and for a short interlude, Lindy blissfully forgot about the unfortunate news awaiting her twin sister.

LILAH SLIPPED THE KEY into the lock and pushed the door open of Heath's childhood home and walked in.

The small cottage had been completely rebuilt from the shack it'd been when Heath was growing up, and now it was a gem with hardwood floors and an open floor plan that was pretty enough to land on the pages of some Bay Area magazine featuring small homes with big appeal.

"Nice," observed Justin. "And where are we?"

"My soon-to-be brother-in-law Heath's place but since he lives at Larimar now with my sister, it pretty much sits empty. I come here sometimes to paint and

Heath doesn't mind. However, I'm more interested in the bedroom than the veranda at the moment," she said, pulling Justin toward the master bedroom.

"Lead the way," Justin said, grinning.

They laughed and tumbled to the bed, sending pillows bouncing to the floor. Lilah heard a muffled rip as Justin caught her sarong.

"Oops," he said, looking chagrined as she wiggled free of the thin material.

She met his mouth with voracious hunger, pushing his shirt from his shoulders. "It's cheap. I can buy a new one," she said against his mouth. "Clothes. Off. Now."

He helped her pull his shirt free, followed by his shorts. His erection bobbed free and Lilah didn't hesitate to curl her hands around his warm length. He sucked in a tight breath and groaned as she palmed him without reservation and inhibition. With Justin she felt free, not locked away inside herself, watching the world from the sidelines as it passed her by. A ravenous hunger raged in her and her touch became more insistent, more demanding. "I want to feel you inside me," she said, arching as Justin slipped her nipple into his mouth and sucked the pebbled tip, teasing the sensitive skin until she writhed beneath him.

His touch was something she craved, needed like air, and she refused to give up even though she should.

Justin's touch became fevered, desperate and she understood his urgency because it rode her nearly as hard. Within moments she was urging him to push himself deep inside her, plunging into that hot core so she could lose herself in the feel of being taken and devoured by the man she couldn't get enough of.

"Your skin is like smooth honey," he murmured

against her rounded shoulder, pausing to nip at the soft skin. "I could touch you a thousand times and never tire of it."

"Sweet talker," she gasped as he entered her. She wasted no time in wrapping her legs around his torso, pulling him closer, burying him deeper. A low moan escaped her mouth as he pumped into her, grinding against her pubic bone until she shuddered at the carnal pressure. "Yesss, Justin, yesss!" she cried out, clutching at his back as he moved above her. Justin's face was screwed into an intense expression as he tried to hold back but she clenched her internal muscles and his eyes popped open as they both hurtled toward a bone-melting orgasm that had each gasping for breath, chests heaving as they tried to find their senses again.

It was a long-drawn-out moment before either could speak. The sound of their breathing filled the room as sweat covered their bodies from the oppressive humidity that the languidly twirling ceiling fan couldn't hope to abate. Lilah's nipples, still hardened to tiny points, tingled as the last rush of sensation from her orgasm slowly receded. She languidly turned her head to regard Justin who was still breathing as if he'd run a marathon and looked dazed by what had just happened between them. He met her gaze and a slow, cocky grin teased the corners of his mouth as he said, "You know I'm totally going to want to do that again and again and again. We might be here all night."

She giggled and rolled to her stomach. "I don't have any plans," she said, but added coyly, "Do you think you can handle me all night?"

Justin rolled to his knees and quickly straddled her, bending to nuzzle her ear. The soft touch of his mouth moving along the sensitive shell, as well as the weight of his still-hard member dragging against her backside, made her shudder with want and need. "Darling, stamina has never been my problem," he whispered. "By the end of the evening, you'll be ruined for any other man."

She sucked in a tight breath. Oh, baby, she bit back the words, he'd already done that.

But that was something he didn't need to know.

Lilah laughed softly as Justin's mouth traveled the ridge of her spine. "We'll see," she teased, casting him a daring look, "if you can *rise* to the occasion."

His grin deepened. "Challenge accepted, sweet island girl. Challenge accepted!"

CHAPTER SEVENTEEN

JUSTIN SAVORED THE FRESH coconut as he and Lilah watched the waves roll in and out with the tide and the sun sink into the horizon. The house overlooked the beach, providing a breathtaking vista as they took a break from their exhausting and voracious bouts of carnal activity. They were both nude, completely comfortable in each other's presence like an old married couple with hot bodies and young minds, and Justin wasn't immune to his own surprise that he'd never been happier.

It was as near to heaven as Justin could imagine.

"Tell me about your life in New York," Lilah said, scooping a spoonful of coconut and glancing at him. "I bet it's a lot different than here."

"It's colder in the winter and perhaps not quite as humid in the summer," he answered with a smile before adding, "I tend to wear more clothes."

She laughed. "I should hope so."

"Well, it snows a lot in New York so it wouldn't be prudent to go around in the buff."

"Okay, joker. Seriously, tell me about Justin Cales when he's home in his own environment."

"You really want to know? It's not very interesting, I promise you."

"Somehow I doubt that."

He sighed when he realized she wasn't going to let it

go. He supposed this moment was going to come eventually, but he'd wanted to preserve his connection with Lilah for as long as possible. Besides, he didn't have much more time left on the island and he wanted to squeeze every last moment with her into that remaining time frame. Somehow telling her of his life back in New York seemed a contamination of something perfect and pure.

"Suddenly you're shy?" she teased. "It can't be that bad."

He offered a chagrined laugh. If she only knew the full extent. His situation seemed something out of a TV movie of the week, not someone's real life. How many fathers openly manipulated their sons for political gain? Actually, probably a few. But he never imagined his own father would sink so low.

"Well, I grew up privileged, I guess you could say," he began, wondering how much to share, how much to censor. "Which came with the usual perks. Private school, tutors when I needed them, vacations in the South Hamptons. God, are you sure you want to hear this? I'm embarrassed just hearing the words fall from my mouth."

"Why would you be embarrassed of your upbringing? There's nothing wrong with being well-off. I mean, I know it's considered bad form these days to admit to that, as if being poor is some noble thing, but trust me, I've seen plenty of poverty here on the island and there's nothing noble about a child starving because his parents can't afford food. It's no more a poverty-stricken child's fault that he's poor than it is a rich kid's fault that he's been born into wealth. It's how you handle yourself that matters."

"Ah, yeah, that's true," Justin said, hiding his dismay at her clearheaded assessment. He hadn't always handled himself with any discernible level of responsibility. Sometimes he'd acted the epitome of spoiled, rich and selfish. But he sure as hell didn't want Lilah to know that. It made him distinctly uncomfortable when he realized that Lilah's respect for him would likely plummet if she knew how he'd been in the recent past. Very recent past, actually. Surely, it had to count for something that he was beginning to see that his behavior had been something of an embarrassment. Of course, he wasn't willing to test that theory at the moment. He offered a bright smile and pocketed his personal discomfort. "You're one smart girl," he said. "Must be the clean island air."

"Or common sense," Lilah retorted. "Just as people shouldn't judge by their pocketbooks, neither should people assume that they are better or worse because of them. My Grams used to tell me that when I was growing up."

"Ah, the infamous Grams. I wish I could've met her. Do you think she would've liked me?"

Lilah cocked her head as if considering her answer, then nodded. "Yeah, I think she would have. She was a sucker for a cute smile and a sharp wit."

"Then she would've adored me because I'm known for those very things," he said with mock seriousness.

"I bet," Lilah said wryly. "Tell me more. How did your family come to be wealthy?" When he hesitated, she apologized with a flush. "I'm sorry. That was way too personal. You don't have to answer."

"Lilah, we're sitting here naked together, covered

in each other's DNA and you think that question is too personal?"

She giggled as she realized the irony. "Yeah, I guess you're right. But we really don't know much about each other and I don't usually do this with strangers. I mean...I'm not really a one-night stand kind of girl."

"Thank God, I was beginning to feel as if you just wanted me for my body," Justin said, pretending to flick his hair back like a girl. Lilah laughed and the sound warmed him, filling him with light and something else not quite easily defined. He shook off the foreign feeling and refocused on his storytelling. "Even though I went to Harvard, I wasn't a great student, not compared to those who really applied themselves. Too social the teachers said. I mean, I did well enough but, I was too busy having a good time to focus on the serious stuff. I figured there was plenty of time for that when I was too old to have fun."

She smiled. "And that was fine with your parents?"

"No. Not exactly. My mom's a socialite so she likes to brag about my accomplishments to her circle of friends—"

"Do you have any?" she cut in with an impish smile.

"Have what?"

"Accomplishments?"

He barked a short laugh. "No, not really."

"Then I guess she didn't do much bragging."

"No, I guess not."

They laughed together and Justin felt completely at ease for the first time in a long time. If it weren't for the hovering specter of the knowledge that his time with Lilah was short, he would've considered this day the best ever.

"Have you ever...thought of visiting New York?" he asked, holding his breath. When Lilah shook her head, he wasn't surprised but he was disappointed. "Why not? New York is a fun place with the right person."

The laughter faded from her eyes and a wistful expression replaced her former joy. "I'm not cut out for the city. My sister Lindy lived in Los Angeles for a time and was constantly asking me to move there but I knew it wasn't the right place for me. I need my island. It's my haven from the world."

He considered her answer and frowned when he came to realize something. "Your haven? Are you hiding from something?"

"Of course not," Lilah said quickly but when she realized she may have given away more than she'd intended, she clarified. "It was just an expression. What I meant was, this is my home. I don't have any need or desire to leave."

"Not even for someone that rocks your world over and over," he said, nudging her thigh with his foot, wearing a suggestive grin. "Come on...imagine this— you, me and a penthouse view. Have you ever made love up against a huge glass window overlooking the city at night?"

She blushed as she laughed. "No."

"Then you're missing out. I'd be willing to give you that experience."

"You own a penthouse?"

He shrugged. "My family does."

"Tempting but I'll pass," she said. "But I appreciate the offer."

He shouldn't have been bothered by her refusal. It should've bounced off his back without notice. But it bothered him. Mostly because he knew her refusal meant that he'd likely never see her again unless he came here, and with the schedule his father had set in place for him when he returned, that was damn near impossible. "So what keeps you here aside from family? There doesn't seem to be too many jobs available."

"My job is with Larimar, helping my family run the resort."

"Yeah, but that's not a career," he said, suddenly hating what he was saying. He sounded like his damn father, harping on him to find a direction in life. Determined to redirect, he said, "I'm just saying, someone with your talent... Shouldn't you be where an artist can be seen? No better place on earth for that purpose than New York."

"Who says I'm talented?"

"Plenty of people," he lied. In truth only Donna at Rush Tide had mentioned it, but Lilah didn't have to know that. Besides, somehow he sensed it was true. Lilah had an artist's soul; he could see it in her eyes. She had more depth than a thousand cultured artistic snobs who fancied themselves critics and connoisseurs of every medium. He'd be willing to bet Lilah's art was something special. Just like her. "Let me see your art and I'll see if it stands up to the praise," he challenged.

"I don't think so," Lilah said, abruptly standing and collecting their used utensils and empty coconut shells. "I don't need anyone's validation. My art is my own, whether it's crap or not."

He followed her back into the house, intrigued by how prickly she became over the subject. "I doubt it's crap."

She smiled with false sweetness. "You'll never know. My art is private."

His brow rose, and he watched as she made short work of cleaning what they'd used and throwing away the coconuts. "Again, need I remind you that we've just spent hours worshipping each other's bodies in the most intimate way possible?"

Her cheeks pinked. "No. But my art is different."

He sensed he ought to let it go. He was on the verge of ruining the evening. Even though he wanted to pursue answers, he dialed back the impulse to chase her down. Instead, he came up behind her and pulled her to him. "Aww, our first fight. I like playing house with you," he murmured against her bare skin, kissing the column of her neck. "Too bad it can't last."

"It's better this way," she answered, her voice dreamy as he continued to gently kiss and suckle the flesh on her neck, causing goose bumps to erupt along her skin. "This way we never bore of each other's company, or become disillusioned by the daily grind of life. We're both perfect in each other's eyes."

"There would never come a day that I didn't see you as I see you right now."

She turned and looped her arms around his neck. "We'll never have to test that theory."

He stared down at her. "No, I guess we won't," he agreed but he found no satisfaction in the agreement. An irrational part of him wanted to do anything to convince her to go with him to New York, even to the point of lying to achieve his goal. But at least he recognized the impulse as highly irrational and irresponsible and resisted the urge to do or say something reckless. His father would have a fit if he brought Lilah home. Likely

Vernon Cales already had a suitable debutante in mind for his son's future wife. She was probably a respectable woman with an impeccable pedigree and dull as day-old white bread in the dollar aisle. She'd be nothing like his island orchid girl with her soulful eyes and smoking hot body, not to mention killer wit and bright mind.

Hell, there was no one who would ever compare to Lilah Bell.

And he already knew that with a certainty that he didn't question.

The knowledge filled him with a desperation that felt worse than his father's manipulation and he never imagined anything would feel worse than that betrayal.

Lilah, sensing a difference in him, pulled away. "What's wrong?" she asked, her eyes full of concern.

He hated to see the light of desire fade from her eyes, particularly when he hated himself for wallowing in morose self-pity. He forced a smile, one that he knew was charming and filled with sexual promise, and surprised her when he lifted her in his arms. She wrapped her legs around his torso and he lifted her to the countertop. She squeaked when her bare bottom touched the cool granite and his heart melted just a little. "Break's over, little bird," he said, taking her mouth and reminding her of what he was capable of with his tongue while his hands reached up to cup her pert, perfect breasts, filling each of his palms as if they'd been made for him. He'd never get enough of her. Ever.

Holy hell, he should've walked away the minute he'd laid eyes on her.

Now, he was completely lost—and royally screwed.

But at the moment?

He didn't give a rat's ass.

CHAPTER EIGHTEEN

LILAH'S AND JUSTIN'S MATCHING smiles faded as they stepped into Larimar and found a firing squad of tense sisters awaiting them.

"Where have you been?" Lora asked tersely. "We were worried."

Justin frowned at the tension flowing between the sisters and Lilah's cheeks burned at being openly chastised like a runaway teen when she was an adult. She flashed Lora a cool look that said, *stand down or else,* and then said to Justin, "I'll see you at lunch?"

"I'll meet you in the lobby." But he didn't move. In fact, he looked ready to fight her sisters for her honor, which she found ridiculously romantic, if not ill-advised. She laid a hand gently on his shoulder and smiled, communicating that she'd be fine and he reluctantly moved on. "Call me if you need me," he said finally, and left the lobby.

Lilah turned to glare at her sisters. "What the hell was that all about?"

"We were up all night worrying about you," Lindy said quickly, hoping to calm the storm building inside Lilah. "We called your cell but you didn't answer. What happened? You were gone all night. We were...scared."

Lilah heard the worry in her twin's voice and she immediately lost some of her bristles. "I'm sorry. I didn't

mean to worry you but I spent the night with Justin—
and, Lora, before you start lecturing me on the inappro-
priateness of dating the guests, just save it. I don't care.
I'm sorry I didn't call. My phone died and I honestly
didn't realize how worried you'd all be or I would've
used Justin's phone to call. We were at Heath's."

"This is really unacceptable. What if we'd needed
you or there'd been an incident with Pops?" Lora asked,
still angry. "Life does not revolve around you."

Lilah opened her mouth to defend herself but then
snapped it shut. They were right. She should've called.
She couldn't defend the indefensible, but she was just
tired of being babysat. "I'm sorry. It won't happen again.
I didn't mean to put everyone in a bad spot but I like
Justin and for the first time in a long time, I feel normal. And it's addicting. I just wanted to go with the
flow and see where it took me."

She expected her sisters to understand and even look
relieved but what she received was the exact opposite.

"He's not a good guy," Lindy said in a jumbled rush,
then clapped her hand over her mouth with an anguished
expression. Lilah was too stunned to respond and simply stared. "I'm so sorry, Li, but I did a Google search
and found some things about him that aren't good. I
mean, really bad," Lindy said, looking miserable for
being the bearer of such bad news. "I'm so sorry. I wish
to God it wasn't true but you know I'd never lie to you."

Lilah felt punched in the gut. She found her voice to
ask, "What kind of things did you find?"

"He's a notorious, rich playboy who is a man-whore
of the worst kind. He runs with this bunch of guys who
are known for their shenanigans and not in a good way.

Spoiled, egocentric and if that wasn't bad enough...
he's in *politics!*"

Lora dismissed the last part but agreed otherwise.
"It appears that he's the son of New York Senator Vernon Cales. And he's gearing up for his own campaign
as he prepares to slide into his father's spot. They've
been in politics for generations. Sort of like a Kennedy
family. But that's not the part that bothers me. It's the
bad press he's gotten. There are some objectionable pictures floating around the internet that I'll let you take a
look at. I forwarded the links to your email."

"Thanks," Lilah said, her lips feeling numb. "Anything else?"

"Isn't that bad enough?" Lindy asked.

"Well, that remains to be seen. I mean, everyone has
skeletons in their closet. I sure have a doozy."

"He's not the right kind of person for you right now
while you're healing," Lora said, gentling her voice.
"I'm sure you know that. Your recovery is the most important thing right now, Li. I know you like him but...
he's not the kind of guy who will stick around...*at all*."

"One of my girlfriends who took a sitcom gig on the
east coast said she ran into him at a club and had the
misfortune to go home with him. After he'd shagged
her, he kicked her out of his penthouse without cab fare.
What kind of D-bag does that?"

Lilah flinched privately at the information, hating
hearing such ugliness about the man she'd just spent
an entire night curled up with. She also had difficulty
reconciling what she knew of Justin with the man who
would do something so rude and uncaring.

"I know this is the worst kind of news but we thought
it wouldn't be smart to keep what we'd found from you."

"Thank you," Lilah murmured, still a bit shocked. She was tired and it was hard to process everything at once. "Would you mind if I went to my room for a bit? I need some time to think about this."

"Of course," Lindy said, rushing to Lilah and embracing her tightly. "Take the whole day. We can handle things here."

Lora nodded in agreement and Lilah offered a wan smile in thanks.

Her intention had been to go to her room and go to bed. Surely things would be clearer once she'd gotten some rest. But her feet took her straight to Justin's room, where suddenly she was banging on his door as if the devil were inside and she was an avenging angel bent on retribution.

Justin opened the door and his frown turned into a happy grin until she pushed past him with terse instructions to shut the door behind her.

"What's wrong?" he asked as soon as he saw her expression.

"I just got some really upsetting news and I need some clarification from you," she said, going straight to the point. "Are you Senator Cales's son?" Justin's expression dimmed under the weight of her question and she had her answer. "Why didn't you tell me?"

"I didn't know it mattered," he retorted stiffly. "And I don't see how it does. So my dad's a politician. I told you I grew up with money. Why should it matter that our wealth came from politics?"

"It doesn't. I don't care about your money. It's the other stuff that bothers me."

"Such as?"

"Such as the fact that you have a reputation for being

a man-whore, for being a notorious, coldhearted player who does whatever it takes to get girls into bed and then kicks them out when he's finished."

"Who told you that?" he demanded.

"Who told me doesn't matter if the information is true. I believe in going to the source. So tell me...is it true?"

JUSTIN STARED INTO THE FACE of the woman he was fairly certain he was falling in love with and his stomach pitched with roiling unease. She'd only scratched the surface of his bad behavior. Previously, he'd been proud of his reputation. But now, faced with the open confusion and hurt reflected in Lilah's eyes, he felt deeply ashamed.

"Lilah, I'm not perfect and I wouldn't pretend to be. We've all made mistakes, right?" He tried to move toward her with the intent of pulling her into his arms but she reacted by putting more distance between them. "What's going on? Remember last night? Remember what an amazing time we had together? Let's go back to that. That was real. This bullshit is just stuff from my past that doesn't reflect who I am now. Are you really going to judge me so unfairly on stuff I did before I met you?"

"Depends," she said. "How far ago in your past are we talking?"

He quieted, not wanting to lie but knowing his transformation was so new he was still getting used to it himself. He answered carefully, saying, "Not that long ago. But," he said quickly when Lilah looked away in disgust, "I can tell you that meeting you changed my life."

"Don't patronize me," Lilah said. "And don't treat

me like some naive girl who will believe whatever falls from your mouth."

"I would never treat you like that," he said stiffly. "What do you want me to say? I could've easily lied but I chose the truth."

"Would you like a pat on the back?" Lilah asked, her gaze hard. "My Grams used to say that you could measure a person's character by their actions. So you chose to be truthful to a direct question, you don't get an *attaboy* for doing what you should've done without thinking."

Justin pushed his hand through his hair, agitated at being cornered. "Oh, so you're always honest? Is that right?" he shot back defensively.

She started to retort but then pink crawled in her cheeks and she said nothing. Although one might count that as a point in his favor, Justin took no pleasure in the victory. The ugliness squatting between them was in direct contrast to the bliss they'd been enjoying hours ago and he wanted nothing more than to forget all this conflict and return to the cuddling and kissing. But judging by the sudden tears welling in Lilah's eyes, that possibility was about as remote as anyone ever finding the Holy Grail. "C'mon, Lilah," he said, gentling his voice as he took a step toward her in the hopes of holding her but she shook her head wildly and stepped farther away. "What? What's going on? Are you really that mad that I didn't share my every shameful and dirty secret the minute we met? I mean, it's hard to impress someone you really like when you unload all that garbage on them," he said, trying to use a smidge of humor to lighten the mood but the attempt fell flat as her eyes began to fill and his hope died.

"Of course not," she responded, sniffing back tears. It killed him to see her cry but she wouldn't let him get near her so he had no choice but to stand there like a douche watching her cry.

"Then what's the issue?" he asked, exasperated.

"The issue is that this incident has proven to me that I don't really know you at all and that makes me uncomfortable. I'm in a place in my life where I need to minimize certain kinds of stress and right now, I'm feeling very stressed and sad and…blindsided." She drew a deep breath and regarded him with a brittle stare. "And I don't like it."

A sense of loss followed her statement and he could almost feel her withdrawing from him emotionally if such a thing were possible. He'd never been a touchy-feely type of person but his heartbeat had begun a panicked beat at the look of goodbye in her eyes. "Lilah… let's talk this out. It's not a big deal—"

"It *is* a big deal. I don't like surprises and I don't like the feeling that I'm with someone with dirty secrets. But you know, maybe this revelation is a blessing. I knew we shouldn't start something as ill-fated as a relationship when you are plainly not interested in staying and I'm not going so this is just the most reasonable decision to arrive at when it comes to you and me."

"What are you saying?" he asked, though he knew. God, he knew. He could feel it in his bones.

"Come on, Justin. You're a smart guy. This was stupid to start."

"Yes," he agreed, surprising her with his answer. "But sometimes things happen that take us by the neck to get our attention and that's what happened when I met you. I can't explain it, Lilah. I wouldn't be able to if I tried because I don't fully understand what's happening, but I think I might be falling in love with you because I haven't once thought of being with another woman since that first day. It's been you, the whole time."

"It's not love, Justin. It's fascination and infatuation. It'll fade."

"Really? You think so? Is that what you're hoping?" he demanded to know. "Because I think you're wrong."

Lilah avoided his gaze. "We were stupid and irresponsible and I'm tired of being that person everyone has to look out for because she's always making dumb mistakes in her life."

"We were not a mistake," he disagreed hotly. "We were great together. Trust me, I've made plenty of my own mistakes and I'm pretty well-acquainted with how regret feels and I don't regret a second with you."

Lilah's gaze sparkled with more tears and for a wild, fleeting moment he thought, perhaps, he'd gotten through to her, but the moment passed and all doors of opportunity slammed shut behind her eyes with a finality that jarred his soul. "Good luck with your career," she murmured in a tear-choked voice. "I wish you the best."

"Lilah, wait!" Justin chased after her but she was quick on her feet and out the door before he could stop her. He nearly ran after her but he didn't trust that he wouldn't muck things up even more. So, he gritted his teeth and bit back the hot words that bubbled to the surface that were half anguish and half anger over her rejection and slammed the door because it was all he could do.

All the crappy things he'd done in the past—that he hadn't thought twice about for a long time—came rushing to the forefront of his memory, reminding him in bright Technicolor that he'd been naive to think that he could shield Lilah from the truth of things if they continued to see each other. But he hadn't cared. His gut rolled and his hands shook. God, was this what a broken heart felt like? Sort of like the flu without a fever. He definitely felt ready to puke.

Two hours ago he'd been making plans to spend the day with Lilah around town, possibly taking a charter boat to St. Croix. Now…he was ready to bawl like a damn baby who'd been pinched.

He'd gone from heaven to hell in the space of twenty-four hours.

And he had no freaking clue as to how to put things back the way they were.

It'll never be the same, a small voice whispered in his mind. He didn't have the heart to argue.

CHAPTER NINETEEN

CELLY WIPED AT THE SWEAT sliding down her temple and resumed chopping at the overgrown flower garden that had gone to pot since she'd become involved with the Bells.

"Stubborn lot," she groused under her breath as she pulled at the invading tropical plants that were choking out her orchids. "Jus' doin' as dey please, no matter what de consequence." She leaned back and surveyed her progress, frowning unhappily when she realized the job was much bigger than she imagined it would be when she started. It'd seemed a good idea at the time when she'd cast a sour look across her yard and found the overgrowth to be the most offensive. Heath had come and fixed her leaking toilet and a host of other annoyances that she hadn't realized were such a problem, but the truth was, she'd had no reason to really care about this place when she was with the Bells. That ridiculous, messed-up bunch of whackadoodles had become…her family.

And now they had tossed her out like day-old bread.

Well, not everyone. Just Lora.

"Dat girl needs a swift kick in her behind," she said, struggling to her feet after kneeling for too long on the hard ground. She thought of Lilah and immediately worry crossed her mind. Was she being looked after?

Lilah certainly wasn't a child but she had a childlike sweetness that called to Celly's heart, reminded her of her own daughter she'd lost so long ago.

Celly blinked back the sudden sting of tears as the memory of her daughter, Hattie, sprang to mind. She'd been a quiet girl with private demons that Celly hadn't been aware of until it'd been too late. Hattie with her dark hair and eyes hadn't been a beauty like Lilah, but their souls felt the same. Celly had recognized the sadness hiding behind Lilah's smile from the moment they'd met. The painful shock had sent a zing straight to Celly's heart and she'd almost walked away but she just couldn't, not when it'd been obvious to Celly that Lilah had been hurting inside and everyone else was too blind to see.

As if conjured by her thoughts, Lilah drove up and Celly could see through the hazy windshield that her face was splotched with tears.

"What's wrong, chile?" Celly asked, immediately ready to slay dragons for the girl. "Tell Celly what troubles yah."

Lilah went into Celly's arms without hesitation and sobbed on her shoulder. Celly clucked and cooed, comforting her until she could form words.

"It's stupid," Lilah admitted, pulling away and wiping at her running nose and eyes. "I shouldn't care. I knew it was temporary and he was going to leave anyway but it hurts to know that he's such a jerk. I mean, he's a total D-bag."

"What is D-bag?" Celly asked, confused. "Is he *clung?*"

Lilah shook her head. "No, he doesn't do drugs—that I know of—but he's a player and he's a politician's son and Lindy said he's bad news and I know she wouldn't lie to me. So, I told him I didn't want to see him anymore and he left the resort this afternoon and it kills me that he didn't even try to say goodbye. I mean, I know I told him to leave me alone but he should've tried a little harder to see me before he left. Right?"

Lilah looked to Celly for validation and Celly chuckled. "What we need is fresh papaya. Settles de nerves and calms de tummy."

Lilah's hand went to her stomach just as it gurgled. Celly knew Lilah struggled with a nervous stomach and whenever she was upset, it would send her racing to the bathroom. Lilah nodded and followed Celly into the house.

"Yah like dis boy dat much?" Celly surmised as she cut the papaya open and scooped out the seeds.

"Yes," Lilah confessed miserably. "I know all the reasons why I shouldn't but I couldn't seem to stay away from him. There was just something about him that I liked."

"Such as?" Celly asked, handing her the papaya slices.

"He made me laugh," Lilah answered with a sad smile before biting into a slice. "He made me feel normal. Like I was just like any other girl he might've met while on vacation."

Celly frowned. "What makes yah tink yah not?"

"Celly…I'm not normal. You know that."

"I know no such ting," Celly said stubbornly. "Yah seem normal to me."

"You're being kind."

Celly barked a short laugh. "Yah know I'm not. I call what I see. Yah had some trouble a little while ago, but yah changed. It's all in de past now, time to move on. Stop dwelling, chile," she admonished gently.

Lilah nodded but there remained a hopeless blanket of misery draped around her small shoulders that Celly knew would take time to shrug off. In the meantime, all anyone could do was be there for her. "Yah know…if he is as good as yah say he is, he will not leave yah. If he doesn't come back—" Celly shrugged "—den he is not de man yah tink he is and it's a blessing he be gone."

Lilah drew a deep, halting breath and her eyes sparked with fresh tears, but she nodded again and Celly knew Lilah heard the wisdom even if she didn't want to. Celly handed her a tissue and Lilah wiped her nose and eyes like a good girl. Celly smiled until Lilah asked, "When are you coming back to Larimar?"

Celly pursed her lips. "Yah know I'm not."

"I know no such thing," Lilah retorted, some of her spirit returning. "We need you and this spat between you and Lora has gone on long enough. I'm tired of not seeing you around. We all miss you. Even Lora but you know she'd rather chew off her own foot than admit it."

"How is Jack?" Celly dared to ask, though she probably didn't want to know. The old man didn't do well with change. She supposed her leaving had thrown him for a loop and she felt right bad about that but she wasn't one to stay where she wasn't wanted.

"Pops needs you more than ever. He's…" Lilah sighed unhappily. "Becoming harder to keep track of. He wanders and we have to keep him occupied at all times. Lora is running out of ideas to keep him corralled. I'm afraid we might have to put him in a home."

"Jack would not like that," Celly said ominously. "A cage is no place for a mon."

"I know that, Celly, but we don't have a choice. What if he wanders off and gets hurt or worse? We have to do what's best for his welfare. I don't know… It's a mess. My problems are certainly small compared to what Larimar is going through."

Lilah rubbed at her eyes and surprised Celly with a yawn. Lilah laughed derisively and shook her head as she said, "It used to be that I had insomnia but now I can't seem to keep my eyes open. I wish there was a happy medium."

Celly eyed her speculatively but said nothing. It could be the stress of everything. Or it could be… Well, no it couldn't be that. Celly knew Lilah was a smart girl. No sense in worrying over maybes and what-ifs. Celly patted Lilah's knee. "Yah need rest. Can't save de world if yah can't keep yah peeps open. Everyting will work out. It always does."

Lilah nodded but didn't look convinced. Celly could see the longing in Lilah's eyes for her to come back to Larimar but Celly needed to think about things for a while before walking back through those doors. Lora had the disposition of a harridan and Celly wasn't of a mind to dance to her tune.

But Celly knew that was only half the problem.

Celly had a soft spot for Jack—which was the most ridiculous of situations given the fact that the old man was still in love and having regular conversations with his dead wife.

There was no future for her with Jack Bell.

But her heart was tied up in an awful tangle with that family. Lord, it'd hurt to walk away but she wasn't going to spend half her time defending herself against a family member who'd rather see her backside than accept her.

But honest to God's truth, her heart cried every night, battering at her poor stubborn dignity for refusing every plea that came from every person except the one it needed to come from.

Damn yah, Lora Bell. Yah harder than petrified stone and just as unyielding.

JACK RUBBED AT HIS EYES and followed his wife out onto the patio. The shimmer of her image confused him and spiked a shaft of fear into his heart. He didn't understand why she was there and then gone. As if his mind was playing tricks on him. Everything seemed out of whack but he couldn't put his finger on exactly what was missing or wrong. The knowledge that slipped in and out of his grasp heightened his irritation and general grouchiness but at the core, he was scared.

A part of him knew that he was slowly losing it.

Some days were worse than others.

It seemed his Lana came to him on the worst days. Today must have been a bad day, because Lana was there smiling at him, gesturing for him to follow her.

If this was losing it, he didn't mind. She was always so lovely. Prettiest girl he'd ever seen and in all the years they'd spent together that'd never changed.

"I'm an old lady," she'd announced with an unhappy sigh as she'd finger combed her fine gray hair from her temple one morning. "When'd that happen?"

"You're not old," he'd said, countering with, "You're simply vintage."

"Ugh. I sound like a car," she'd responded, but he'd coaxed a smile out of her. He'd always been able to do that. Oftentimes it'd been his saving grace, his ability to make her laugh. "I used to be beautiful," she said wistfully.

"And you still are," he replied indignantly. "As if I'd squire around an ugly lady on my arm. I have a reputation to protect you know."

She laughed, the sound full of light and love. "Jack Bell, you're such a joker. The only reputation you have is that you're an excellent judge of character but a terrible birdhouse maker." Her statement caused him to double take in surprise but she soothed his wounded ego by wrapping her arms around his middle and holding him tight. He rested his cheek on her crown and she smiled against his chest. "Well, I guess you're stuck with me even if I'm old and gray."

"I guess so. But I want to take a second look at the warranty. I think I was suckered by the fine print."

She gasped in mock outrage and swatted him on the arm. "Just for that, no broiled pineapple for you."

"Aww, I take it back," he said, smiling to add with total sincerity, "You're a classic, Lana. No need for a warranty. You were built to last."

The voices from that memory faded until they were a distant echo and Jack found himself alone, standing on a section of beach he didn't recognize. He turned and gazed down the long expanse of white sand and realized he didn't recognize anything. His lip began to tremble and he fought tears of frustration. He wiped at his brow, not quite sure where to go. Then, a flash of sunlight caught his eye and there was Lana, shimmering in the humid heat, smiling. Only this time, she was beckoning for him to join her in the water.

A smile cracked his face. His Lana had always been

part fish. He shucked his flip-flops and followed his wife into the warm, tepid Caribbean waters.

"Wait up!" he called out to Lana who was already making clean, swift strokes away from shore. She'd always been a better swimmer than him and eager to show off her skills. He struck out with more vigor. He'd show her that he could still keep up with his mermaid woman. Just wait and see. "I'm coming after you. This time, I *will* catch you!"

Light laughter floated on the breeze and Lana disappeared but Jack knew she was there. He just had to catch up.

CHAPTER TWENTY

JUSTIN LANDED IN NEW YORK with the disposition of a man caught by the IRS cheating on his taxes: angry, scared, frustrated and defensive.

So when his father was in the Town Car sent to the airport to pick him up, he wasn't in the mood to chit-chat.

"I must say, I'm surprised you came home early. I thought you'd wring every last minute out of your vacation. Eager to start your new career, eh?" Vernon Cales seemed pleased. "Did you enjoy St. John?"

Justin sent a cold look to his father. "It was adequate for a last meal."

His father's easygoing pleasantry chilled in the face of Justin's open disdain. "I see your attitude hasn't improved. I'd hoped you would've returned with a renewed sense of purpose. You disappoint me."

"Then we're even. You disappointed me a long time ago."

His father stiffened. "Oh? And how is that? By providing you with a top-notch education for you to piss all over? For providing you with a privileged lifestyle so that you could be ultimately useless? Tell me, how did I disappoint you?"

"By being a shitty father," Justin answered without pulling punches. "Kids need more than someone who signs the checks. You know, I met someone over in St. John and I saw how *her* family operates. They don't have as much money but they are tight and they openly love each other. It's not about the privilege or the things that you can buy. It's about the people, *Dad,*" he said, sneering, too hurt inside to censor himself. "But you wouldn't know anything about that."

"Are you going to start sniveling because you didn't get enough hugs as a child? Grow up. There is no place in politics for someone so soft."

"I never wanted to be in politics," Justin muttered.

"You have the choice. If you choose not to follow the path I've outlined for you, you simply have to accept that I will no longer fund your lifestyle. No one is forcing you to do anything. But it's easier for you to blame me for coercing you rather than accept the fact that you aren't willing to fend for yourself. You do love your lifestyle, don't you, son?"

Justin looked away, his face hot. Could he give it all up? The idea scared him more than he wanted to admit. But he hated that his father knew his weakness and exploited it. "I still have a week available within my vacation. I don't want to discuss this on my time. I will schedule a meeting with you on Monday to discuss my new career path. Until then, stay the hell out of my life."

"Very well." Vernon Cales drew himself up. "One week. Monday I expect to see a young man ready to work, not this petulant child who still blames his problems on everyone else."

Justin couldn't listen to this sanctimonious bullshit a moment longer. He'd rather walk. "Pull over," he instructed the driver.

"What are you doing?" his father asked, irritated.

"Getting away from you."

He didn't even grab his luggage. They would deliver it to his apartment. He didn't watch as the Town Car pulled away; he simply walked into the throng of people and hoped to disappear.

LORA'S SENSE THAT SOMETHING was wrong intensified when she couldn't find Pops. Lilah was working the front desk and hadn't seen him but it was her hope that Heath was keeping Pops occupied in the shop with him.

But when she entered the shop and found Heath alone, bent over a glass fusion project, her hope plummeted.

"I can't find Pops," Lora said without preamble, the flutter of fear becoming a familiar sensation as Pops's mental acuity had continued to deteriorate. "He's not in Larimar."

Immediately abandoning his piece, Heath dropped the glass into the bucket without regard. She winced knowing the piece was ruined and he'd have to start over but she didn't have time to worry about that right now. "Last I saw him he was going to have a snack and then take a nap. Are you sure he's not puttering around in the private section?"

"I looked three times. He's not there," Lora said, her voice rising with panic. "He could be anywhere by this point."

"Let's try and stay calm," he said, grabbing her by the shoulders and holding her gaze with his own. "He's probably fine. We just need to use a process of elimination to find him. There are only so many places he could be and he hasn't had time to jump the ferry to

St. Thomas so he is here on this island. I'll call Billy and tell him to keep an eye out for him near the docks."

Lora nodded and wiped at the tears oozing from her eyes. If anything happened to Pops she'd never forgive herself. She knew it was probably time to hire a care-giver at the very least or at the worst, put him in a man-aged care facility but she'd been stubbornly holding off, citing the expense but that wasn't really the reason. If she did any of those things it would only make the sit-uation that much more real. Their Pops wasn't coming back to them, no matter what they did. And that killed her deep inside. God, how it hurt. But it was nothing compared to the guilt that would crush her if her stub-bornness ended up hurting Pops.

Heath returned a moment later, his expression de-termined. "I'm calling Celly. She knows of all the little places Pops likes to wander off to."

Lora opened her mouth to refuse that idea but a voice sounding a lot like Grams chastised her soundly, say-ing, *Stop being such a donkey, little Bell. This is bigger than your ego and you know it.*

Lora swallowed her comment and nodded jerkily to Heath. "Hopefully, she can help" was all she managed to say before her throat closed. If Celly had been here, perhaps this wouldn't have happened. They'd never had so many problems with Pops before Celly had left. Per-haps Pops hadn't gotten worse, it was just that Celly had always managed to make it seem not so bad because she handled Pops so well.

Damn it. What a fool she'd been. Hot, shameful tears rolled down her face as she realized how her pride had, once again, bitten her in the ass. She wiped at her eyes and made a promise. If they managed to circumvent disaster with Pops, she'd make things right with Celly.

"I promise, Grams," she murmured, hoping her grandmother could hear her and approved. "I promise."

LILAH RAN OUT TO THE PATIO and scanned the private beach. Nothing but gorgeous blue skies and clear waters met her gaze. She searched her memory for anything that might provide a clue as to where Pops might've gone and at first, she came up with nothing. Frustrated, she thought harder, determined to find something— anything—that might help.

"Grams…where is he?" she whispered, closing her eyes, praying for a miracle. She opened her eyes and something caught her eye. No…it couldn't be… She stared harder, the air evaporating from her lungs. She fished her cell phone from her pocket and called Billy.

"Billy, I need a huge favor, can you bring your boat around to our private beach? I think I see Pops and he's way out there, too far for me to swim but I can see him and he's heading for Dead Man's Breach."

"Dat plenty far from de Larimar beach," Billy said, worried. "Yah sure?"

"I can see him. Quickly, Billy, I'm afraid he's going to drown!"

"I'll be there in two minutes," he promised, and then he was gone. Lilah spun on her heel and ran back into the resort, yelling as she went. "I've found him! He's swimming to Dead Man's Breach!"

"Dead Man's Breach?" Lora repeated with horror. "That's impossible for a man his age! He's going to drown!"

"I have Billy going to get him. Do you think he'll remember Billy? What if he refuses the help? Oh, damn, maybe we should call the authorities and have search and rescue get him instead."

"There's no time." Heath looked just as fearful. "We'll just have to hope and pray that he remembers Billy or just plain wants to get out of the water."

"Oh, God, this is a nightmare," Lora said, wringing her hands in an uncharacteristic move. "I feel like I'm going to throw up."

That made two of them, Lilah thought as her mouth watered in a warning sign. She wiped the sweat suddenly beading her brow as she swallowed hard. Oh, dear…

"Are you all right?" Heath asked, noticing her distress. "You don't look very good."

"It's my nerves, I think," Lilah answered, her hands shaking as she wiped away the sweat. "I feel…nauseous."

"Go eat some crackers or something. We'll keep an eye out for Pops and Billy," Lora assured her, gesturing for her to go. "We don't need you fainting or passing out because you haven't eaten or something like that."

"It's probably just my medication disagreeing with me," she said faintly, feeling sicker by the minute but she was determined to stick it out. There was no way she was leaving until she knew Pops was okay.

It seemed the longest two minutes of their lives but soon, they saw Billy's charter boat, *Jumbie Moon,* sailing past their private beach. Heath's phone buzzed and it was Billy giving them the thumbs-up.

"Thank God," he said, hanging up. "Billy has Pops and he's okay. Exhausted but okay. Seems he did remember Billy—another blessing—and was happy to see a familiar face. I'll go pick him up at the dock."

"I'll go with you," Lora said quickly, and they hurried out the door. Lilah smiled with relief but her stomach hadn't yet received the news that everything was in the clear. She wrapped her arms around her middle and groaned. Her stomach had always been sensitive to her nerves but this was going to another level. Oh, no, she was definitely not feeling better. Not even the thought of fresh papaya made her feel better.

In fact, she wasn't sure she was going to make it to the bathroom. A bubble of ickiness propelled her into action and she ran to the bathroom to bury her head in the toilet.

Somewhere between bouts of ralphing her guts out and groaning she realized something that made everything so much worse than it already was.

Her period was officially two weeks late.

And she was barfing her guts out.

Oh. Shit.

CHAPTER TWENTY-ONE

LILAH STARED AT THE STRIP, uncomprehending. "How is this possible?" she groaned, looking to her sister for answers though she knew Lindy was just as shell-shocked. "I'm on the Pill...I never miss a day. I swear!"

"No birth control method is one hundred percent," Lindy murmured with a pained expression. "I can't believe this..."

"*You?* I'm freaking out here!"

"Okay, first we need to calm down—it's not good for the baby all this freaking out," Lindy said, although she still appeared bewildered. "Maybe we read the strip wrong?" The hope in her voice mirrored Lilah's panic. Lilah knew they hadn't read the test wrong but she was willing to give it a go. She grabbed the box and read the directions again. After a minute of staring hard at the strip, she shook her head and threw it in the trash. "You're p-p-pregnant, aren't you?" Lindy said, barely able to say the words.

"It would appear so," Lilah said, tears filling her eyes. "What am I going to do?"

Lindy cast a look filled with uncertainty, then asked in a timid tone, "Are you going to keep the baby?"

"That's a dumb question. Of course I am," Lilah shot back with irritation. "How could you even ask such a thing?"

"I'm sorry. I didn't want to assume and you know, that's like a really personal thing," Lindy said, clearly out of her element and turning herself inside out in her attempt to be calm, rational and supportive. "Li...this is... Oh, my God, I'm going to be an auntie! I will be the coolest auntie I just know it because I'm a pretty awesome stepmom."

"Almost stepmom," Lilah reminded Lindy. "You're not married yet."

"Hey, I wash that kid's clothes. I think I qualify."

Lilah slumped down onto the sofa and stared at the ceiling, overwhelmed and scared but mostly wishing Justin was there with her instead of hundreds of miles away completely clueless as to how both their lives were going to change.

"So now what?" Lindy asked.

"I don't know."

"We should tell Lora and Heath."

"Yeah, I suppose so. Maybe we should wait given all the excitement with Pops. I don't know if Lora's sanity can take another hit."

"You might be right but if we wait...she'll be pissed to be finding out last."

Lilah sighed. "Whatever. I guess you're right. It's a lose-lose situation no matter how you slice it."

"What about the father?" Lindy ventured. "What are you going to tell him?"

Lilah thought of Justin and her heart ached. Telling him wasn't high on her list of desirables. What would he say? Would he accuse her of trying to trap him because she knew that his family had money? Ugh. What an abhorrent thought. "I don't know," she hedged, still uncomfortable over the very idea that Justin might think something so reprehensible about her. "Maybe I won't tell him at all."

Lindy looked shocked. "You can't do that. He deserves to know."

Lilah focused a speculative look on Lindy. "Really? Says who? Maybe he wouldn't care or want this baby. Why would I subject a child to his rejection?"

"But then again, maybe he'll want to be a part of this child's life and it's not your place to deny him that right."

Lilah scowled and looked away. "You sound like Lora. What happened to my twin sister? You know, the one who was flippant and nonchalant about most things and certainly didn't make moral judgments?"

"She grew up."

"More's the pity. I need *that* sister back. I already have a stick-in-the-mud sister," Lilah muttered.

"Well, one thing's for sure, those pregnancy hormones are doing absolutely nothing for your disposition," Lindy huffed, getting to her feet. "Should we call a family meeting?"

"God, no. I will tell Lora privately."

"Okay. I still think you ought to tell Justin."

"What makes you think it's Justin's baby?" Lilah said, shrugging. "Maybe it's someone else's."

"Good try," Lindy said, not buying her act. "I know you, Li, and one thing you are not is promiscuous."

"People change."

"Do they?"

Lilah hoped they did. She wanted to tell Justin about their baby but…she couldn't push from her mind the information she'd received before he left. He was a player of the worst kind. And honestly, she couldn't fathom the pain his rejection would cause in her heart if she told him and he pushed her away.

She'd rather just raise the baby herself. God, when had she turned into such a coward? She squeezed her eyes shut to keep the tears from oozing out. How could she explain she hadn't truly gotten pregnant on purpose? She knew how it would appear and she cringed at the thought of defending herself. Why hadn't he worn a damn condom? Why hadn't she insisted? Because most times they were both so eager to tear each other's clothes off that neither had been thinking of anything aside from the moment.

"Justin doesn't need a baby in his life right now. His father has big plans for him in the political arena and I'm sure a baby mama wasn't on the agenda."

"What kind of big plans and how do you know that?"

Lilah glanced away sheepishly, embarrassed that she'd scoured the internet looking for news on Justin and had stumbled on a news article with the senator officially announcing his plans to step down so that his son could take his place on the campaign trail. Justin had looked strong and confident standing there, shaking his father's hand with that wide, easy grin that she'd come to adore. "I found a news article announcing the plan for Justin to follow his father into politics," she finally admitted to her sister. "That's how I know. And nowhere did it mention plans to expand the Cales family anytime soon."

"Plans change."

She sighed. "Not this kind. I don't know what to do," she cried, grinding out the moisture from her eyes. "I'm the exact opposite of what a politician's wife should be."

"Who said anything about marriage? I didn't say you

ought to run out and marry the guy, just let him know that he's going to be a father. Two separate things," Lindy said firmly.

"I know, I'm just saying…" Her voice trailed as she thought of the kind of person Justin would probably marry. Likely some pale-faced respectable girl with a pedigree as polished as his own; not a barefoot island girl with her head in the clouds most times who hadn't even attended college.

Embarrassment flooded her as she pictured herself stacked up against all the other women Justin was more suited for and realized with a certainty she was making the right decision. "Well, I don't have to decide today," she murmured, although she already had.

Justin wasn't ready to be a father.

She swallowed a lump of fear.

But was she ready to be a mother?

She supposed she had eight more months to figure it out.

JUSTIN'S MOOD HADN'T improved in spite of his buddy's ardent and well-intentioned attempts to lighten his spirits by dragging him from one club to the next.

They were in their usual spot at Martini, the upscale bar that catered to the rich and elite of Manhattan, but whereas Keenan and Benny were admiring the eye candy with open appreciation, Justin was just ready to go home.

"What is wrong with you?" Keenan asked when Justin failed to blink twice at the sexy redhead giving him a few sultry stares brimming with invitation. "That woman is practically sending out a smoke signal saying she's into you. Are you sick or something? Go after it, man! It's a moral imperative that you nail that tail!"

Justin looked sharply at Keenan, irritation in his voice as he said, "Not interested in just chasing after nameless women for a meaningless romp in the sack."

"Yeah? Since when?" Benny challenged. "Two months ago you'd have been halfway down her dress by now. Suddenly you're all Mr. Morals and shit? Who do you think you're kidding? We know you, Cales. You're as horny as a goat and just as eager to stick it to whoever is willing."

Justin couldn't hide his discomfort at Benny's derisive comment. Was it true? Had he truly been such a pig? He remembered times when he'd been less than chivalrous. He also remembered times when he'd been downright cruel. Damn, this self-examination wasn't improving his mood any that was for sure. He drained his beer and reached into his wallet to throw down a few twenties. "I'm out of here," he announced, much to the surprise of his buddies.

"Hey, man, what's going on?" Keenan said, following him to the curb where Justin was hailing a cab. "You're acting weird. Did you get too much sun while in the tropics?"

Ordinarily, Keenan always made him laugh but he didn't find anything funny at the moment. Maybe he was just drowning in self-pity but honestly, his father's manipulations weren't first and foremost on his mind. His mind was focused on his last moments with Lilah. He could still see her look of disappointment as her faith in him shattered. He could still hear the echo of her anguished tone as she left him in that room without even allowing him to explain.

Not that he would've been able to explain his behavior.

But she hadn't wanted to hear it anyway.

At night he was overcome with the urge to board a plane to see her one last time, to make her understand that he'd never meant to withhold information, but he'd savored their time together as something pure and magical and sharing all the sordid details of his true life would've contaminated everything.

He wasn't even sure if she'd care.

The fear that she'd reject him again kept him from following through with his impulse but it left him feeling out of sorts and angry.

Which was why he wasn't in the mood for silly games or nights of chasing tail.

"Keenan, I'm not good company tonight. I'd just bring everyone down."

"It's your old man, isn't it?" Keenan said with sympathy. "He's a right bastard for forcing you into politics. At least my old man isn't that bad."

"Yeah, well, he says he's doing it for my own good," Justin said. "Says I was made for this career, even if I don't realize it just yet."

"You think he's right? You looked the part the other day, that's for sure. I never thought I'd see the day when Justin Cales wore a politician's smile for the camera."

He agreed. "You and me both but I guess now's as good a time as any to get on with my life, right?"

"Yeah, I guess so. Still, sucks how it came about," Keenan said with open sympathy. "Listen, politics can't be all bad. The perks are nice," he said, waggling his eyebrows. "Just make sure all your interns are hot chicks and you're golden."

Justin smiled but there was no true humor in it. He didn't want hot interns. He wanted Lilah. He stifled a groan and scrubbed his hands over his face, before saying, "I'll catch you later, buddy," eager to put a cap on the day but Keenan stopped him with a clap on his shoulder.

"Listen, just go through the motions for now. Put a good face on it and then when the old man kicks it, get out," Keenan advised in all seriousness.

Good God, Justin thought with irritation. When had Keenan turned into such a douche?

Keenan closed Justin's cab door and then brightened and said, "All right, man, you take it easy. I'll call you tomorrow. Maybe we can take the boat out?"

"Maybe," Justin said in a noncommittal manner. He didn't want to go spend hours on a boat, either, but he knew Keenan was just trying to be a good friend in the only way he knew how. "Catch you later."

Justin gave the cabbie his apartment address. As the familiar sights of the city flashed by him, he thought of how he'd love to show Lilah the city and all its urban glory. He imagined her shy smile and heard her soft sigh when he closed his eyes. God, he missed her.

How was it possible that he'd fallen so quickly for a woman so wildly unsuited for his lifestyle?

Lovesick. That's what he was.

He'd never imagined such a thing actually existed but he believed it now.

His brain was mush; his gut twisted.

But worst of all?

His heart felt punched to pulp.

How was he going to survive the knowledge that he'd likely never see Lilah again?

To his surprise, a tear slid from his eye.

Ahh hell. This was just great. Now he was blubbering in a taxicab.

Focus, Cales.

Lilah was in the past. Get over it. He had bigger problems. He'd already signed on the dotted line; his life was officially a Cales commodity in the political market.

The only good thing? Likely, he'd be too busy to think of Lilah any longer with the grueling campaign trail his father had already scheduled. He was going to spend the next few months hitting every little pocket town and urban city within the New York sphere in the hopes of gaining votes. It'd definitely keep him preoccupied, to the point of mental and physical exhaustion.

As another spasm of pain rocked him, he clenched his fist and lightly tapped the window.

And he'd welcome it.

CHAPTER TWENTY-TWO

"I'M SORRY, COME AGAIN?" Lora said, blinking hard and shaking her head as if her ears had suddenly malfunctioned the minute Lilah shared her bomb. "Did you say...?"

"Yes," Lilah answered, eager to get this scene over with. "I went to the doctor yesterday to confirm. I'm about four weeks. So, barely pregnant but pregnant all the same."

"Are you sure? Sometimes the tests give out false positives, right?" Lora said, the strained hope in her voice chafing at Lilah's nerves.

"Yes, I'm sure," Lilah said, still grappling with the implications. "And even if I hadn't gone to the doctor's the fact that I can't seem to walk ten feet without burying my head in a toilet would've been a big tip-off."

"Crap," Lora muttered, closing her eyes and leaning her head against the headrest of the desk chair. "What about the father?"

"What about him?"

"Don't be coy, Lilah. Just tell me. Is he going to help support your baby?"

"No, because he's not going to know about the baby."

"As much as I agree it would be easier in the short term to leave him out, you and I both know it's not right."

"I wish people would stop pushing their morality judgments down my throat when it's not their situation," Lilah snapped. "I will handle things on my own."

"How?"

Lora's blunt question made Lilah realize she didn't have all the answers just yet. "I don't know," she admitted. "But I will."

"That's not good enough, Li. Taking care of a baby requires more than just good intentions."

"I know that."

"Well, Justin Cales should be held responsible, at least financially for this baby. Don't cut your nose off to spite your face. Of course, we'll all help as much as possible but honestly, Li…we didn't need one more financial commitment on top of everything else."

"I didn't get pregnant on purpose. I was on the Pill," Lilah said in her own defense, though it sounded pretty pathetic. "I guess my antidepressants monkeyed with the effectiveness of the Pill. I didn't realize that would happen. I wasn't planning to be sexually active so I guess I didn't pay much attention to that part of the instructions when Dr. Veronica was telling me all the dos and don'ts with the meds."

Lora sighed. "Well, live and learn. Speaking of the meds…can you take them while pregnant?"

"I've already taken steps to wean myself from the medication," Lilah answered, shocking Lora. "I don't want any chemicals going to my baby, no matter how safe the doctors say they are, there are always risks and I'm not willing to take the chance."

"Lilah, that's not a good idea. You need your medication," Lora said, worried. "What did Dr. Veronica say when you told her?"

"Don't worry, I talked with Dr. Veronica about it and she's conditionally supportive."

"What does that mean?"

"Well, I told her I was going to implement yoga and meditation into my routine, which will help with my anxiety and of course, I will still be going to my sessions. Dr. Veronica says I've been a model patient and she's cautiously optimistic to try this new approach and so…yeah, I'm going to go for it."

"Aren't you worried about a relapse?" Lora asked, concerned. "It's not like your condition will just go away because you want it to."

Lilah nodded, having given this very possibility a lot of thought. "The difference is that I'm aware of the problem. I know what to look for. I think it's going to be okay. And…you know what…I know I always have my family to be my support system. I'm really not worried," she said, trying to ease the concern in her sister's expression. "Frankly, I'm more freaked out about giving birth," she said with a delicate shudder. "Scary stuff."

"You're not kidding," Lora agreed. "You might never be the same down there, if you know what I mean."

Lilah gasped and gave her sister a playful push. "Thanks a lot. That helps. *Not.*"

They laughed but beneath the laughter lurked apprehension on both sides. Lilah knew Lora was worried about her relapsing but all Lilah could do was continue to show her that she was getting better every day and maybe someday that fear would ease. Adding her unexpected pregnancy on top of everything else they were dealing with was a burden Lilah never would've purposely thrown on the pile for her family to deal with but there was no turning back now.

A moment of silence fraught with the heaviness of their thoughts passed between them and Lilah suffered an attack of extreme guilt over the situation she'd found herself. "I'm sorry, Lora. I didn't mean to make things worse for everyone," she sighed.

Lora straightened and pulled Lilah into a tight hug. "Enough of that. Grams used to say that babies were the highest blessing and she's right. We'll figure it out. We'll love that baby as much as we love any of our crazy Bells, right?"

Lilah nodded, squeezing her eyes shut as she clung to her older sister. "I'm scared," she whispered. "What if I'm a terrible mother?"

"Impossible. You're the most caring, sensitive person I know. You'll be a natural."

Lilah wanted to believe that but her recent past sneered at her, making a mockery of her brave intentions. She pulled away from Lora and smiled in spite of the fear quivering in her gut. "Thank you for being here for me." Then she admitted, "I just wish Celly was here, too. She's kind of like a surrogate Grams." At Lora's quick look, Lilah said, "I don't mean she's replacing Grams of course. It's just that, I don't know, she always made me feel like Grams did…protected and loved. And I miss that."

Lora bit her lip, then drew a deep breath with a self-deprecating smile. "Yeah, I know what you mean. I've been doing a lot of thinking lately and I've come to realize I was blaming Celly for trying to slide into Grams's spot when that was never her intention. The fact is, Grams is gone but Celly did a lot to keep our family running smoothly. I guess I didn't want to see that because I was threatened by it."

"You ready to talk to Celly?" Lilah asked, daring to hope. "Because you know she won't come back until the air is cleared between you. Trust me, I've tried."

Lora chuckled. "Yeah…I've been working up the nerve. Everything with Pops has pretty much opened my eyes to a few things. I'm not sure what I was hoping to accomplish by getting rid of Celly. I'm just going to chalk it up to a huge misstep in judgment."

"You always were the smart sister," Lilah quipped, smiling. "Glad to hear I'm not the only one who makes mistakes."

Lora draped an arm around Lilah as they walked from the office. "Honey, I make plenty of mistakes. It just takes longer for mine to catch up. Let's go get something to eat. All this heavy talk has made me hungry."

Lilah chuckled until a wave of nausea hit. "Oh, God…don't talk about food." And then she was running to the bathroom.

At this rate, she'd spend half the summer with her head in the john.

CELLY NEARLY SWALLOWED her tongue when she saw Lora in her driveway. "Took yah long enough," she muttered as she met her outside. "What yah want?"

Lora winced and drew a deep breath. "I want…to apologize and ask you to come back to Larimar."

Celly certainly hadn't expected a surrender from the mighty Lora Bell quite so easily. She eyed the woman with suspicion. "Why?"

"Are you going to make me do this? Beg?" When Celly remained stubbornly quiet, Lora sighed and said, "I guess so. Okay, so here it is. I was wrong to let you go. I shouldn't have interfered with your system when you plainly had things running smoothly without my interference. I guess I've been struggling with something that had nothing to do with you and I'm sorry for that. The fact is, you have become a part of this family and I'm difficult with change. But you have done an amazing job with Pops and we need you. Please come back."

Celly broke into a pleased grin and gathered Lora into a fierce hug that shocked the young woman. "Now was dat so hard? Yah a stubborn mule of a girl but yah remind me of mahself when I was full of piss and vinegar. Only yah nicer dan I was back in de day."

Lora laughed ruefully. "Really? So I guess there's hope for me yet?"

Celly chuckled. "Maybe," she said, then walked staunchly to the house and strode inside to pack. Lora followed her into the house. "I seen a lot of people come and go on dis island but Jack and Lana Bell had island blood even if dey weren't born here."

"You knew my Grams before she died?" Lora asked, incredulous.

"Of course I knew her," Celly said. "She was my friend. Good woman."

"Why didn't you tell me that?"

"Yah never asked. Yah made assumptions and I let yah have dem. Why do yah tink Jack is so easy with me? He knows I was close with his Lana."

"I don't remember you coming around when I was growing up."

Celly chuckled. "Yah never were much for anyting aside from yah books. Besides, I didn't come round too much to the resort until Lana died. I noticed Jack was having troubles and Lilah was at a loss of what to do.

So I slipped myself into the front desk and stayed until yah come along and boost me out."

Lora's cheeks flushed with embarrassment and Celly patted her shoulder. She was Lana's blood true and because of that Celly would always care for Lora, but lord she be hard and stubborn. "Now, enough of dis. I've had just all I can stand of dis place. Have yah completely destroyed my desk wit your fancy filing and methods?"

"Probably," Lora admitted with a wince. "But whatever you need to put it right, I'll get for you. Even if it means hiring another part-timer."

"Bah, we don't need anyone else poking their noses into Larimar business. I can fix tings, never yah mind."

Lora's shoulders sagged with relief. "You're a lifesaver. Did you hear what happened to Pops the other day? He tried swimming to Dead Man's Breach! He nearly drowned."

At that Celly broke into a wistful grin. "Prolly following his Lana out for a swim. Yah know she was half fish he used to say."

"Yeah, I remember him saying that."

"Well, de secret to keeping Jack occupied is to keep him occupied like Lana used to. She was always putting him on task so as to keep him out of her hair when she needed to do busy work for the resort."

Lora chuckled. "No, I didn't know that. Well, I'm curious as to what we can have him do that won't endanger him or others at this point."

"Leave him to me," Celly said, smiling. She'd been managing Jack for years, much longer than any of them realized. She managed to make it work because she cared for the old coot. More than she should but that was her secret to keep and there was no reason to burden the girls with the knowledge. Deliberately switching mental gears, she said brightly, "I fancy myself some boiled bananas tonight. What do yah tink of dat?"

Lora grinned. "I think it's the best thing I've heard all day." As they climbed into the Jeep, Lora suddenly grimaced and said, "Oh, and there's something else you should know...Lilah's pregnant."

Celly surprised Lora with a chuckle. "Chile, I already knew dat. Yah'd have to be blind not to see it. Come, we'll stop by the fruit stand to pick up some coconut. Coconut water will fix her right up. Island girls been drinking it for ages to calm a baby kicking up a fuss in de belly."

The ache that'd been in Celly's heart since walking away from Larimar had eased and her step was spry. The Bells had never known it, but Lana had always tasked Celly with watching over her sugar birds and Celly had done so in her own way. Lana's sugar birds were her own.

And now there was another sugar bird on the way? Joy, that's what was in her heart. Pure joy.

Lilah was going to need her. She knew it in her bones.

All the Bells would need her, just as they'd needed Lana.

I won't let yah down, Lana girl, Celly promised silently. *I promise.*

JUSTIN HAD STRANGE DREAMS the night before. He'd tossed and turned on the bed, finding no comfort on the expensive mattress designed to give him a perfect night's rest when previously he'd always slept like a baby.

Maybe it'd been nerves. As he awaited his father inside his office, he drummed his fingers on the brand-new briefcase his father had instructed that he purchase, and his eyes burned with the need to catch some shut-eye. But just as he knew sleep wasn't on the schedule, he also knew it wasn't nerves.

He couldn't stop thinking of Lilah and last night had been the height of pain and longing. It was as if she was everywhere in his mind; there were no safe passages that he could travel without running into some reminder of his time with her. Maybe she was some kind of is-land witch, he mused darkly. Because how else could he explain the constant and unrelenting obsession he had with her? Keenan suggested a carnal cleansing.

"Just screw someone else right away, wipe away the memory, man," he'd said with the confidence of a man who believed in the method. "Remember when I got hung up on that waitress? I mean, I was totally into her in the worst way, but when I knew it wasn't going to work out, I made sure to jump in the sack with as many chicks as possible. Before too long, I couldn't even re-member what it was that had me so hung up on her." He made a rude sound. "Like, I can't even remember her name. Okay, that's a lie. I remember her name, it was Alicia, but she wasn't so special that she couldn't be easily replaced with a little effort. That's what you need, bro. I promise you this."

He'd nodded and briefly considered the idea, but it came down to this: he didn't want to screw some other chick to wipe away Lilah in his memory—not that it would work—he wanted to make more mem-ories. Lots of them. He wanted to take her to Times Square on New Year's Eve and watch as her eyes lit up with awe as the ball dropped. He wanted to take her to art museums and galleries and fine restaurants just to experience each from her perspective. There was a sweetness to Lilah that couldn't be replicated but even more alluring than her sweetness was that raw, primal animal lurking beneath the surface that she unleashed in private moments. He shuddered with the memory and his groin ached as his pants suddenly tightened. God, he missed her. The smell of her skin, an intoxicating blend of coconut-scented sunscreen and island wildness, was permanently etched in his scent receptors and he knew nothing short of burning out his nose would ever change that.

He had to go back. He had to talk to her again. If even just to get some kind of real closure.

He rose to stalk from the room, intent on booking a plane that very second when his father entered the room with his team of campaign advisors and general minions who worked expressly for the senator.

"Ah, the man of the hour. Gentlemen, you remember my son, Justin Cales? Soon to be Senator Cales if we play our cards right," he said, winking at his senior advisor, Rudy Bench.

"Of course. The resemblance is striking. I'd pick him out of the crowd as your son any day," Rudy said smoothly, reaching out to shake Justin's hand vigorously. "I just want to say, it's an honor to work alongside you to help continue the Cales political tradition. Your father has created some very big shoes to fill but I'm sure you're up to the job."

"Rudy will be your right-hand man. He will handle your press conferences and campaign appearances. He will also be your go-to guy for anything that needs massaging. But seeing as you won't be having any more of those unfortunate incidents happening, I'm sure that particular skill set will not be needed. Isn't that right, son?"

He was referencing the stripper incident. Justin gave the man a terse nod, irritated all over again, but good manners wouldn't permit him to make a caustic comment in front of the team. "I'm pleased to represent the Cales family," he said, the words tasting like ash in his mouth. "I hope to do your faith proud."

"No worries there," Rudy said, smiling. "However, we should talk about any dust that might spring up on the campaign trail. We need complete honesty if we're to campaign you successfully. You know your competitors will do whatever they can to dredge up dirt that might aid their own candidacy." Rudy looked him square in the eye with the gaze of a sharpshooter. "Is there anything else we should be made aware of?"

"No...not that I know of, aside from the stripper picture that was already splashed across the newspapers and internet blogs."

"That's already been handled," Rudy said briskly. "The official story is you suffered an unfortunate fall in the darkened club and landed in an embarrassing position just in time for the paparazzi to snap their picture. It was all an unfortunate misunderstanding, blown up in sensationalistic style to sell advertising for the various outlets. But we can't have more of that, you understand. From now on, you're the picture of moral and healthy living. Do you work out?"

"Yes," he said. "An hour a day."

"Good. We'd like to see you running in Central Park to show that you're the everyman's politician. We're running your platform on the steam of the everyman's man. You eat at the same restaurants, enjoy the same entertainments and you're there to look out for the ordinary citizen. You're young and capable, handsome to boot. Are you dating anyone? No? Good. We have a few suitable women you might be seen squiring around town."

It was all moving so quickly that Justin barely had time to voice a protest before he was being whisked away for a new wardrobe—his official campaign wardrobe. He was to appear smart and capable but down-to-earth and very approachable.

In between a tailor getting up close and personal with his balls—or inseam, as the man snippily put it when Justin growled at him to stop copping a feel—he realized with a sinking heart, there was no way he'd be able to board a plane now that he had his entourage firmly in place. Rudy would wrangle him before he could step foot in the terminal.

Justin briefly shut his eyes and swallowed the odd lump that rose in his throat as he mentally said goodbye to the woman who haunted his heart.

It was probably better this way, anyway.

Who was he kidding?

Lilah would hate New York.

CHAPTER TWENTY-THREE

LILAH WALKED INTO THE ATRIUM and smiled as the familiar warm and sultry smells of lush greenery assaulted her nostrils. Perhaps it was all in her head, but since becoming pregnant smells seemed so much more vibrant than before, almost alive under her nose. Unlike other smells, such as the aroma of popcorn, which made her want to puke, this one made her want to sink down and roll around in it. She went to her secret closet as she liked to call it and pulled out her painting supplies. Her mind was brimming with something that needed out, something that itched at the confines of her brain and demanded air or else. Even though fatigue dragged at her lids, she made a point never to ignore that creative impulse. She needed to paint as much as she needed to breathe, and when her mind was troubled, painting was her only salvation.

She moved on autopilot as she set up her supplies. The fresh creamy canvas beckoned and she savored the familiar thrill at facing a blank template. It was this point that seemed magical, where anything could happen and the world was full of possibilities. She closed her eyes and drew a deep breath. Here she found solace from the world, the problems that chased her down, and from the fear that rode her dreams.

A part of her had hoped—like a foolish girl—that

Justin would return to her and everything would be perfect. Of course, in her daydream, when she told him of their baby, he swooped her in his arms and professed his undying love for her, pledging his heart to their little family.

And they lived happily ever after.

Okay, so that was a little melodramatic, she supposed, but it was her daydream and she could make it as improbable as she pleased.

Besides, if a girl was going to dream, she might as well dream big.

Lilah rarely knew what she was going to paint when she started off, but soon enough a picture always emerged. Sometimes Lilah was shocked by what appeared, though why she didn't know. It all came from her head, right? But somehow, it didn't always seem that way. Sometimes, frightfully, it seemed as if she were two people living in one body. And she never knew which one was taking over.

She knew how that sounded and thus, it seemed only right she'd been medicated but it wasn't that she was split personality or anything like that. It was just that when she created something, she never set out to do so, it just happened and that's when she felt that other half took over. Call it her muse, or whatever, but when that happened, it was as if she'd slipped into a trance and when she emerged, she'd created something masterful and scary, evocative and raw.

Her heart bled onto the canvas with each stroke, leaching the pain that would certainly crack her soul in two if she didn't find a release valve.

Swipes of the brush, dipped in midnight-blue,

slapped against the canvas, melded with vibrant splashes of spring-yellow and married with bloodred.

An image emerged as it always did.

That lonely girl. The same girl who walked into the sea and yearned to sleep at the bottom stared off into a dark and turbulent distance, that familiar sense of longing and sadness draped around her thin shoulders as she lifted a slim hand as if to say, "Come back." The skies roiled in an angry clash of the gods, commanding an equally dangerous sea. Gone were the normally placid waters; now they churned. The green jungle pressed at her back, supporting her, curling around her ankles in thin, searching root tendrils, anchoring her to the ground. Protecting her from anything that might try to rip her from the land.

Her face, slightly turned in profile, was lifted to the sky, as if daring it to bring its worst, or perhaps she was simply resigned to her fate yet not afraid.

By the time Lilah put the finishing touches on the painting, she was exhausted. Time had flown and darkness had begun to fall. She stepped away and surveyed her work as if seeing it for the first time. She was the lonely girl.

She always had been.

Only this time, she wasn't going to walk into calm waters and hide. She was going to face the storm with courage, no matter how fierce the wind howled.

At least she hoped.

This was her chance to show everyone that she could handle big things. She wasn't fragile or weak. She had to be strong for her baby.

JUSTIN WAS RIDING A HIGH. He'd just finished his first campaign tour and he'd acquired a taste for victory in the five months he'd been hitting every town and city within New York. He'd gathered a respectable following and he was hungry to win.

Hell, he had every expectation to win. And he wanted it.

"Son, I'm real proud of you," his father said with a warm, approving smile that nearly shocked Justin out of his high. Over the past few months Justin and his father had slowly stopped snarling at each other, and what had started as fake smiles for the camera, had evolved into genuine respect and admiration as Justin had learned firsthand all the good work his father had done over the years while in office. The memory of all those missed birthdays and baseball games seemed to fade under the weight of the reason his father had been too busy for him. When he wasn't so royally pissed off at the old man, he'd had the opportunity to see that his father was, in fact, a good man. Still, it was a shock to the system to have his father standing behind him with full support. Made him wonder how things might've been different between them if Justin had realized this fact much earlier in his life. Justin swallowed and accepted his well-earned beer from Rudy as his father did the same. They clinked beer bottles and his father said, "That was a singularly spectacular speech. If I wasn't already voting for you, you'd definitely have my vote."

"He's got enough charisma to convince people that a useless swamp is prime real estate," Rudy commented with open glee. "The people want to believe in him. It's a good sign, I can tell you that."

Pride shone in his father's eyes. Justin had to admit,

it felt good to be on the same side for once. He couldn't remember the last time they'd been able to sit around enjoying a beer together like this. Hell, if ever.

"I knew you would be a natural, son," he said. "The people already believe in you. First stop, the Senate, then...who knows?"

Justin laughed ruefully. "I don't know about that, Dad. Let me win this first and then we'll see. But you know it's easy to sell what you believe in. I never realized how important health care reform was until I took a tour of that children's hospital. It's ridiculous that fat-cat bureaucrats have full coverage when kids go without. I aim to push as many health care reforms as I can manage. I grew up with everything I ever needed. I never realized that for some people they have to make the choice between taking their child to the doctor and buying food for the week because they don't have insurance and a trip to the doctor will cost an arm and a leg. Health care shouldn't be a privilege," he added quietly, still feeling the impact of the hospital visit. "If I'm ever able to do anything worth remembering, I hope it's something that will help future generations and I can't think of a better place to start than ensuring kids have access to quality health care."

"It's an excellent platform, but be judicious about it. We don't want to alienate your campaign supporters who might be considered one of those 'fat cats,' as you called them," Rudy warned.

"I'll try," he said, but that was the part about politics he didn't like. The idea of kissing ass to gain favors rubbed him the wrong way. Still, he'd cross that bridge when he came to it. At the moment, he was doing well on his own, but he knew eventually he'd run up against that moral wall.

"Listen to Rudy, son. He knows his stuff," his father advised with a final swig of his beer. "Passion is good but you have to temper that passion with reason or else you'll lose all the ground you've gained. Well—" his father sighed and rubbed his hand over his stomach "—I'll leave you to talk shop. I promised your mother dinner at her favorite restaurant," he said with a heavy exhale, adding with chagrin, "Some fancy French place that will probably give me indigestion. The things I do for love. Good night, boys."

"Night, Dad."

"Evening, Vernon."

After his father left, the discussion wandered across various topics until Rudy hoisted himself free from the chair and said, "So, you've earned yourself some R & R, what do you plan to do with yourself for the next two weeks?" His gaze was sharp and alert as he awaited Justin's answer. It wasn't only polite interest that spurred the question. For all intents and purposes, Rudy was his wrangler and it was his job to approve all of Justin's adventures.

"Take a much-needed nap," Justin quipped lightly before lifting his beer to his mouth. He swallowed and shrugged. "I don't know. I haven't decided yet."

"Well, whatever you do, keep in mind you're always in the voters' line of sight. Keep your nose clean and stick to your mantra—"

"If I wouldn't do it in plain sight of my mother, don't do it," Justin finished for him. Rudy smiled in approval. "I'm not that crazy playboy anymore. This campaign has really opened my eyes to a few things and I want to help become the change this city needs."

"I love your idealism. It's refreshing, even if a little naive. But no worries. Let's get you into the Senate seat first and then go from there."

Justin nodded and finished his beer. His thoughts drifted to Lilah and as always his heart sped up. He'd hoped distance and time would dull his obsession but there were nights all he did was clench his fists to keep from calling her at ridiculous hours of the night. Now he had two weeks to kill and the one person he should've forgotten about by now was the one person he couldn't shake.

"So who's in St. John?" Rudy asked casually, startling Justin with his keen-eyed question.

"What makes you ask that?"

"You've booked a plane ticket to St. John. Wasn't that the place your father sent you to, to sow your wild oats as they used to say? Just wondered if there was anyone in particular you left behind."

"Not really," Justin answered as casually as possible. He didn't want Rudy knowing about Lilah. Somehow he knew he wouldn't approve and Justin would never subject Lilah to that kind of scrutiny. "But I found the place really relaxing. It's quiet and the pace is slow. After the breakneck speed we've been traveling, I'm looking forward to a little peace and quiet in a place no one knows."

"Sounds lovely. Maybe I'll tag along?"

"No," Justin said firmly. "I need a break. Even from you, Rudy."

"Ah. I understand." Rudy stood and collected their empty beer bottles. "Well, enjoy your two-week sabbatical. When you return we hit the trail hard. I also have a few ladies for you to consider for the fund-raiser dinner. It would look good to have a nice lady on your arm, someone with impeccable pedigree and possibly well-connected parents. Voters trust a man who is in a committed relationship. A bachelor is too loose of a cannon. Besides, tying in an engagement could be good press. Think about it."

"Yeah, sure," he said in a noncommittal manner. He really didn't want to discuss his romantic life with Rudy. It felt wrong and fake, which it was. In his heart, he belonged to Lilah, which was a fatal flaw he knew, but he couldn't help it.

By this time tomorrow he'd be walking into Larimar. It was for closure, he told himself. Closure that he needed to move on.

But a small voice in his heart was too busy singing to listen to the brain's lies.

All that mattered was seeing Lilah one last time.

"You have the cutest belly I've ever seen," Lora remarked wistfully as she gazed at Lilah when she crossed the lobby to double check if an art piece was still available for an internet order that came through this morning. "You hardly look pregnant at all."

"Are you kidding me?" Lilah said, rubbing her round belly. "I'm huge. I'm already waddling. I can't imagine what I'll do when I'm nine months. I might have to get a wheelchair and have Heath push me around the resort."

"He'd do it in a heartbeat," Lora said wryly. "You've ignited baby fever in that man. Do you know how many times he's asked if I'm ready to have kids?"

"What do you tell him?" Lilah asked, curious.

"I tell him not now. Not until I know Larimar is on firmer footing. I mean, we've been very lucky with our bookings but that's not stable. We need something bigger, more reliable."

"We're in the tourist business. I don't think anything will ever be stable. Maybe this is as good as it gets."

"Don't say that. I might cry."

"It'll be okay. We're already doing better than we ever were before. Steady bookings, corporate retreats and internet commerce from the new site Heath had built... I'd say we're doing much better than we dreamed."

"We even have a little saved," Lora admitted. "I guess I'm just paranoid. One crisis and we'd be wiped out again."

"Don't think like that. Think positive."

Lora smiled. "Look at you all Miss Bright and Sunshiney today. No more morning sickness?"

Lilah laughed. "Not since the fourth month. I'm good, actually. Aside from my feet swelling at night. And the constant craving for watermelon at odd hours of the night. And the night sweats from the hormonal surges. Oh, and the weird hairs that sprang up out of nowhere on my stomach...yeah, I'm great."

Lora made a face. "Now I definitely want to wait a bit longer to have kids."

"It's not that bad. Besides, I've just started really feeling the babies move and that's pretty amazing."

"What does it feel like?"

"Like little bubbles fluttering around in there. Or gas."

Lora barked a laugh. "Gas? Cute." She smiled as

Celly walked in with a banana smoothie in her hand for Lilah.

"Here yah are, yah breakfast. Drink it all up. Those babies need their protein. All island girls eat lots of bananas…good for growing kids."

"It's a good thing I like bananas," Lilah said, accepting the smoothie. "Otherwise, I'd be in big trouble with the sheer number of smoothies you've made for me to drink."

Celly winked and walked back out of the room to check on Pops.

Since Celly had returned, Pops had settled down and was wandering less. It almost seemed normal, whatever normal was these days, and they'd slipped into a comforting routine.

Everything seemed calm and relaxed.

Except her mind at night.

She never stopped thinking about Justin.

Maybe it was because his babies were growing inside her—two perfect individuals who were an equal part of them each—and she wished he were there to share it with her. But each time she considered calling him, the words dried up on her tongue. What would she say to him? How would she explain? Would he believe her? Likely by this point he'd demand a paternity test. She wouldn't blame him, but she'd be a liar if she didn't admit that such a requirement would hurt.

As time wore on, her courage dwindled. And soon, her justification for keeping the knowledge of his impending fatherhood to herself was that he was better off not knowing.

Which was total crap and she knew it but she was too afraid to face what she knew was coming eventually.

She just had no idea when she woke up that morning that the moment would come so soon.

In fact, if she'd known…she might've stayed in bed with the covers pulled tightly over her head, because the one person she desperately missed yet hoped would never return to Larimar had just gasped her name in shock, and she, like a ninny from an outdated movie, simply slid to the floor in an ungainly heap.

CHAPTER TWENTY-FOUR

NO SOONER HAD HER NAME slipped from his lips in a shocked exclamation, than Lilah's face had blanched and she'd crumpled to the floor, igniting a firestorm around them.

Justin ran to her side, but he was pushed rudely aside by Heath as he maneuvered Lilah's body into his arms and lifted her from the lobby.

"You stay here," Heath bit out to Justin.

"Like hell I will," Justin shot back, following Heath as closely as a shadow. "What's going on? Is she okay?"

"She's fine. Probably just shocked to see you," Lora answered.

Heath placed Lilah gently on the sofa in the private section of the resort and everyone, including Justin, awaited the flutter of her lashes. When she awoke a few seconds later, she groaned when she saw Justin.

"Why are you here?"

"Why are you *pregnant?*" he countered, unable to stop staring at her rounded stomach. He was no expert but her belly seemed a bit big. Had she been pregnant when they'd first started seeing each other? Perhaps that'd been the complication she'd been referencing...

Lilah's hand covered her eyes and she looked green around the gills. "Can you guys give us a minute?" she asked her hovering family.

"Are you sure?" Heath asked, looking distrustfully at Justin. "What if you pass out again?"

"Then I will be here for her," Justin said sharply, hating that everyone was looking at him as if he were the enemy when clearly some key information had been withheld from him. As far as he was concerned they were all accessories to the crime.

"I'll be fine," Lilah promised, and struggled to sit up. Justin tried to help but she pulled away from him. He sat back on his haunches beside her, angry and perplexed at what was happening. Lilah waited for everyone to clear from the room and then took a moment to compose herself. "Just so you know, I've never actually fainted before. I just... Well, the shock of seeing you..."

"I can imagine," he said darkly. "What's going on?" His attention focused squarely on her stomach as she defensively rubbed her belly with both hands as if reassuring the baby and herself. "Please explain."

Lilah glared. "Isn't it obvious? I'm pregnant."

"You know I'm asking for more than the obvious. Is it mine?"

Lilah's expression paled and her hands fluttered over her belly again, as if struggling with how she wanted to answer. He held his breath, not quite sure how he hoped she would answer. Here was the woman he'd fallen in love with all those months ago, and yet, she seemed different from the girl he'd left behind and he wasn't just talking about the basketball she was cradling. "Does it matter?" she asked.

"Of course it matters," he exploded, unable to take the tension. He rose and started to pace. "This is...bad timing for me. I'm actively campaigning and this could be very damaging to my career. Everything was going really well. I have a good chance of winning. I could be the next New York senator. And I never really thought that I'd want that, but since starting my campaign, I've come to realize that I could make a real difference out there. It's ignited a passion I never knew I had…" He glanced helplessly at her stomach. "And that…I mean, a baby…it's just not…"

"It's not your baby," Lilah cut in, stopping him cold.

"Are you sure?"

"Of course I'm sure," she said. "Don't you think I might've told you if I were carrying your baby?"

Her cheeks crawled with color as she made her casual announcement and his gut questioned her honesty. But why would she lie about something like that? Wouldn't it benefit her to ring him as the father? He regarded her with open speculation and she lifted her chin, daring him to call her out. "I want a paternity test," he said, folding his arms across his chest.

She startled at his statement. "But why?" she protested. "You're off the hook. I'm not trying to get anything from you. I just want to raise my babies—"

"Babies?" he gasped, his eyes widening. "What do you mean 'babies'? There's more than one?"

"Damn it," she muttered, angry with herself for the slip. "Yes, babies. Plural," she answered with a dark scowl. "I'm a twin, remember? The chances that I would produce twins are pretty high and I got lucky."

That explained the bigger belly. He couldn't stop staring. He wanted to touch it and feel his babies beneath her bronzed, sun-kissed skin. Tears pricked his eyes but he held them back. Now was not the time. First, they had to iron out some details. "Let's try this again… When were you going to tell me that I was going to be a father?"

"I told you they aren't yours," she maintained stubbornly, but her gaze slid away.

"I know you're lying. When were you going to tell me?"

"Never, okay?" she blurted out, wiping away angry tears. "I wasn't ever going to tell you. You just said yourself, this is bad timing and I wasn't going to be the one who derailed your career because I trapped you into something you weren't ready for. I don't need you or your money. I will raise my babies on my own."

"Like hell," he said simply. "Those are *my* babies, too. I have a say in how and where they will be raised."

She paled. "What do you mean?"

"I mean, my home is in New York. So it will be theirs."

"Well, my home is here and they're presently in my belly."

"I will fly you to New York to give birth of course. I want my babies to have the best medical care available and I don't think a little island hospital is going to fit the bill."

"Women give birth every day. It's nothing that can't be accomplished right here in this living room, if need be," Lilah countered with a glare. "And I'm not going to New York."

"We'll talk about this later. Right now, I want to know everything about your pregnancy. You've cheated me out of the first few months of their existence and you're not going to take another moment from me."

He was being harsh. He could hear it in his tone but he was angry. White-hot angry, but also hurt. Why wouldn't she have called him the minute she found out? He would've been here in a heartbeat. To think she was going to let him go on without ever knowing… Well, it pierced him to his core. Perhaps he didn't know her as well as he'd thought. To keep something as big as his babies from him? It seemed downright cold and he'd never imagined Lilah was capable of being so cruel.

"Twins… Do you know what they are? Girls? Boys? One of each?" he asked.

"No, I don't know yet," she snapped. "I wasn't going to find out."

"Oh. Don't you think it'd be nice to know? For planning purposes?"

Her gaze cut away. "No, I wanted to be surprised."

"Well, I've had a big enough surprise already. I want to know."

Tears sparkled in her eyes and for a second he felt an apology trying to push past the angry wall he was surrounded by, but in the end, he just couldn't let it go and he hated himself for it, but this was damn near unforgivable.

LILAH WANTED TO SOB but she held back her tears through sheer force of will. It helped that she was percolating with indignant anger. How dare he start making demands? She ignored the voice of reason providing irritating counterpoints to her justifications. Of all the scenarios she pictured in her head of telling Justin about the pregnancy, she never imagined it going so wrong.

He wanted to take her babies away from her. He was acting as if she didn't have a say. Panic made her heart flutter like a caged bird. "Why are you doing this?" she managed to ask. "I gave you an out. You don't want to be a father. You said so yourself. You're not ready and it's bad timing. I won't come after you for money. I won't pester you, I promise. I just want to raise my babies in peace."

Justin turned and regarded her with a chilly expression. "You didn't have the right to make that choice for me. Forgive me if I was a little shocked and didn't act as you rehearsed my reaction. Let me make myself clear…I will be a part of my children's lives. End of story. Get used to it."

"Get out." When he refused to budge, she screamed, "Get out!" and everyone came running.

Heath stood with clenched fists, looking more than ready to plow Justin's face into a squishy mess if he so much as dared to breathe an errant word and Lora stood not far off with the same expression. Celly watched everything unfold with a speculative stare, as if seeing something no one else did.

"You've been asked to leave," Heath said curtly. "I suggest you do so."

Justin hesitated for a moment, as if debating the merits of picking a fight. Then he turned to leave. "I'll be back. Be ready to discuss this."

Lilah waited until she heard the door slam and then she broke down and sobbed. "He hates me," she cried into her hands, shaking with each breath. "His eyes were so cold and mean. I've never seen him so cruel. I don't even know that man." She looked up to regard her family wildly. "And he wants to take my babies away. Oh, God…I'd die if he tried!"

"No one is taking de babies," Celly said calmly, surprising them all with her ability to remain cool and collected. In fact, she seemed vaguely amused by the whole situation, which baffled Lilah. "Time will work tings out. Yah gave him a start and he reacted badly. Give him time to adjust. He will come around. I have a feeling, it'll be fine."

"No disrespect, Celly, but I disagree," Lora broke in, concerned. "He has access to a litany of attorneys that we don't. With his connections, he could hire the best money could buy. We need to get an attorney right away."

"Give him time to do de right ting," Celly advised, looking past Lora and speaking directly to Lilah. "Yah know dat boy's heart. Trust dat. And stop worrying. Bad for de babies."

"It's not that simple," Lora disagreed, but Celly shrugged and started walking away.

"I have to go check on Jack. It's his snack time and he gets right ornery when he doesn't get his grilled pineapple."

Lilah watched Celly leave, confused by Celly's comments. How could she say that everything would work out? Hadn't she heard what Justin said? There was nothing soft or giving about the man who'd just stared her down as if she were beneath him, tossing out demands as if it were his right to do so.

Lora rushed to her side and clasped her hand. "It's going to be all right. I promise. If we all have to pool our resources to hire the best attorney out there, we'll do it. Justin Cales is going to have one helluva fight on his hands when he takes on a Bell."

Lilah nodded, grateful for her family's unflagging support but her heart was weeping in misery. She kept seeing the anger and hatred in Justin's eyes and it was as if he was stabbing her in the heart.

Why'd you have to return, Justin? Why?

CHAPTER TWENTY-FIVE

JUSTIN STRODE INTO THE room he'd booked at the Worchester and tossed his keys onto the bureau with agitation. His world had just tipped upside down and he was still struggling to discern which way was right side up.

A baby? Two babies?

He sat heavily on the edge of the bed and cradled his head in his hands. Lilah was going to have his babies.

He was going to be a father.

The words seemed nonsensical in his head. The entire plane ride all he could think of was how he was going to convince Lilah to return to New York with him, screw his original idea of closure.

Now there was no closure in sight.

Was he crazy that a part of him was relieved? Lilah would always be a part of his life now. But he hadn't wanted it like this—tense and angry on both sides.

Didn't he have a right to be pissed? She was going to deny him the right to know his children. That wasn't something that could be easily forgiven. But he supposed he'd have to find a way. For better or worse, Lilah Bell was going to be the mother of his children.

Would the babies have her fair hair? Her beautiful blue eyes?

Or would they favor him? He tried picturing himself cradling two babies in his arms, and it was fortunate he was already sitting because his knees would've given out and landed him on the floor.

It was all happening so fast. This changed everything.

What was he going to do about his political career? He'd have to do some quick maneuvering to make this a positive instead of a negative. He fished his cell from his pocket with the intention of calling Rudy, but he hesitated, staring at the phone. If he told Rudy, his campaign manager would kick into damage-control gear and possibly ruin any chance he and Lilah had to get through this. He'd already bungled things. He didn't need anyone's assistance in that regard. He pocketed his cell phone and fell back on the bed to close his eyes and regroup.

He was going to be a father.

How was he even remotely qualified for such a responsibility?

Six months ago he'd been a total idiot with little more on his mind than the next party and the next conquest. He hardly recognized the image of himself from then. That person embarrassed him. He certainly didn't want to be that kind of person as a role model for his kids.

A small flutter of nerves jumped in his gut when he let the knowledge truly sink in how his life was about to change.

Babies.

He didn't even know where to start.

"HE WANTS TO TAKE THE BABIES," Lilah sobbed into the phone to Lindy, nearly hysterical. "As soon as he found out, he was so mad, and he looked at me like I was the worst person on the planet! He hates me now and he's going to punish me for ruining his career by taking my babies!"

"Okay, calm down, Li," Lindy said, trying to calm Lilah down, but Lilah was beside herself with fear and regret. "It's going to be okay. Justin isn't that bad of a guy, right? I mean, you wouldn't have fallen for him if he was bad."

"I never fell for him," Lilah protested. Was she truly that transparent? If so, the knowledge only compounded her misery. "But he's different now. He's not the man I knew when he was here before."

"Of course he's different. Cut the guy some slack, sweetie. You just told him that he was going to be the father of twins—twins that he didn't even know existed until today. Imagine how that must've thrown him for a loop. And the fact that he wants to be a part of the babies' lives… Well, I gotta say, that's pretty honorable."

"Fine time to be honorable," Lilah groused. "Why couldn't he have stayed a happy memory?"

"You know that's kinda selfish, right? I mean, you know I'm on your side but I can't believe that you would purposefully keep a man from his children just because it's more convenient for you," Lindy chided gently. When Lilah didn't respond, she added with a pinch of logic, "Besides, it's truly better this way. He should take responsibility for his children. The fact that he's adamant about being a true father…that's a good thing. Once you get past the hurt from the initial shock, I think you guys can work this out."

"Work it out how?"

"I don't know. How do you want it to work out?"

Lilah hesitated, the words trapped in her throat. Before he'd shown up unannounced she'd dreamed of him every night, wished he was here with her, and fantasized of their life together, but now that she was faced with the reality, she was too scared to hope for anything that resembled the landscape of her dreams. "I just want what's best for the babies," she whispered.

"Then, stop fighting him and find out how you can do this together," came Lindy's reasonable advice. "Try to be friends."

Friends? She suddenly hated the word. She didn't want to be Justin's friend. She wanted to be his...? Well, she didn't know exactly but it definitely wasn't in the friend zone.

"I don't know how to be friends with Justin," she admitted. "What if I'm terrible at it?"

"You'll make it work because two perfect little halves of you and Justin will require it. I know you can do this, Li. Have faith in yourself. You're going to make an amazing mother, just be yourself."

That started the waterworks anew and it took several moments before Lilah could speak again. How did Lindy know she'd make a good mother? She'd messed up every major project she'd ever undertaken. How could she possibly handle raising two human beings? She longed to rest her head on Justin's shoulder with the privilege of sharing her fears with the father of her children. But that wasn't an option. She'd been terribly selfish and kept a secret that wasn't entirely hers to keep. It was little wonder he thought she was the devil.

"He wants me to go to New York to have the babies," she said, wiping her nose on a tissue. "I don't want to go."

Lindy sighed. "I'm sorry to say that you're going to have to work on compromising with each other. He has a right to his opinions and desires, just like you. And, like Grams used to say, you catch more bees with honey, so stop putting out vinegar."

Lilah rolled her eyes although she understood the sentiment. She'd felt attacked and so had gone on the defensive. She supposed she could've handled things better. "Do you think he'll ever forgive me?" she asked.

"I think once he holds those babies in his arms, nothing else will matter. Give him a chance to show you he can be the man you thought he was when you first met before you write him out of your life and start a war you never intended to fight. I mean, think about it, Li, you fell in love with him for a reason, right?"

"Yeah," she agreed reluctantly. "But what if he hasn't really changed? I don't want to get on that roller coaster of wondering if he's lying to me or sleeping around. Don't you remember what you said he was like? A playboy. The worst kind. Remember? What if—"

"Don't play the what-if game," Lindy admonished. "No one wins that game. You have to trust your heart and hope for the best. Otherwise, you're just resigning yourself to living in fear of what *may* or *may not* happen."

Lilah chuckled bleakly, yet was silently amazed at how wise her twin had become in such a short time frame. "How'd you get so smart?"

Lindy laughed. "I'm just channeling Grams as much as possible. She was the best woman I knew. I figure if I just did what she would do in any given situation, I couldn't go wrong. So far, it's worked out. And considering I've jumped into the deep end of the parenting pool with a teenager, I'm still treading water and that's pretty amazing."

"You're just lucky because Carys is a lot like you and there's nothing she could do that you haven't already done," Lilah quipped.

"True story."

"I wish you were here," Lilah remarked with a hitch in her voice. "I always feel more secure when you're around."

"Li, you're going to do just fine. You're so much stronger than you give yourself credit for. You don't need me as your security any longer."

Lilah was warmed by her twin's statement but it didn't quell the nervous roil of her stomach as she considered everything that lay ahead. "I miss you, still."

"And I miss you. But if you end up following Justin to New York, I can fly over and see you and the babies. Gabe has an apartment in the city for when he's on the east coast on business."

The way Lindy casually talked about her going to New York shocked her, as if it weren't a huge concession on her part to leave the island. "I hate the city," Lilah said churlishly.

"You've never really been to the city so you can't actually say that," Lindy reminded her. "Besides, I have a feeling there are a few things about the city that you will enjoy."

"Such as?"

"Such as being with the man you love."

Lilah actually growled and glowered, irritated that Lindy kept trying to remind her that she had hidden feelings for Justin. Fat lot of good those feelings had done for her lately. "Just because you hooked up with a Prince Charming doesn't mean I'm going to end up with one. I'd rather not set myself up for failure. You didn't see how he looked at me. It wasn't nice. Or filled with love."

Lindy sighed. "Okay, grouchy pants. See it your way. I have to get going. I have a teenager who likes to sleep in on school days, which means I have to drag her butt out of bed when the alarm goes off and it's never pretty. Sleep tight, Li, and keep me in the loop."

They wrapped up their conversation and Lilah disconnected. A sea of used tissues surrounded her from her cry fest and she was hungry as usual. She discarded the tissues and made her way to the kitchen where she found a bowl of strawberries freshly cut and waiting for her. She smiled. "Bless your crafty heart, Celly," she murmured, and grabbed the bowl. She didn't waste time with another smaller bowl or plate; she planned to eat them all.

She didn't know how to fix this situation with Justin but she did know how to polish off a flat of strawberries.

So that's what she did.

CHAPTER TWENTY-SIX

"WHAT BAD LUCK," Lora said to Heath as they lay in bed. She tightened her hold across his chest and snuggled deeper against his side. "I feel terrible for Lilah. Why'd Justin have to show up now?"

"As opposed to when? Would there really be a better time for him to reinsert himself into her life? I look at it as a blessing."

"How so?"

"He can still be there for his kids from the very beginning, which is his right. He's not really missing out on anything and thus, it'll be easier for him to forgive Lilah for keeping the knowledge from him."

Lora fell silent, digesting Heath's reasoning. She supposed Heath had a point, but she didn't know if Lilah needed yet another burden to deal with. "Yeah, but my initial misgivings about him remain. What kind of father is he going to be when he hardly qualified as a good boyfriend?"

"People change if they are motivated to do so," Heath said, his voice a reassuring rumble against her ear. "But you have to give him the chance to prove himself. And so does Lilah. I don't think he's so mad at Lilah that he'll hold this against her for the rest of their lives. I think he still cares for her."

Lora frowned. "What makes you think that?"

"I saw it in his eyes the second before he saw her belly and the realization hit that she was pregnant."

"What did you see?" Lora asked, intrigued.

"Love. Pure, wild and uncontainable love."

Lora was shocked. "Really? How do you know?"

"Because I recognized it. It's how I feel when I look at you and when Gabe looks at Lindy."

Lora warmed all over and tears sprang to her eyes. God, how she loved this man. "You know, you're an amazing individual, Heath Cannon," she said as her throat closed. "I'm so lucky. I want that for Lilah, too."

"Me, too."

"So if you saw all this, why'd you want to punch his lights out?"

She heard the smile in his tone as he said, "Because Lilah is like my little sister and he'd made her cry. I figured, he deserved a punch in the nose at the very least for leaving her behind in the first place."

Lora secretly agreed but she felt obligated to point out, "Well, we kind of chased him away."

"I don't consider that a viable excuse. Look how hard you tried to chase me away. I didn't budge."

"No, you didn't," Lora recalled with a giddy smile. "And I'm so grateful."

"The way I look at it is this—if you want the privilege of calling a Bell yours, you have to earn it. And that's what Justin has to do right now."

Lora was silently struck by how wise Heath was. He'd always had a firm grasp on what made people tick, something she'd paid a lot of money in college tuition to learn and yet still managed to miss the mark at times. "Your glass fusion is really starting to take off," she said, switching subjects. "Your wedding ring centerpieces are truly beautiful. I hope our kids have your artistic talent," she said with a sigh. She felt Heath still and she glanced up at him. "What?" she asked, concerned she'd said something wrong.

"You said, 'kids,'" he observed, breaking into a grin.

"Yeah," she admitted, almost shyly. "I've been thinking a lot about having babies. It's all Lilah's fault."

"Every time I've brought it up you've quickly switched the subject or put me off. I didn't want to pressure you but...I want to start our family. I want to hold our child in my arms. It's kind of all I think about these days," he said with a pinch of embarrassment. "I know that's not very manly, right?"

His admission sparked a hunger inside her that she didn't realize was so strong. She rose up and straddled him. His body was warm and strong beneath her and she reveled in the familiar feel of each curve and ridge. This man was her *everything*. How could she possibly want to hang on to an image from the past when the future was so much sweeter? For too long she'd been trying to preserved the identity of the woman she'd been—corporate shark and ballbuster—but it was distinctly at odds with who she was becoming and it'd been confusing and stressful trying to embrace both identities. She realized in that moment, she no longer needed to be the corporate shark. She cupped his jaw with both hands and pressed a kiss to his lips. "I'm ready for it all, Heath Cannon. I want to be your wife and the mother of your children. I don't know what I was waiting for but I'm done waiting."

Heath rose up and met her mouth with a hungry kiss that devoured her from the inside out. She felt his answer and his joy in the fervent touch of his hands as he roamed her body and demanded an equal and arousing reaction from her. He pulled her panties down and off, tossing them from the bed as he rolled her onto her back, his gaze darkening with desire and love—a heady combination. "Then let's get on with it, sweetheart," he said in a husky murmur against her neck that sent shivers dancing across her skin. "By the end of tonight, if there's not a baby in your belly, it won't be from lack of trying!"

She gasped and clutched at him, closing her eyes as sweet bliss followed. *Yesss...*

JUSTIN TOOK CARE in his presentation that morning, taking time to pick out an outfit he thought Lilah would like, rehearsing what he wanted to say to her so that he didn't find himself tongue-tied when it mattered most. But the tension in his gut told him that no matter how he prepared, he was going to remain a nervous wreck because there was so much at stake.

Lilah had tentatively agreed to meet him at their favorite beach, a meeting point he'd purposely selected in the hopes that it might spark tender feelings for him and increase his chances of success, because he'd certainly need any advantage possible.

He arrived early and when he saw Lilah pull up in the Jeep, he ran to meet her when it seemed she struggled to clear the high lip of the Jeep's frame. "I got it," she said, warning him off with a cool look.

Justin stiffened. "I just want to help."

"Well, I didn't ask for your help."

He sighed, not liking the sour beginning to what he hoped would end happily. "Lilah, I'm really not the enemy here. Can we try not to fight?"

She looked away, somewhat guiltily, and then jerked a nod. Justin held out his hand as a peace offering and he held his breath, waiting to see if she would continue to rebuff him or if she would accept the gesture. To his relief, she slipped her hand into his—however reluctantly. The minute he felt her small hand fit into his, a shiver passed over his body and he was reminded in excruciating detail how it felt to be inside her, to feel her beside him, and he ached for the loss. He shouldn't have waited so long to come back. He should've listened to his instincts and returned that very day and patched things up between them, forced her to listen to his side. Now he didn't know where to begin but the fact that she was there with him gave him hope.

"When'd you find out?" he asked as they walked the beach, hand in hand.

"Two weeks after you'd left. I couldn't stop throwing up."

"I'm sorry," he said, feeling like a toad that he wasn't there for her. "Are you feeling better now?"

"Yes," she said with a short nod as she stared ahead. "Why'd you come back?"

He drew a tight breath. "No small talk, huh?" he remarked, only partially joking. Already his chest felt as if he couldn't quite get a deep enough breath and it was going to be a bitch getting the words out yet she wasn't making it any easier on him. He tried to remember that she was probably just as freaked out as him at the prospect of parenthood, though she'd had considerably longer than him to adjust to the idea. "I'm sorry, Lilah, for leaving like I did. I should've stayed and explained everything that was going on."

"You didn't need to explain. It wasn't my business," she murmured with a subtle shrug.

"No, I wanted to explain but it was and still is complicated. I was sent here by my father to get my party days out of my system because he was going to stop my allowance if I didn't go into politics. I know that sounds shallow and stupid for a grown man to rely on his parents for his livelihood, and trust me in the past few months I've realized I was pretty ridiculous, but the thing is, I didn't know when I came here that I would meet someone like you. I wasn't looking for love."

She stopped and pulled her hand free abruptly to stare at him with wide eyes. "Love?"

He swallowed. "Yes. It's taken me this long to realize that I fell in love with you."

"Why didn't you say something then?" she asked, her tone mildly accusatory, as if she didn't believe him. "You don't have to say these things just because I'm pregnant and you think that's what I need to hear."

"I'm not saying these things because of either of those reasons," he said, trying again. "I'm saying them because I mean them. My feelings for you haven't changed. Not one bit. And in fact, they're stronger than ever."

She blinked and tears filled her eyes. "Do you mean that?"

"Of course I do," he said, stepping in front of her and reaching for her hands. "I reacted badly last night and I'm sorry. But I'm not about to walk away from my babies or you again. Please say you'll forgive me for being an idiot."

She opened her mouth, then snapped it shut as she wiped her tears away. "This isn't fair," she whispered.

"Here I am trying to work up the nerve to tell you that I'm willing to be friends for the sake of the babies and you're telling me that you love me?"

His heart stuttered to a painful stop and he stared, unsure he'd understood her correctly. "You want to be friends?"

"No," she answered, confusing him. "I can't be your friend. I don't know how we can be friends when we've never been friends before. I don't know you, Justin. The guy I thought I knew, he doesn't really exist. He was a figment of our collective imagination and you're a stranger to me."

Justin's first reaction was to pull away angrily, but he pushed down the impulse, determined to make this work. He could see her distress, could understand her frustration at his lack of sharing when it would've been appropriate and he didn't want to blow this by allowing his temper to get the best of him. "Lilah, my father is New York Senator Vernon Cales. He's very connected and our family has been in politics for many generations. It's in our blood, if you will. I wouldn't have believed that kind of nonsense until my father forced my hand and sent me on the campaign trail. I never thought I'd say this, but I enjoy what I'm doing. I can really make a difference and for the first time in my life I have a serious purpose. It's changed me for the better. The reason I didn't say anything when you confronted me with my past was because there was nothing I could say in my own defense. I *was* that guy. I was a jerk. A real asshole who used people and didn't care about their feelings after I'd gotten what I wanted. And so I just left. But the reality is, the time I had with you was magical and I wouldn't trade it for the world."

He dared to softly touch her belly and she stilled when his hands gently caressed the rounded skin. "And now I know that I was right. It *was* magical. We created life together. And I could never regret that."

Tears slipped down her cheeks. "I didn't get pregnant on purpose," she whispered in earnest. "I want you to know that. I—" She stopped. Something in her eyes that looked like fear made him want to hold her tight but he sensed she was holding back and wouldn't welcome his embrace just yet.

"I believe you," he said, trying to soothe her fears but the minute shake of her head caused a knot to form in his stomach. "What's wrong?"

Her hands became clammy and she pulled them free. "Justin…I…need time to think about this," she stammered. "It's a lot to take in and I need… I just need to talk to my sisters first."

Frowning, he bracketed his hips, as his frustration peaked. "Why? Talk to *me,* Lilah. I'm the one affected by whatever it is you're holding back. Trust me, I won't judge if that's what you're afraid of. Even if you did get pregnant on purpose, *I don't care.* What matters is how we feel about each other. I know you still care for me. I can see it in your eyes." When she remained stubbornly silent but tears continued to dribble from her eyes, he said a bit sharply, "Come on, Lilah. Let me in. *Tell me* what's wrong."

"I didn't get pregnant on purpose," she snapped, wiping at her eyes. "That's all you need to know right now. I can't talk about this right now. I need time." She turned and walked back to the Jeep, the deep sand making her trek slow and ungainly but he knew she wouldn't accept his help.

"Lilah," he called out in irritation but she ignored him. "Damn it, girl, I want to marry your stubborn ass!"

At that she stopped and nearly toppled over when her center of gravity tipped. She wobbled and then turned to stare at him, her mouth open.

"What?"

"You heard me," he bit out, not liking how this had turned out. It certainly wasn't the romantic declaration he'd envisioned. Now he was so agitated, he just wanted to scoop her into his arms and haul her to the first justice of the peace that he could find and be done with it. "I want to marry you."

"Marry?" she gasped, her hand going to her belly. She stared as if he'd told her that he wanted to fly to the moon and make angels in the moon dust. She certainly didn't look overcome with elation. *Aww crap.* He winced as his worst fear started to materialize right before his eyes. "Marry?" she repeated incredulously. "Absolutely not."

CHAPTER TWENTY-SEVEN

LILAH COULDN'T THINK STRAIGHT. She needed to get away from Justin for just a moment. Everything was moving too quickly. One minute she was daydreaming about him, the next he was at Larimar and yelling at her, and finally, he's professing his love and wanting to marry her. He didn't even truly know her!

"Lilah! Wait up!"

She heard him but she wasn't stopping. She had to get to the Jeep; had to get back to Larimar so she could talk to Lora. This was insanity. Marry him? Six months ago they'd been strangers having a bit of fun; now she was his baby mama.

But he wants to make you his wife!

The voice in her head was practically shrieking at her to get a grip and face this situation like an adult, but her feet weren't cooperating with her brain. He didn't want her for a wife. That was the reality of it. He was making a grand gesture because she was pregnant and that was the last kind of proposal she wanted. In her dreams when she envisioned her wedding, it wasn't like this. In her mind, she wore a beautiful, flowing dress that drifted around her feet like a designer cloud of white and creams like sea froth on the sand and she was surrounded by her friends and family as she pledged her love to the man who made her life worth living. In her daydreams, she certainly wasn't bulging in the middle and huffing and puffing with every labored step because she was carrying around two extra people in her body. And in her daydreams, she certainly didn't have a groom who felt obligated to do the right thing. When she married, she wanted to know that she was the only woman for him and he was marrying her for love and forever. Tears stung her eyes and she dashed them away, refusing to cry. But worse than the shattering of her dream wedding was the fact that she wasn't fit to be Justin's wife. Who was she? Nobody. With a nobody career of doing nothing of use. She leaned against the Jeep and in the midst of trying to catch her breath, she started to sob, much to her horror, but she couldn't stop.

Within seconds, Justin had folded her into his arms and he held her while she soaked his shirt and made a general mess of everything.

When she thought she could speak, she pulled away with a bleak sadness in her heart. She was suddenly tired and worn out. The humidity and the emotional upset was just too much to handle. She decided to just let it all out. She didn't have the strength to dance around the truth. "Justin...I can't marry you. I do love you. But marrying me would be political poison to your campaign and I would never do that to you. You deserve the best and I can't give you that."

"What are you talking about? What do you mean political poison? Are you a secret drug runner or a trafficker in black market babies?" he asked, trying to lighten the mood with a touch of his signature humor but Lilah's countenance didn't change.

"Justin, trust me when I say I'm doing you a kindness when I refuse your offer. I would never sacrifice your future for my happiness in the short term. I didn't tell you about the babies because I didn't want to burden you with a family you never asked for. Now, with your political position, I'm the least appropriate candidate for a wife that you could possibly find. I say this, not entirely altruistically, either. I don't want to subject myself to the scrutiny that would undoubtedly come with the job of being your wife. I'm sorry."

"So are you asking me to choose between you and my career?"

"No, of course not," she answered, aghast. "I'm telling you there is no choice because I'm not an option. The best thing we could do for each other is to find a way to become friends and then work out a joint custody schedule when the babies are old enough."

"No. I won't live apart from my children."

"I don't see how that's going to work out seeing as you live in New York and your career is in New York, as well."

"Good point. Which is why you ought to move to New York."

"That's not going to happen," she said seriously, wishing they didn't have to hash over this particular argument again. "My home is here and this is where I'm happiest. The babies will have a wonderful home here with me. You will always be welcome in their lives, of course."

"Lilah," Justin growled when she turned to climb back into the Jeep. "This matter is not finished."

"Yes, it is," she retorted as she buckled up, trying to ignore the vicious pang in her heart as she continued to maintain her position even as her soul railed at the decision. It was lunacy. She wouldn't blacken his political career with her past. If the press chose to dig into her life they'd discover her suicide attempt and subsequent commitment. They'd have a field day ripping Justin's candidacy to shreds. And she simply wouldn't bear that burden.

"Lilah, do you hear yourself? You've admitted that you love me but you just want to be friends? That doesn't make sense."

"Justin, please just let it go," she pleaded, her eyes filling again. When he saw how agitated she was becoming, he backed down but it looked like it was killing him to do so. "I'm sorry for making such a mess of everything," she said quietly, and truly meant it. Someday he'd realize her rejection was a blessing.

Justin refused to look at her and simply backed away from the Jeep so she could pull onto the highway.

As she drove away, she let the tears flow. There was no need to wipe them away. She was alone and there was no one to hide them from.

LATER THAT NIGHT AS Justin nursed a beer on his private patio he ignored the call from Rudy. His campaign manager was the last person he wanted to talk to right now. He was confused and soured by the day's meeting with Lilah. She'd admitted that she loved him, yet she wanted to remain simply friends? She'd said something about being political poison. What did that mean? Clearly, whatever it was, Lilah wasn't going to share with him. He needed to find out what the big bad secret was and then decide for himself whether it was something he could handle or not.

Honestly, he didn't know what to think. He didn't rightly care what she thought was so horrible that he couldn't handle because there was nothing he could think of—short of murder—that he couldn't overlook for her.

No one was perfect. Hell, if anyone understood that fact better than him, he'd eat his shoe.

He needed answers. How to get them was the question.

Justin doubted that her sisters would give her up. And Lilah was such a private person he doubted anyone in town would know what was eating her up. As he finished his last swallow of beer, he remembered the bartender at Rush Tide—Donna.

She'd seemed to know a bit about Lilah and had even given him a clue as to her artistic talents. Maybe she'd know more about her personal life, too.

And maybe with a little luck…she'd clue him into what was so scary in Lilah's proverbial closet.

It couldn't be half as bad as the skeletons rattling around in his.

At least that's what he hoped.

He found Donna easily enough. The bar was hopping and a reggae band played on the small stage. He took a seat at the bar and smiled as he hailed her for a beer.

"Remember me?" he asked with an engaging grin. He didn't want to seem as if he were flirting with her but he needed information so he played up the fact that he remembered her, as well. "Donna, right?" he asked.

"That's right," she said with an impressed smile. "How's it going, handsome?"

"Could be better," he admitted. "I was hoping you could help me or at the very least point me in the right direction."

"Sure, sugar. I'd be happy to help. What do you need?"

"Well, I was hoping you could tell me something about Lilah," he said.

"You're still hung up on Lilah Bell? You poor thing. That girl has her head in the clouds most days so unless you can fly, I'd let that one go."

He smiled but otherwise kept on course. "Here's the thing… She's been acting pretty strange lately."

"Pregnant girls do that," Donna remarked wryly, and then her eyes lit up with avid curiosity. "Are you the father?"

For a split second he considered lying, only because he hadn't told anyone in his sphere and he wanted to protect Lilah for as long as possible from the press, but he realized he'd probably have to part with some juicy tidbits before Donna would feel safe sharing what she knew. "Yes, I am," he said, watching her reaction closely.

Donna whistled. "Lucky girl, that Lilah. Always did manage to catch the best ones, though I have to admit, she never liked to hold on to them."

"What do you mean?"

Donna started but then thought better of it, saying, "I shouldn't gossip. Besides, Lilah is my friend and I don't talk about my friends to strangers. You feeling me? Can I get you a drink?"

He gave Donna a sardonic look. "Lilah is carrying my babies. I wouldn't call me a stranger."

"Where you been this whole time then?"

"It's complicated but I'm here now and I don't plan to leave again without her. We have some issues to work around but I love her, Donna. I really do. And I need some help here because I'm drowning. She's got it in her head to just be friends but I want to marry her. I want to put my ring on her finger and give her my name. Does that sound like someone you can trust with a little personal information about your friend?" he asked in earnest.

Donna regarded him for a long moment as if weighing his declaration, and Justin felt the seconds stretch by with agonizing slowness as he held his breath waiting for her answer.

A sudden grin broke out on Donna's face and Justin nearly sagged against the bar in relief as she said, "I'm a sucker for a romantic that's for sure. Okay, here's what I know but you'd better not break that girl's heart or you're going to have to answer to me. Got it?"

Justin nodded vigorously. "Deal."

"Okay. I always considered Lilah a 'catch and release' type of girl. She could catch the guy no problem but she never really found keeping them all that interesting. Sort of like her twin, Lindy, but less in your face about it. Lilah, for as long as I've known her, has always been the type to drift. Most times she's in her own world, which honestly given what happened last year, is not surprising."

That piqued Justin's attention. "What happened last year?"

"You don't know? Well, if you don't know, you probably ought to if you're of a mind to marry her." At the shake of his head, she leaned forward to whisper in a low tone, "She tried to kill herself. Walked right into the sea and tried to take a water nap. It was quite the scandal for the sleepy town of St. John. I mean, you just don't hear that every day. People drown, sure, but they don't simply walk into the ocean with the intent to end it all. And then of course, because she was deemed a danger to herself, she was committed. It was crazy. No one saw that one coming. Scary, too. I mean, you think you know someone and then pow! They go and do something completely crazy."

Justin stared, unable to believe what Donna had shared. He continued to listen and nod at the appropriate spots but his mind was still spinning over the revelation about Lilah.

That was one helluva skeleton.

If Rudy found out, he'd advise Justin to steer clear of Lilah. He'd call her a danger to his success. Or as Lilah put it, political poison. He might as well resign his candidacy if he continued to pursue Lilah.

Logic and reason demanded that he cut ties and even sue for custody. No doubt he'd win given her recent past. But the idea made him feel wretched. His heart didn't care about her past. Whatever was happening in her life then, certainly wasn't an issue now. She was committed to being a good mother and in her own way, she was trying to protect him, too.

He couldn't walk away. Not even if she wasn't pregnant. The fact that there were babies involved actually simplified things.

He would stand by her.

No matter what.

He just didn't know how to make her see that he wasn't going to walk away.

CHAPTER TWENTY-EIGHT

"HE ASKED YOU TO MARRY HIM?" Lora repeated slowly as if trying to make sure she'd heard Lilah correctly. When Lilah nodded, Lora collapsed against the sofa with her hand over her eyes and groaned. "What did you say?"

"Of course I said no," Lilah answered miserably. "He has no idea how having me as a wife would be terrible for his career."

At that Lora dropped her hand to stare at Lilah. "Wait…why'd you say no? To protect his career?"

"Well, yes. Mostly." Lilah fidgeted with the fringe on her sarong. "I mean, I don't want to be given a marriage proposal that's based on the fact that I'm pregnant, but aside from that he has a good shot of becoming the next New York senator and I couldn't possibly ruin that for him without dying inside from guilt."

"Lilah…do you have feelings for this guy?"

Lilah bit her lip, hesitant to admit her private thoughts about Justin Cales, but she supposed her sister had a right to know seeing as she was standing so staunchly behind her in the matter. "Yes. I—I think I love him."

Lora groaned and rose from the sofa. "Why didn't you say so in the first place? That changes everything, wouldn't you say? He loves you, you love him… Why are you pushing him away? And don't give me that line of bull about his damn career. If he's willing to take the risk, then you ought to let him."

Lilah stared at her older sister, hating that she so easily stripped away her defenses and left her bare and shivering in the open. "He deserves better than me, okay?" she answered stiffly, hating how pathetic she sounded.

"Better?" Lora repeated. "What a crock. You're scared. This is real stuff. Time to grow up, honey. We've always protected you, thinking that you're the fragile one in the family, and you've always chafed at that protection. Well, now is the time to show your strength. Show us all that we've been spending all this time and effort for no reason. Heath has always maintained that you're stronger than we give you credit. Here's your moment. Stop giving up. Fight for your man, girl! When Heath fell off the roof and cracked his head open, I sat by his bed every moment, baring my miserable soul in the hopes that he'd hear me and come back to me so I could spend the rest of my life showing him how much I love him. Stand up to the people who dare to say you're not good enough to be a senator's wife. We all believe in you. It's time for you to believe in yourself."

"If the press finds out about my suicide attempt...it'll be a massacre. I won't be his Achilles' heel."

"What if you already are? I'm pretty sure he's not going to leave without you."

"Damn straight I'm not."

Justin's voice startled them both as he stood framed in the doorway of the private section. He had eyes only for Lilah, and Lora's mouth tipped in a small, almost approving smile.

"I'll leave you two to talk," Lora said, exiting the room quickly.

Lilah's traitorous pulse quickened at the sight of him. Perhaps it would've been easier to ignore him if he hadn't been so damn handsome. That mischievous smile could do her in.

"What are you doing here?"

"Talking some sense into your stubborn head."

Lilah sighed. "I don't want to go over this again. I told you—"

"I know what happened last summer."

His flat statement stopped her cold and the air squeezed from her lungs in a horrified wheeze. He strode toward her and without giving her a chance to protest, simply kissed her until she was unable to remember the good reasons she was pushing him away. She clung to him, desperate to feel him against her again, buffeted by the sweet memories of their time together. All too soon, he pulled away and she nearly whimpered with disappointment.

"Lilah," he murmured, pressing his forehead to hers in a tender gesture. "It chills my blood to think that I might not ever have met you. That these babies—" his hand slid down to caress her belly "—might not have been. You're the most amazing gift in my life and you're gracing me with two little people with half of you as part of them. I don't care what anyone says. I will quit my campaign and walk away. I have a master's degree in business, I can get a job doing something else. If you're worried about me being able to support you, don't. I will always find a way to support my family."

Her breath hitched and she openly wept, unable to hold back the tears. "No, Justin. I can't handle that guilt.

Someday you might resent me, or the babies. I won't let you sacrifice your life for us."

"My life is with you. It isn't a sacrifice."

She threw her arms around his neck and sobbed, not sure what to do, although his ardent declaration warmed her heart.

"I can't ask that of you. It's too much but I love you for it," she admitted against his warm skin. His scent enveloped her and she sank into the comforting aroma that was all Justin. She reluctantly drew away and sucked a halting breath as her tears slowed. "What will your family say? You're quitting a promising career because you got a girl pregnant while on vacation? That's no better than a high school kid quitting college because his girlfriend got knocked up. How am I supposed to meet your family and stand by your side knowing that deep down inside, your family is judging me for taking down your career? I mean, think about it, Justin. You know I'm right." His silence was answer enough but even so her heart broke. "There's a reason bad timing is the driving force behind breakups—sometimes there's just no way to circumvent the obvious truth that's staring us in the face."

"Damn it," he muttered, turning away as he pushed his hand through his hair. "There is far more at stake here than just an ill-fated romance. We have kids coming and I'm not going to be an absent father."

The vehemence with which he delivered his last statement sent a shiver dancing down Lilah's back. She sensed there was a raw nerve somewhere and she hated that their situation was jumping on it. He wanted to be a father to his children but the reality was that it would be difficult to do so unless they were in the same geographic location at the very least. She swallowed, knowing that she could help ease the stress between them if she agreed to move to New York but when she considered the option a cold, greasy knot of fear coagulated in her stomach and she just couldn't do it. In the end, she just fell silent, unable to say the words that might make a difference.

CHAPTER TWENTY-NINE

JUSTIN COULDN'T ARGUE Lilah's logic. His parents would never accept her given the circumstances. He pictured his society-driven mother falling over in a horrified swoon if he brought Lilah home with her obviously pregnant stomach, and his father would bellow and rage about the family's reputation going down in flames all because Justin couldn't keep his pants zipped for one bleeding second. Justin realized with a heavy heart, this one thing had the power to destroy all the fence mending he and his father had done in the past six months. But even knowing that, Justin knew he wouldn't forsake Lilah and the babies for the world.

On one hand Justin could understand their dismay; his situation wasn't ideal but there was no way in hell he was going to walk away from Lilah or his children.

He'd never known how much he wanted to be a father until the moment he realized Lilah was carrying his babies. Something inside him bloomed and spread, branching out like a wild, mystic root that wrapped itself around his heart and took hold with a death grip that nothing would shake. He didn't want to miss a minute of their lives and no political career would ever replace what he would miss if he walked away right now.

Not to mention, he wasn't sure it was physically possible for him to leave Lilah. Everything about her made him want to be with her, even when she was driving him nuts.

Immediately, his thoughts went to his apartment and how unsuited it was for kids. He had sharp-cornered glass tables and cold, granite flooring that looked beautiful but would provide little cushion for toddling twins. His place was a bachelor pad made for impressing the ladies in the short term, and providing him a lair for hiding out to nurse hangovers. He couldn't bring Lilah and the babies there.

Justin owned the apartment, one of the only smart purchases he'd made with his trust fund. He could lease it out or sell it, though the market hadn't rebounded from the crash just yet. However, he'd be willing to take a loss if he had to. He needed to find something that was conducive to family life if he was ever going to convince Lilah to move with him. He thought of his family's vacation cottage in upstate New York near Lake Hunnicut and wondered if Lilah would be willing to swap country air for sand and surf. He supposed there was only one way to find out.

For the next week, he knew his mission: get Lilah to agree to go to New York with him.

"THANKS FOR LETTING ME GO to the doctor's appointment with you," Justin said, gracing her with a warm smile, which she returned as she drove the short distance to the clinic. Today was the ultrasound and even though she didn't want to know the sex of the babies, the ultrasound was necessary to ensure they were growing as they should and that there weren't any problems with the placentas. The fact that Justin was going with her made her a little giddy, though she tried to tell herself not to get used to it. Justin had to leave and that's just how it went. But she'd enjoy today.

"So far the doctor has said we're right on track with growth and whatnot so this is just to make sure the placentas are placed in good spots and there aren't any problems in that regard."

"When are you due?" he asked. "By my calculations, sometime in September?"

"Yes, that's pretty good. September 17."

"Right before the November elections," he murmured, and her smile faltered. Always that reminder hanging between them. She focused on the road and tried not to let him see that her mood had dimmed. To her surprise, he changed the subject abruptly. "Did I ever tell you that my family owns a cottage on Lake Hunnicut in upstate New York?"

"No, I don't think so," she answered, mildly perplexed by the subject change.

"It's beautiful up there. Fresh air, trees all around and the prettiest lake around with the cleanest waters. Some of my best memories were made up at that cottage. Have you ever caught fireflies?" he asked.

She shook her head, entertained by the plain nostalgia in his tone. He looked younger, more relaxed. "My dad used to insist that on one month out of the year we get out of the city, and although the cottage wasn't my mom's idea of getting away—she preferred Europe or some other expensive vacation—my dad was adamant, it had to be Hunnicut. Eventually, even she started to like it. There's a certain charm to the place that's hard to ignore. Very peaceful. I used to love our time there and looked forward to the trip every year." His smile changed as if he just remembered something. "It was the one time me and my dad actually got along. He taught me to fish and catch fireflies, make s'mores and start a campfire. It was as if he was a different person than the man behind the desk."

"You and your dad don't get along most days?"

"We didn't, until recently. Before I returned from St. John and started on the campaign trail, I thought he was an overbearing control freak. Now I've had the chance to walk a mile in his shoes and realized he was trying to make a difference in the world. Actually, it was a humbling realization and it also made me see that I'd been a selfish, spoiled jerk for a long time. Kinda embarrassing, really," he admitted with a flush, but Lilah's forgiving smile smoothed away the lingering frown lines creasing his forehead.

"So it was the job that made him seem that way," Lilah guessed.

"Yeah, I guess so. I've only just realized how much pressure my father is under. When you're in politics, everyone wants something from you and they're not willing to help you unless you agree to help them. And often, their interests are in direct opposition to your interests but you have to ignore that little fact in order to get their contribution or assistance."

"Sounds tediously confusing," she said.

"It can be. But I've started to recognize there's a rhythm to the dance and I think I might be good at it."

"I don't doubt it," she said. "You have charisma. When you turn on the charm, it's hard to ignore," she admitted. This was something she knew firsthand. "All the greatest leaders were like that."

He chuckled with self-deprecation but glanced at

her with something akin to curiosity. "Do you think I could be a good leader?"

"I don't know," she answered honestly. "But I do know that you can probably get people to do what you want them to. Whether that translates into being a good leader or not probably depends on how you use that power, right?"

"I guess so," he agreed. "I want to help people. That's what I want to use my influence for."

"Then you will be a good leader if you let that sentiment drive your decisions."

"The mother of my children is a wise woman," he said, reaching over to caress her cheek. She leaned into his touch but pulled away before she became too comfortable accepting his presence as normal.

"My Grams was the smart one. I just listened more than most."

They pulled into the parking lot of the tiny clinic and Lilah read the misgivings on his face. She clasped his hand and tugged him forward. "Don't judge a book by its cover. We have excellent doctors here. I promise."

"It's no bigger than a matchbox," he grumbled, glancing around at the ugly little building that housed the clinic. "And it looks as if it's going to fall down."

"Bigger is not necessarily better," she quipped with a grin.

"That's what men have been trying to tell women for ages. So far it hasn't stuck," he retorted, causing her to laugh out loud.

She returned with a coy smile, "Well, I'm sure you've had no complaints in that department."

"Oh…" he said. The fact that she could make him blush just a little gave her a silly thrill. But just as she reached for the door, he slid in front of her and kissed her soundly. "That's what you get for reminding me about the times I had the privilege of making love to you," he murmured against her lips. "If you keep it up, I'm going to need a refresher course."

She gasped and sank into his kiss, her hormones were already going crazy, but Justin's comment had just kicked them into overdrive. God, she was…um… well…hungry for something other than food and she wasn't embarrassed by her desire, only ready to shuck her clothes. "I could reschedule," she said, her hands curling against his back as he held her to him.

"Such an impatient little thing," he said softly with approval. "But your appointments are important. Business first, fun later."

She pretended to pout. "Fine. But the way my hormones work, I might not be into you within the next ten minutes. You might've missed your window."

He laughed. "Fortunately, I think I can figure out how to flip the switch. I've had months to fantasize about exactly what I'd do to get you back into my bed."

She couldn't help the grin that followed his statement. "You did?"

"Hell yes. It's all I thought about when I wasn't shaking strangers' hands and kissing up to rich old men for their campaign support."

"I bet you didn't imagine that there'd be a big belly in the way, did you?"

"Sweetheart…your belly is sexier than anything I've ever seen. If I didn't worry you'd think I was a pervert, I'd have thrown you down a long time ago."

Now it was her turn to blush. How was it that his comment had just made her the happiest woman on the planet? He thought her big, ungainly stomach was sexy? If she hadn't been so deliriously happy, she would've called bullshit but as it was…she just wanted to bask in the happiness. Lord knows, it wouldn't last.

JUSTIN STARED IN AMAZEMENT as the doctor moved the ultrasound wand over Lilah's stomach through a layer of goo. Immediately a snowy image came onto the screen, though he couldn't for the life of him see anything that resembled a human being.

"Two hearts beating strongly," the doctor observed with a smile, but his focus seemed on something else that gave Justin's nerves a pinch of alarm. But the doctor straightened and nodded as though confirming something he already suspected. "Lilah, you have fraternal twins, not identical. So each baby has its own placenta and sac, which alleviates some worry over placenta issues. Both are right on target and growing perfectly."

"Fraternal? So…they could be a girl and boy?" Justin swallowed, tears springing to his eyes. The doctor looked to Lilah for permission and when she nodded her assent, the doctor grinned and nodded, as well. Justin swallowed, staring harder at the screen. "Can you… can you tell if… I mean, what the sex is?"

"Let's see," the doctor said, moving the wand around as if searching. "Ah. There's one of them…" Justin held his breath and looked quickly at Lilah, aware that she didn't want to know. She seemed to be holding her breath, her eyes wide. "Ah, yes. Okay. Would you like to know the sex of the babies?"

He wanted to shout, *yes!* But he held back, waiting for Lilah. He forced himself to settle his anticipation into a more manageable emotion for fear of crushing poor Lilah's hand clutched in his.

"You really want to know?" Lilah asked.

"Yes," he admitted. "But I'll wait if you want to. It'll be a nice surprise in three months I suppose." Her reluctant expression told him that she had her heart set on waiting. He surprised her with a kiss to the hand he was holding. "Never mind, Doc. I've decided it'll be an awesome surprise for us both."

"All right," the doctor said, smiling. "We'll wait for the big reveal at the birth. You know, back in my day, that's all we had. I like not knowing. It was always such a huge thrill discovering if it was a boy or a girl."

"Are you sure?" she asked.

"Yeah," he said as if he weren't dying inside knowing that the knowledge was right there yet he was denying himself. "It's only three months. I can wait."

She blinked and looked away, presumably to watch the screen but Justin could've sworn he caught the sparkle of tears. The doctor printed out a few pictures of their babies and handed them to Lilah until she said, "Doctor, would you mind printing two sets? Justin works out of town and I'm sure he'd like a picture or two to keep with him to remind him of us."

Now it was Justin's turn to choke up. He managed to jerk a nod to the doctor but he couldn't manage words. Thankfully, no words were necessary.

Justin and Lilah left the clinic with their pictures and each took turns gazing at the snowy, indistinct alien-looking creatures that were in the process of changing their parents' lives before they'd even been born.

"They're…beautiful," Justin said.

"Really? I thought they looked like lizard people," Lilah confessed with a small giggle. "You should've seen the first scan at twelve weeks. They kinda looked like fish."

Her blithe statement just hit home how much he'd missed. Sure, they weren't here yet but the fact that he'd missed anything chafed and he made a mental vow not to miss another minute. "How about dinner tonight?" he asked, striving to sound casual.

"You mean, like a date?"

"Yeah, if I recall, I never really got the chance to wine and dine you properly. As the mother of my children, I believe you've earned it."

Lilah laughed. "Well, when you put it that way... okay. I will meet you for dinner but I'm going to make you spring for something expensive because I'm starving most of the time and you have no idea what it's like carrying around two people who do nothing but use your bladder for a trampoline."

"I will bring my platinum card," he said with mock seriousness. "You can eat out the whole restaurant if you feel the need."

Her laughter filled the cracks and crevices of his heart with light that was only slightly dimmed at the knowledge that he had ulterior motives for the dinner.

Somehow, he had to convince Lilah to go back to New York with him.

Now more than ever, he knew he wouldn't allow a day to go by without his children with him.

And so, the solution was quite simple: he'd have to get Lilah to marry him.

The bigger question was how to marry Lilah without sacrificing all he'd built in his newfound political career.

He thought of the sonogram photos in his possession and their images renewed his resolve; failure wasn't an option.

CHAPTER THIRTY

LILAH FOUND CELLY IN the gift shop moving some merchandise around while she kept Pops busy sorting shells that'd gotten mixed up. Lilah smiled and pressed a quick kiss to Pops's forehead and then went to Celly, unable to suppress her grin.

"Yah look like yah de cat dat ate de clumsy bird," Celly observed with a keen eye. "What's put dat silly grin on yah face?"

"Oh, it's just a beautiful day and I'm loving life," Lilah answered, going to the T-shirts and straightening. Then she remembered her sonogram pictures and fished them from her pocket to thrust at Celly. "Look! New pics of the babies," she said.

Celly gazed at the pictures and grimaced. "It's a good ting we don't always see what's growing. Looks like an alien. I wait until de babies get here, when dey no longer raw."

Lilah chuckled. "Okay. No more sonogram pictures for you."

"Is dat all you singing about?" she asked.

"Well, mostly," Lilah said.

"Yah a bad liar, girl. Spit it out."

"Okay, I'm going to dinner with Justin tonight. He's taking me to Allamanda."

Celly whistled her approval. "Fancy eatin'. What's the occasion? Yah agree to let him be yah mon?"

Lilah colored and laughed uncomfortably. "Unfortunately, it's not so simple as just allowing him to be a part of my life. We love each other but sometimes you have to look at the bigger picture. He has a promising political career that he has to protect and knocking up an island girl probably wasn't on his agenda."

"Agendas change," Celly said stubbornly with a glower. "He's not being a mon and standing up to his responsibility?"

"Oh, no, not at all," Lilah exclaimed, defending Justin. "I won't let him throw everything away for me. Sure, it sounds good in the short term because selfishly, I want to be with him, but that's a recipe for resentment later. I'd rather practice at being friends and that's why he's taking me to dinner. We're going as friends."

"Friends?" Celly repeated, not buying it for a second.

Lilah felt the heat crawl into her cheeks as the memory of the sexual tension that exploded between them before the doctor's appointment returned full force, and she remembered how easily it would've been for them both to simply tear each other's clothes off. That's definitely not what a friend did to another friend. But Celly didn't know that and there was no reason she should have to know.

"Yes," Lilah maintained stubbornly. "Friends. It's better this way."

"So, let me understand…he wants to be in yah life wit de babies, but you're pushing him away so he can be a politician? Girl, yah a bigger donkey dan I took yah for. Dat's plain crazy talk and foolish to boot. Yah never push away a good mon. *Evah*. A good mon don't just fall from de sky and land in yah lap. If a mon comes along wants to be a right mon and do well by his woman…yah let him!"

Lilah scowled a little, surprised by Celly's brusque manner. "He wants to live in New York. I want to live here. It's not going to work out anyway. We might as well admit to that now before things get messy. This way, we remain friends and Justin is always an active part of his kids' lives."

"How active can a mon be when he's so far away?" Celly demanded to know. "Can a mon trow a ball to his son from New York? Can he teach a boy to ride a bike or swim from hundreds of miles away? Can he keep de boys away from his little girl from New York?"

"Of course not. I will do those things for the babies," Lilah answered, stung. Pops surprised them all by chiming in with a growl.

"That no good man of Lisa's…I knew he was a bad apple from the start. Do you know how I knew?" he asked without looking up from his task as he took great care in separating each colored shell. "When Lisa got pregnant with Lora, he wouldn't even take time off for the birth. As it was he was damn late. Lora'd been born and bathed by the time he sauntered in, acting like he'd been the one to do all the work. Worthless, I tell you. I always thought he was worthless and Grams didn't think much of him, neither." He nodded as if listening to someone else who'd just validated his statement and then went back to his shell-sorting. "A real man makes sacrifices for the people he loves."

Lilah was a bit stunned. Pops had never said a bad word against her father, although she'd always wondered how Pops had managed such restraint given how her father had broken her mom's heart.

Celly gave a short nod of approval. "See, girl? Even yah Pops is saying yah mon is worth holding on to. He's making plenty sacrifice for yah. Stop being a donkey and go after him."

Lilah stared after Celly and Pops as they left the gift shop. Celly had always been so protective of her. Now she was practically thumping her on the head for being protective of herself. She told herself she was doing all this for Justin, but was she actually being selfish? Justin had the most to lose yet he was willing to risk whatever it took to have her and the babies around him.

Her elation slowly deflated. Was Celly right? The thought weighed heavily on her mind as she left to get ready.

JUSTIN HAD OFFERED TO pick up Lilah but she'd insisted on driving herself, which only made him realize his uphill battle was a steeper incline than he previously thought. But when she entered the upscale restaurant, wearing a pretty white linen sundress that molded to her rounded curves and distended stomach, he couldn't help but stare. Her hair was twisted up in a messy twist, but the heat and the subsequent ride in the Jeep had already loosened a few strands to curl against the nape of her neck and frame her jaw. She looked delicate yet strong, a sexy contradiction that summed up Lilah perfectly. He immediately rose and pulled her chair out for her.

"Thank you, you didn't have to do that," she said with a shy smile that bordered on embarrassment.

"I didn't have to, I wanted to. A woman should always be treated like a lady—that's something my mom tried to pound into my head. Unfortunately, for a time I'd forgotten the lesson."

"That's sweet. Do you get along with your mother?" she asked, sliding into the seat and placing the napkin in her lap, though admittedly, there wasn't much room for the napkin because of her belly.

Justin pulled his attention away from her body and busied himself with his own napkin, if only to have something to do because his mind was conjuring all sorts of activities that didn't include a fork and spoon. How was it that she was becoming even more beautiful to him? He was spiraling deeper and deeper and there seemed no stopping his descent.

Last night, he couldn't help his thoughts from wandering into X-rated territory, which certainly hadn't helped his ability to sleep. Now, after the sonogram experience and the tease of sexual innuendo between them, he was burning hot with the desire to once again feel her close around him. Surely, this wasn't normal. Her stomach was no longer flat and taut but it didn't matter. He wanted to caress and kiss that rounded belly and hold her tightly each night. He wanted to coax those sweet little mewling noises from her throat as he touched her in intimate places and swallow her sharp breaths as he plunged inside her. He wanted to taste the nipples of each rapidly swelling breast until she writhed helplessly against her rising desire.

"Justin?"

Lilah's gentle inquiry snapped Justin back to the present and he realized he'd gone on a mental walkabout as he'd fantasized about what he desperately wanted to do to her. "Ah, um, I'm sorry," he stated with a flush. "Yes, you asked if I got along with my mom…yeah, mostly. She's a proud woman with a soft center. She likes to organize charity balls and fancy dinners with seven-course meals and she loves to decorate for the holidays. Any holiday, actually. When you walk into her house, you have no doubt what season you're in. She has a full decorating staff to help her transform her house into a wonderland of expensive furnishings."

"Oh," Lilah said, a little subdued. "She sounds terrifying."

Realizing he'd said the wrong thing, he tried to clarify. "My mom is very sweet. You'd probably like her a lot. I just don't fully appreciate her talents because I'm a guy. To me, there is no difference between green and teal. And peach is not a color it's a fruit." At that Lilah giggled and he relaxed. "You know, now that I think about it, you and her would probably get along because of your artistic talents. My mom loves the arts. She can spend hours staring at dusty old paintings at the museums."

"You don't like art?"

"Yeah, I do. I just have a short attention span. I don't want to analyze and discuss it for hours. I like what I like and I move on…unless it's something I love. Then I purchase and put it on my walls but I still don't want to have a discourse on form, shadow and light. I just want to enjoy it." He paused, then took a chance that he knew could backfire. "I'd love to see your art."

Lilah stilled, her expression becoming deadly serious. Or perhaps it was fear lurking in her gaze. Either way, somehow he knew if she were to show him her art, it would mean something to them both. "Why?" she whispered.

"Because I fell in love with an artist. Her art is a part

of her and there isn't a part of that woman that I don't want to know and love." Tears filled her eyes and she seemed to struggle with the words she wanted to say. He knew this was a turning point, something tremendously momentous between them. He pushed a little harder, not willing to give up any ground he'd gained inch by inch. "I think that woman I'm madly in love with is afraid of showing me her true self, and because her art is painted with her soul, and she's afraid if I see the real her, I'll run away." She swallowed, her eyes becoming luminous. He reached out to grasp her hand from across the table. "But she doesn't have to worry. Everything about her I love. There is nothing that could scare me away. *Nothing.*"

HER HEART HAMMERED AGAINST her breastbone almost to the point of pain. He'd seen her naked yet she'd never allowed him to see her. What he was asking…she nearly collapsed under the weight of it. He had no idea how right he was. Her art was a tangible expression of her soul and to let him see…would render her totally bare to his scrutiny. The fearful voices in her head whispered all the reasons why she ought to shut him down—self-preservation, sheltering fear and crippled self-esteem—but another voice, one that was growing stronger, almost shouting above the fearful chorus, urged her to take that leap and fly, to let go of the past and run with open arms into her future.

A future with Justin.

"What if you don't like it?" *What if you don't like me? The real me?*

"Impossible. I've caught glimpses and you're amazing."

She didn't know how to respond. All her life she'd run away from anything that resembled commitment, whether it was romantic, personal or just responsibilities. She didn't mean to run, she just ended up doing it and then regretted her actions later. Her instinct in this situation should've urged her to run, to remind him that they ought to simply remain friends. But that option wasn't appealing in the least. She hated the idea of smiling and shrugging nonchalantly when Justin inevitably moved on with someone else because she'd continually pushed him away. She loathed the idea of not seeing him walk through the front door with a smile on his face reserved for her. And she particularly detested the idea of watching as someone else helped raise their babies when it was his visitation week or month. The cold hard fact of the situation was staring at her in the face, daring her to ignore what was plain: she loved him and she was willing to take the risk.

"If you're not ready…" Justin started, disappointment in his tone, but Lilah cut in breathlessly, forcing the words out before she chickened out.

"Yes! Yes! You can see my art. I want to share that part of myself with you."

Just please, please handle with care, she prayed fervently. There was so much riding on this one thing.

But she was going to leap—and hope she didn't fall flat on her face.

Again.

CHAPTER THIRTY-ONE

LILAH LED JUSTIN TOWARD the atrium through the lighted path that provided a dim glow in the sultry night. The humidity was like a warm caress on her bare shoulders, an air kiss she'd come to love. Justin wiped away the sweat on his brow but otherwise didn't complain; he was too focused on her.

Dinner had been exquisite but she felt mildly guilty for not enjoying the experience to its fullest. Her mind had been going in different places, but mostly she wondered how Justin would react to her art.

And now the moment was here.

She pushed open the glass atrium doors and walked inside. The closed heat was nearly stifling and so she left the doors open. Within minutes she had a few lights on and then led Justin to her secret room where she stashed her art.

As Justin watched her produce a door out of the wall, his brow arched. "A secret door?" he remarked, impressed. "That's very cool. I always wanted to find a secret door in one of our houses. Never happened."

"You poor thing," she murmured with a small smile. She flicked the light and breathed deeply before reaching on her tiptoes for the rolled-up pieces that were her best. Justin was surprised by the sheer number of paintings she had rolled up in the small space and commented on it.

"I think you've outgrown this secret spot," he observed with a wink to keep things light.

He had no idea how true his statement was. She'd begun to realize that she couldn't hide in a closet her entire life—partly due to the sessions with Dr. Veronica, but also due to Justin and the babies.

She unrolled the painting carefully and attached it to the easel. It was her first painting when the depression had hit. Just looking at it again brought out a feeling of desolation and loneliness but she knew it was simply an echo and not a true reflection of what she was feeling now.

Justin gazed at the piece and his silence frightened her. She was afraid to ask so she also remained silent. When he finally spoke, it wasn't anything she expected.

"You're a master." His simple, yet shocked statement floored her and she didn't know how to react. She frowned with disappointment, believing he was being effusive in his praise to spare her feelings. She started to reach for the piece to roll it back up again but he stopped her, cupping her face and regarding her with serious awe. "Lilah…I'm not saying this to feed your ego. I came here prepared to love whatever I saw, but I never expected to see such quality."

"Justin, I know that's not true even though I love you for trying," she said, through a wash of tears. "I've had masters evaluate my work and they called it, 'infantile at its worst, moderately adequate at its best.' I was rejected from the most prestigious art school in Florida and it nearly destroyed me. I vowed never to subject my art to that kind of criticism again. And I haven't.

You're the first person I've let see my art, aside from Carys, but she's a child."

"Lilah, I don't know what your art looked like ten years ago or whenever you submitted your application, but what I'm looking at right now is the work of someone who can not only nail the technical aspects of the medium but has the artistic talent that gives a piece that extra something. Just looking at this…makes me want to cry and that's what art is supposed to do right? Evoke an emotion?" At her halting nod, he added without reservation, "I want to buy this. Right now. How much?"

"I—I don't know," she stammered. "It's not for sale. I can't sell it."

"Why not?" he asked.

She wondered why she was reluctant to part with it. It felt like selling off a piece of her but artists sell their work, that's what they did to make a living. How was she ever going to change and grow into the artist she wanted to be if she didn't start somewhere? She supposed selling a piece to Justin would be a gentle start to that change. But how could she charge the father of her children? "How much do you think it's worth?" she asked with uncertainty. Maybe a hundred dollars?

"Easily two grand," he assessed with a critical eye, startling her. At her expression, he misunderstood and amended his offer. "You're right, that's lowballing. Would you take three thousand for it?"

"God, Justin, that's too much," she gasped. "I can't let you spend that on my painting. I just can't."

"Fine. Then let me take it on consignment. Artists do this all the time. I will pay to have it framed and hung. And then we'll see how it does on its own. Do you have any others like this?"

"I have a whole series," she admitted.

"May I see them?"

She nodded and pulled the rolls. They worked together to hang them on the easels. The growing pride in Justin's expression as he perused each piece caused the air in her lungs to feel constricted. She'd never imagined she could be so dependent on someone else's opinion after the debacle with the Florida art school but here she was, holding her breath as Justin evaluated her work. Fresh tears sprang to her eyes when he announced without reservation, "I want them all."

"Are you sure? Maybe just the one would be better. What if you spend all this money to have it framed and they don't sell at all?" she asked, voicing one of the fears jabbering in her ear, dampening her joy.

"I sincerely doubt that will happen. However, I will keep them all if they don't sell. I want them all anyway but since you don't want to sell to me…"

"It's not that I wouldn't sell them to you…I just don't feel right doing so," she clarified. "I would give them to you."

"And I would never allow you to give away your work. This is…" His voice caught and he paused to collect himself. "Lilah…I can only hope our babies get half your talent. You are…incredible."

The words stunned her, but the sentiment behind them, humbled her beyond measure. She smiled through her tears and reached out her hand. If there was ever a moment that she knew exactly what she wanted, this was it.

And she wanted him.

"Let's go," she said.

He accepted her hand but his brows bunched together in concern. "Are you okay? Are you tired?"

"Not tired but I'm ready for bed."

She sent him a coy look and his Adam's apple bobbed as her meaning sank in. She flipped off the lights and locked the atrium.

There were too many clothes between them.

And judging by Justin's quickened step as they headed to Lilah's room, he couldn't agree more.

By the time they reached her room, their desire had reached a fever pitch as they tore at each other's clothes, eager to feel skin against skin. Would it always be this way with them? She hoped so. Justin's touch ignited a need she'd never experienced and she was greedy for more.

She'd become almost insatiable.

He rained kisses down her neck, to her breasts. He didn't give her an opportunity to worry about her changing body as he worshipped each new curve and valley created by her burgeoning pregnancy. If anything, he seemed unable to get enough of her and his urgency fed her own. She straddled him and he entered her with one gentle push. Their lovemaking slowed to a sweet and gentle pace as Justin made allowances for her condition. Soon, Lilah had reached her peak and she shuddered all around him, crying out as wave after wave crashed down inside her, wrenching a prolonged orgasm from her body that left her gasping for air from the sheer pleasure erupting from her nerve endings.

"God, you're so damn sexy," he said in a tight voice as he soon found his own release, bathing her with his love and gasping her name over and over as his thrusts slowly stilled and his breathing was as harsh as her own.

This was true between them—this connection that defied all reason.

And she couldn't deny its power.

JUSTIN LAY WITH HIS HEAD near Lilah's stomach, pressing intermittent kisses to her rounded belly as he tried to catch his breath. Her gloriously naked body glowed in the dim moonlight as the sweat dried on their skin. She looked like a proud heathen goddess with her voluptuous curves softening her formerly lean body with a little more padding that he found incredibly sexy.

The night sounds buzzed all around them as the ceiling fans whirred to push the hot air from the room. Justin was blissfully content until he heard the muffled vibration of his cell phone tucked away in his discarded shorts.

Lilah lifted on her elbows and frowned. "What is that sound?"

He sighed and rolled to his feet. "It's my cell phone."

"Who would call so late at night?" she asked, puzzled.

Justin knew but didn't want to say. He'd been ducking Rudy's calls. By now the man had probably hit DEFCON 1 on the panic level and was one whiskey away from calling the FBI to report him missing. When Rudy's name flashed on the screen in a frantic pulse, Justin pressed his lips together in agitation but answered anyway. "Hey, Rudy, what's up?"

"Holy shit!" Rudy exploded at Justin's attempt to sound casual. "Where the hell have you been? I haven't been able to raise you on the phone for over a week! I was about to call the authorities and report you missing."

Called it. Justin rolled his eyes and then gestured to Lilah that he was going to take the call outside. Once clear, he said in a low tone, "First, calm down. Everything is fine. I just wanted to enjoy a little time to myself without being harassed about work. What's so urgent that it couldn't wait?"

"You tell me," Rudy said, still heated. "A little bird has told me something that really raised my blood pressure and I hope to God it's not true."

The fine hairs on Justin's neck rose but he remained cool. "Yeah, such as?"

"Why St. John? Why not Tahiti or Fiji?" Rudy countered with suspicion. "I wondered when you told me and it seemed an odd choice. Particularly when you returned early from your first vacation and it was the place of your father's choosing for you. Given your relationship, I would've thought that'd be the last place you'd want to return. So it got me to thinking…"

"Spit it out, Rudy. It's late."

"Who's the girl, Justin?"

And there it was. Somehow Rudy had sniffed out the truth. Or at least some variation of it. He had a choice: lie to gain some time to work up to telling the truth or just let the chips fall where they may and come clean. On one hand it angered him that his personal business was on everyone else's radar, but then he knew that was the price of politics so he couldn't rail too loudly. Still, the reality of it sucked when it worked against you.

"Her name is Lilah and she's…" not a girlfriend, not his fiancée "…someone special to me. I'd appreciate some discretion. I'm not ready to tell my parents yet."

Rudy exhaled sharply but didn't sound too sorry when he said, "Sorry, bud. You should've returned my phone calls. Your parents left for St. John on the 9:00 p.m. flight. My guess is they've already landed in St. Thomas."

"What the hell, Rudy!" Justin whispered harshly, agitated for the intrusion and worried about Lilah. "What did you tell them?"

"Listen, you're not the only one with a life on the line. Your father's reputation is at stake because he's endorsing you, as are all of your father's supporters. We can't have any kind of scandal rock the boat when we're so close to winning! Say goodbye to your island honey and be done with it."

"It's not that simple," he ground out.

"No, it really is. Is she worth it? Who is she? No one that can help your career, therefore, she has to go." At Justin's angry silence, Rudy tried to tone down his harsh words by saying, "Listen, I get it. We've all had someone in our past who felt like something special at the time, but trust me, you don't want to throw everything away over a sweet piece of ass. How about this… after the election you can still hook up. Maybe we can even find a nice little apartment for her in the city, somewhere out of the way or even better, how are her secretarial skills? Maybe we could put her to work as a personal assistant. Don't worry, there are ways around these types of problems. But right now, we need you to focus."

Justin felt sick. And dirty. It was all he could do to keep from throwing the phone into the wild, overgrown foliage lining the walkway.

"You there, Justin?" Rudy asked when Justin refrained from responding for fear of saying something he couldn't take back. "Say your goodbyes. Take my word for it, it's better this way."

"Where are my parents staying?" he asked tightly.

"The Worchester. One of the suites."

"I'll be in touch," Justin said curtly, and then clicked off. His blood percolated with impotent rage. He felt trapped and suffocated. He wanted to take Lilah and run away but there were so many lives connected to his campaign that he couldn't in good conscience screw over. Rudy, he couldn't give a rat's ass about, but there were plenty of good, solid people in his employment who gave up positions with the competitor because they'd believed in him. He couldn't let them down.

But he'd do anything to protect Lilah. And if Rudy so much as breathed a word of his disgusting little proposal to Lilah, he'd put his fist in Rudy's slick, ass-kissing mouth.

"Justin?" Lilah's voice floated through the open window.

"Coming," he answered, returning inside with a false smile.

She turned sleepily on her side, rubbing her stomach as one of the babies must've given her a little kick. "Who was that?"

"Campaign manager, Rudy. There's a bit of a situation he wanted to make sure I knew about."

At that Lilah opened her eyes to stare groggily at him. "What kind of situation?"

He drew a deep breath and then let it out. "My parents are arriving tonight. In fact, they might already be here."

ALL SLEEPINESS FLED from Lilah's body as she sat up. "Your parents? Why?"

Justin looked irritated and just as unhappy about the situation as she but likely for different reasons. "Someone let slip that I was seeing someone here. When Rudy couldn't get ahold of me, he alerted my parents and they thought you were a significant threat to my campaign so they're on their way, likely to talk some sense into me away from the prying eyes of the press."

"Oh, God," Lilah breathed, her hand going to her chest. "I can't breathe. They're going to see that I'm pregnant. I mean, there's no hiding this!" She pointed to her belly and then tried to cover herself with the light sheet. Suddenly, she felt overexposed. He grimaced and helped her cover up. "They're going to hate me."

"They won't," he assured her but he looked worried. "I won't let them."

Lilah groaned. "I don't feel good," she said, rubbing her stomach and then rolling onto her side in pain. Damn her nervous stomach.

"Are you okay?" Justin asked, coming to her side immediately. "Is it the babies?"

"No, it's my nervous stomach. I internalize stress." She groaned in embarrassment as her stomach gurgled. "Get ready for something not so sexy," she admitted as her cheeks flushed with heat. She struggled to her feet and waddled to the bathroom.

Moments later, Lilah reemerged and climbed into the bed. "So what's going to happen?" she asked, trying to be brave when she wanted to run.

Justin bit his lip, contemplating his answer. "I'm not sure," he admitted. "Let me take point on this. Just follow my lead. I won't let them say or do anything that will offend you. I promise."

She believed him but she was worried. Was he about to throw away everything for her? Could she let him?

Her stomach grumbled again and Justin looked at her with sympathy. "Still upset?" he asked.

She shook her head and admitted sheepishly, "No... now I'm hungry."

He chuckled and tucked her under his arm. "Well, let's raid the kitchen, then. Can't let my babies and my girl starve."

Lilah grinned and decided to worry about tomorrow when it came.

JUSTIN'S PARENTS CONVERGED on Larimar early the next morning after receiving a message from Justin to meet him there. Lilah and Justin figured it was better to meet them with home field advantage and if things went south, they could always ask them to leave. It seemed a good plan, though Justin wasn't sure what he was going to say to lessen the shock when they saw Lilah's stomach.

Lora and Heath agreed to take Pops out for a ride around the island to give them some privacy while Celly covered the front desk.

Vernon and his wife, Virginia—or Ginny as her close friends called her—arrived exactly on time as was the senator's habit and walked into the airy lobby of Larimar with stiff expressions on their wilted faces.

Justin thought it best to meet them and bring them into the private section to avoid any altercations with the guests. He happened to catch a look from Celly as she watched them walk past and the Caribe woman did not look impressed with either of them. No doubt, she felt protective over Lilah and seemed ready to give the Caleses a piece of her mind if they so much as looked cross-eyed at Lilah. Justin appreciated Celly's gruff nature. At least he always knew where he stood with her, which was a quality he'd come to respect since entering politics.

"Justin dear, why are we meeting here?" his mother asked, pushing a strand of her hair from her face and pressing a linen handkerchief to her brow. "Good lord, it's hot. There was air-conditioning at our suite at the Worchester. Why couldn't we meet there?"

"You get used to the heat, Mother," he said, gracing his mother with a kiss on the cheek. "Follow me."

Vernon made a sound of barely restrained impatience but followed without a word. Justin's instincts told him this was going to be the battle of his life. He hoped he was up for it.

He'd never gone toe-to-toe with his father before and won. In the past he'd been too weak, too spoiled to risk losing what he felt was his way of life. Now he realized he had bigger purpose. His father would learn that he wouldn't be pushed around. Not anymore. Hopefully, his father would respect that he was finally standing up for something bigger than himself and even more important than politics.

"Mother, Father," he said, pushing open the door to the living room where Lilah awaited. "I'd like to introduce you to Lilah Bell, the woman I hope to marry. Lilah…these are my parents, Vernon and Virginia Cales."

It didn't take long for all hell to break loose.

CHAPTER THIRTY-TWO

"YOU'RE P-PREGNANT!" Virginia Cales exclaimed as she sank into a nearby chair and her husband began to bellow.

"What is the meaning of this!" Vernon Cales shouted, his face turning a florid red as he looked to Justin as if he wanted to throttle him.

Lilah cringed as Vernon clenched his fists and looked ready to punch a hole in whatever was near enough. It seemed useless to cling to the usual social etiquette of exchanging pleasantries so she didn't bother; not that anyone would've heard her attempt anyway as Vernon and Justin had started yelling at one another and Virginia had begun to cry.

Lilah wanted to cry, too, but just as her eyes began to swim, she felt the babies kick and roll around in her womb as if doing somersaults. She straightened and her gaze narrowed. This was ridiculous. There was no way they could hold a decent conversation among all the ruckus. Putting her two fingers in her mouth she blew hard, producing a whistle loud enough to shatter eardrums. Everyone stopped and clapped their hands over their ears, including Justin, as they turned to stare.

She wagged her fingers in a subtle gesture, explaining shortly, "A little trick my Grams taught me. She could whistle and we would come running. Sort of a family thing." Now that she had their attention, she drew a breath and continued in a more pleasant voice, "It's very nice to meet you. I wish the circumstances were different but they're not. The facts are simple—Justin and I met while he was on vacation and I discovered I was pregnant after he left."

"Convenient that you managed to snare a wealthy young politician hopeful," Vernon muttered, earning a black look from Justin. If it weren't for the restraining hand Lilah placed on Justin's shoulder, he might've toppled the old man into the tall plant beside the sofa. "We're going to require a paternity test. You can bet on that."

"Justin…are you sure it's your baby?" Virginia ventured stiffly. "Mistakes happen, of course, but one must be sure it's *your* mistake."

Lilah swallowed, hating that she'd referred to their babies as a mistake but she tried to stay focused and not dissolve into tears. For better or worse, these uptight people were going to be her babies' grandparents. Oh, God, the idea made her shudder.

Justin corrected his mother, saying, "Babies. Lilah is a twin and she conceived twins."

"Twins," Virginia repeated faintly, as if the thought of one baby had been bad enough. Now two? Lord have mercy. "Darling…we should've discussed this in private. These are delicate matters…"

"There's nothing delicate about it, Mother. I want to marry Lilah. Plain and simple."

"Ah, hell," Vernon grumbled to the ceiling. "Now he wants to get married. Son, you've barely begun to care for yourself, much less a wife and two kids. Does your girl know about your exploits back in the city? How you've never held a job long enough to collect a true paycheck? Too busy partying and having a good time to bother with something as menial as work."

Justin's cheeks burned but he said, "What about the campaign, Dad? I've been doing a pretty good job of running my own life since I hit the campaign trail. Remember how proud you said you were of me just last week?"

"That was before—" he gestured wildly at Lilah "—*this!* Now it seems I was hasty in my praise. I never in a million years would've suspected that you'd screw up this big."

Red blotches crawled up Justin's neck. "I've learned a lot and changed even more," Justin said in a steely tone. The tension between the two men was enough to choke a horse and Lilah could only watch apprehensively as they squared off. "It's true I didn't know Lilah was pregnant, but I never forgot her. As soon as I got some time off from the campaign, I came here to be with her. I wanted to marry her then. Learning she was pregnant, well, it just made everything fall into place even more snugly. It feels right. It's what I'm going to do."

Virginia looked pale whereas Vernon's face was florid. Lilah felt obligated to offer something cool to drink. "We have fresh lemonade," she said, in an attempt at hospitality.

Virginia appeared reluctant to accept anything from Lilah but was just miserable enough to overlook that fact and nodded brusquely. "If you wouldn't mind."

"I'll be right back. Try not to kill each other."

Lilah knew the minute she left the room, they'd start

talking about her specifically but she had faith in Justin. He'd stand up for her.

And their babies.

THE MINUTE LILAH WAS OUT of earshot, Vernon turned to Justin, his expression thunderous but resigned to the distasteful business at hand. "We have a fund we can tap to make this embarrassment go away," he said in a low tone. "Admittedly, two babies will be more expensive but we'll do what we must to protect your future."

Justin glared at his father. "The only embarrassment I feel right now is that I'm related to you. My children are not an embarrassment and neither is Lilah. How could you even suggest such a thing? Those babies are your *grandchildren*. Think about it, Dad. You would honestly rather make them go away to save some idea in your head for my career, rather than embrace your own flesh and blood?"

His father's mouth tightened even as his bottom lip trembled, whether it was from rage or something else, Justin didn't know, and frankly didn't care. He looked to his mother. She watched them with a stricken expression that was equal parts horror and bewilderment and he knew he wasn't going to get the support he'd hoped for from that corner. He made a sound of disgust and said, "I'd rather stand with her than beside you if you can honestly stand here and call your grandchildren *embarrassments*."

Vernon swallowed and had the grace to look ashamed but he countered with an emphatic display. "She will ruin you! Is that what you want? How will this look for your campaign? You knocked up some random girl while on vacation and now you've sullied any chance you might've had of landing a decent wife. No one is going to be willing to take on this kind of baggage. It's too messy, too humiliating. People will judge you and they will pass their judgment in the form of their vote. You might as well have just given the seat to Campbell Duncan and have done with it!"

"How could you, Justin?" Virginia asked in a trembling voice as if Justin had betrayed her. "This is… unfathomable that you would be so careless with your family name. We don't know a thing about this girl. I never imagined that you might be so…oh, just so careless."

"I love her," Justin said simply, his heart weighing heavily in his chest for his parents' lack of support. He'd hoped for a miracle; he should've known he wouldn't be so lucky. "If she says yes, I'm going to marry her. End of story. If it ends my political career…so be it."

Vernon threw his hands up. "It's always this way for you, isn't it? So easy to screw over anyone who ever built a bridge for you in your life. Well, that's not going to happen. I forbid you to marry this girl. I forbid it!"

Justin forced a laugh. "You forbid it? You don't have that option."

"I will cut you off so fast, your head will spin," Vernon ground out, nearly spitting the words. "Try supporting your island tramp on the fumes of your love and see how many diapers it buys."

"*Vernon!*" his mother exclaimed, horrified by her husband's coarse words but his father didn't back down, in fact, he refused to even admit he'd overstepped but that was his father in a nutshell. He always rode the course, no matter how far off the track he'd traveled.

"Don't you dare call her that again," Justin warned.

"You can cut me off, I don't care about your money. But believe me when I say, I will also cut you off. You will never see me or your grandkids again. You don't deserve them anyway, you pompous, arrogant, control freak."

Vernon buttoned up his mouth in an angry press of his lips and then gestured to his wife angrily that they were leaving. "Your son has made his choice," he said. "Enjoy your new life in poverty."

Virginia seemed reluctant to leave things as they were, something had changed in her eyes when Justin had counter threatened but she wouldn't go against her husband. Not openly. Justin watched them go.

To his shock, tears began to fall.

When Lilah returned with the lemonade, she found him sobbing into his hands, unable to stop.

VERNON CALES WAS SO ANGRY he couldn't see straight and it didn't help that the roads in St. John were engineered by a drunken crazy person with all the twists and turns and left-handed driving.

"Vernon, slow down," his wife exclaimed when the tires on their rented Jeep Cherokee squealed in protest around the turn. "I don't want to lose my son and die all in the same day!"

Vernon spared his wife a short look but eased up on the gas pedal. He would've paid for a driver but there hadn't been time to find one and he'd been anxious to find out if the rumors had been true. Damn it all to hell! That boy was going to ruin his life!

"Why? Why now? He was just starting to become a son a father could be proud of," he lamented loudly. "No more whoring and late-night parties for the paparazzi to catch at all hours of the night doing who knows what! And now, this!"

"He says he loves her," Virginia said, grabbing on to the armrest as another sharp turn made them lean. "Maybe we were too hasty in our judgment."

"You've always been too soft on the boy," Vernon groused with open irritation. "Turned him into a worthless boy who wants to play at being a man."

"Stop it," Virginia warned, a note of steel weaving its way through her voice. "You're going too far."

Vernon was surprised at her tone with him. She never raised her voice or spoke brusquely. He wasn't sure he liked it. "What do you propose we do? Embrace this girl with open arms?" he suggested, sneering. "She's a nobody, a gold digger who just found a way to get her hooks into our pocketbooks."

"You don't know that," Virginia responded with uncertainty. "She didn't call and tell him when she discovered she was pregnant. In fact, she waited and my guess is that she wasn't going to tell him at all. It was just luck that put him back on this island to discover that fact."

"Maybe she wasn't sure who the babies belonged to and wanted to wait and see who the babies favored," he shot back with ill humor. "Who knows? Fact remains, I want a paternity."

"Husband dear, you're being a royal ass about this. Of course, it was a shock but I've never seen Justin so solid in his conviction. He never wavered. Not one ounce. He truly loves this woman. It doesn't matter what the paternity will reveal. Those are his babies because he loves her."

"It matters to me," Vernon retorted, but he couldn't ignore the logic in his wife's statement. She was right.

Justin hadn't quailed, not even in the face of being disowned. He'd live in poverty with his woman if that's what it came down to. And what would that look like in the press? Former New York Senator Cales's Son Living in Poverty. The headlines would destroy his reputation as a family man. He'd always tried to protect his reputation by quietly dousing fires his son had sparked. From the frat parties to the multitude of women…Vernon had always managed to make those stories go away—usually with money.

But there was no making it go away if Justin didn't want his help.

Or his money.

An odd pang that felt suspiciously like heartbreak followed as he realized that money had been the only thing between them for years aside from animosity. Whatever had happened to that sweet boy who'd smiled up at him with joy and adoration as he'd taught him how to bait a hook and catch a fish?

That boy was long gone.

And the man he'd become looked at him with anger and disappointment.

His lip began to tremble but he stiffened as he said, "He's made his bed. Let's see how long he'd like to sleep in it."

If his own gut hadn't been telling him that he was making a grave error, the mutinous expression on his wife's face would've shouted it.

Mistake or no…he was going to stick to his decision.

The boy had to learn his lessons the hard way.

CHPATER THIRTY-THREE

"It was awful," Lilah said quietly into the phone as she related to Lindy what had transpired earlier that day. Justin had left to go get her a hamburger after she'd professed a craving but she suspected he'd needed a little time to regroup after that disastrous meeting with his parents. "I think he was brokenhearted over what his father said to him. Justin told me their relationship had been strained for a while, but I think deep down, he hoped his father would see the changes he'd made and trust him to make a choice that was right for his life. Instead, he cut him down. Oh, Lindy…my heart broke for him and I didn't know what to say."

Lindy sighed "There was probably nothing you could say. This is between them. They have to hash it out and you have to let them."

"I overheard some of the conversation," Lilah admitted, feeling guilty for cavesdropping but she hadn't been able to stop. "He's giving up his career for me and his parents have cut him off completely. I feel terrible about it. It's as if I've ripped his family apart. I feel sick inside."

"They actually said those things?" Lindy asked, incredulous.

"And worse," recalled Lilah, grimacing. "I think his dad thinks I deliberately trapped him into something.

Like I'm a gold digger or something. I've never been so humiliated in my life."

"What a bunch of jerks," Lindy muttered. "Sounds like Justin is better off without them."

"Yeah, but that's his family. And I know it hurt him deeply even if he won't admit it. I don't know if I can go through with this…"

"What do you mean?" Lindy asked, alarmed.

"I just mean, I don't think I can let Justin throw everything away for me. It sounded romantic and noble when he declared that he would but now the aftermath is just painful and upsetting. Without his parents' support he can't continue to campaign and his political career will die before it's even begun."

"What about his campaign supporters aside from his parents?"

"They're all connected through his father. Basically, he's gaining a lot of support because of the track record of his father. It's easy to back a horse you know comes from winning stock, that's how Justin put it." Lilah heard Lindy shudder and she didn't blame her. It all sounded like a foreign language to her, too. "Nothing is as simple as I love him, he loves me. I was naive to think it could be."

"You can't walk away. You'll devastate him."

"Without me, his parents will support him. I can't ask that he pay that big of a price for me. I know he will resent me eventually and I just can't bear that burden. I know myself. I can't handle it."

"Who's to say that you'd ever have to?" Lindy disagreed. "You're making a lot of assumptions about a future that hasn't even arrived yet. Plus you're all hopped up on hormones and your brain is on baby overload. Just give it some time. Maybe things will change."

"You didn't see their faces," Lilah said sadly. "There's no turning that around. At least not with his father. And I can't go my entire life knowing they hate me. And I shouldn't have to. I don't deserve that, right?"

"No, of course not," Lindy murmured on a sigh. "This sucks."

"Yeah, tell me about it."

"So what are you going to do?" she asked.

Lilah drew a sharp breath and closed her eyes as she answered with a heavy heart. "I'm going to send Justin home."

"And how do you hope to accomplish that?"

"By pushing him away. For good."

JUSTIN HADN'T SEEN IT COMING. Truthfully, he'd still been reeling from his parents' actions that he hadn't realized how much damage had truly been done.

"What are you talking about?" he demanded, staring at Lilah, not quite sure he'd heard her correctly. "What do you mean you don't want to be together?"

She quietly smoothed the light fabric covering her stomach and answered in a cool tone, "After the scene with your parents I've come to realize we were being naive, and there's no room for that now that we're going to be parents. Your parents hate me and will always resent me for getting pregnant. I won't live under that kind of scrutiny and judgment. It's not healthy and it'll ruin all the good work I've done with my therapist to regain my mental health. I'm sorry, Justin. I'm not willing to sacrifice my mental wellness for you. I just can't. I have the babies to think of first."

"Lilah, I will walk away from them forever. They won't judge you—they won't say two words to you. They don't matter. Just you and I matter."

She graced him with a short look. "How will you support your children? The job market is fierce. Without your father's support, your political career will fall. You know this. I think we both know I'm right. It hurts right now to admit it, but someday, we'll both agree this was best."

"Bullshit."

She stared. "Excuse me?"

"You're running scared and this is the easy way. I'm willing to fight but you're backing out the minute it gets tough," he accused, throwing his hands up as frustration and despair ate at his ability to remain calm. He could not lose Lilah over this. He could not! "My parents will come around. I know it."

"I don't want them to bother," she said with a shrug. "First impressions can be a lingering poison if the impressions aren't favorable. They're never going to forgive me for getting pregnant. There will always be a suspicion that I got pregnant on purpose and I don't want to waste my life trying to prove to them that I'm worthy of their love. I have a family who loves me. I don't need their approval." She drew a deep breath and continued even though he'd opened his mouth to protest. "But you do. It's plain to me now that you're desperate for your father's approval. All that stuff you said you did before we met…it was a child's attempt at getting his father's attention. If you're ever going to repair your relationship with your father—and I strongly suggest that you try—I cannot be your roadblock to that success. They will love the babies when they get here, but

I will always be a reminder of what they deem a failure. It's just not worth it, Justin. Not for me."

Justin fought against the rising panic that was nearly level with the suffocating realization that she was right.

"Lilah…I love you," he said, his voice breaking. How could she be so heartless? "We can work this out if we do it together."

She seemed to falter but held to her course. "I'm not going to change my mind. I will send you updates about the babies. I will never keep you from them. I swear. But we should probably talk with a mediator about future custody arrangements. I don't want to fight about the kids. It'll only be worse for them."

"Stop it, Lilah," he ordered, tears filling his eyes. This had to be a nightmare. This couldn't be real. She wasn't leaving him. "You don't mean any of this. You're freaked out and overreacting. This is fixable. Please."

She blinked rapidly and her lip trembled but she didn't cave. The sadness in her eyes told the story. She might love him but not enough to battle his parents and his career.

"Goodbye, Justin."

It was barely a whisper but the words stabbed him in the heart.

Lilah…please…

And then she was gone.

THE URGE TO WAIL AND SCREAM at the injustice of it all was trapped in a bubble of pain and sorrow just under her breastbone but she managed to keep it down until she reached her room at Larimar.

Then, behind the safety of her own walls, she sobbed until it felt her eyes might bleed.

It was for the best, she told herself. It was for the best and someday he would realize this painful moment was a blessing in disguise. He would go on to do great things for many people and she had full faith in his ability to change lives for the better. She knew this because she'd changed and grown by knowing him during the short time they'd shared. And now she carried two small bits of Justin that she could love and cherish her entire life. It would have to be enough.

But still the knowledge gave her no solace. Her heart was a broken, pulpy mess of shattered dreams and naive illusions.

She had to be strong for the babies. She had to be strong to endure in the coming months. To do this alone—without Justin—felt wrong on so many levels but she forced herself to believe that she was making a sacrifice worth making.

In the meantime, she simply let her pain flow from her body in racking sobs as she clutched at the bedding where she and Justin had cuddled together mere hours ago—when she'd dreamed blissfully of a future that would never be.

VIRGINIA CALES HAD NEVER been overly fond of conflict and as such, had endeavored to avoid it. Most people mistook her acquiescence for weakness—including her husband—but Virginia had learned quite early that a person needn't knock down walls when finding a back door accomplished the same goal.

"It's really quite lovely here," she remarked casually as she gazed out across the crystal sea from their balcony. "I can certainly understand the appeal."

Vernon grunted something but otherwise remained

focused on his iPhone emails. He squinted and then gestured to Virginia, saying, "Get me my reading glasses, will you? These damn screens are too small to read."

"Of course, dear," she said, handing Vernon his glasses. They were supposed to leave St. John in the morning. Vernon seemed all too eager to put this place behind him, but Virginia felt there was unfinished business to attend.

The business between two women.

She had no intention of leaving this island until she'd spoken to Lilah Bell. The woman was the mother of her grandchildren—ah, grandchildren, just saying the word, although foreign, held a certain warm appeal—and Virginia believed words had been said that were unfair.

But first…she needed to speak with her son. "I'm going out for a bit. Do you need anything?" she asked solicitously as she grabbed her purse and wide floppy hat.

Vernon barely acknowledged her, which was typical when he was engrossed in his work. She didn't hold it against him but she did file it away for future reference. Virginia had an impeccable memory, some would say almost eidetic, and she always knew what to keep and what to discard. The ability had never failed her and she suspected, it never would.

It'd been several days since the distasteful event had happened at Larimar and they hadn't heard from Justin even though his room was not far from theirs. She'd half expected him to show up so they could hash things out, but his silence was just as damning as the rashly shouted words.

She knocked at his door but when no answer came,

she let herself in using the key card she'd acquired from the front desk.

The mess was appalling. Clothes that looked as if they'd been ripped from the drawers and thrown around in a fit of rage—or grief—littered the floor and the smell of whiskey floated on the stale, closed air, causing her to delicately hold her nose and head straight for the window. Justin, smelling like a distillery, lay facedown on his bed, sprawled as if a giant had tossed him there, and for a horrifying moment, Virginia feared he was dead.

Until a loud, resounding snore followed.

Sighing, she jerked open the drapes and allowed the sunshine to fill the room while she went about tidying and straightening until Justin groaned as consciousness returned. She readied a pot of strong coffee while she waited for him to fully awake.

"Good morning, love," she said evenly, moving swiftly to hand him a shirt and shorts as he was nearly naked. She looked away as he slowly jerked on the clothes with a barely civil expression. "Rough night?"

"What are you doing here?" he asked flatly, rubbing at his jaw and wincing as, no doubt, his head throbbed from a killer hangover. "Who let you in?"

"Don't be rude. I am here to talk with you, that's all that matters. Sit up, please. And drink this," she instructed, handing him a hot cup of coffee strong enough to put hair on his chest. She seated herself on the opposite bed and waited for him to take a sip of the brew. She smiled briefly with understanding when he seemed to appreciate the coffee, at the very least. "What happened?" she asked, assuming by the torn up room and his equally destroyed demeanor that all wasn't well with Lilah.

"She left me," he answered sourly. "Are you happy?"

Virginia digested the information and then asked, "Why?"

"Because she said my parents would never accept her and she wasn't going to fight both you and my career. And you know what…she was right. Damn, if she wasn't right. Dad will always look down on her and you'll never accept her as she is. So, she left me. Nothing I could say would change her mind. You win. *Yay.* Go Team Cales." He ended with enough sarcasm to choke a goat.

A pinch of guilt straightened her back a bit. She supposed she could see how their reaction would've been off-putting. Taking in her son's appearance, she judged he hadn't showered since then, which was days ago, and if she had a guess, his minibar was likely empty. And he didn't seem eager to shower and shape up. She'd never seen her cavalier son so…brokenhearted. "Do you love her?" she asked in the plainest terms. "I mean, *really* love her?"

Justin turned to stare at her with bloodshot eyes filled with bleak sadness. It was answer enough, but when he said in a barely audible voice, "She's my world," Virginia realized this woman had the power to make or break her son. And a good mother would do anything to protect her child. Even if it meant getting to know someone she may have judged prematurely. "Darling, you smell like a drunken pig. May I suggest a shower and some breakfast?"

"I'd rather not. I'm comfortable right like this," he answered, raising his mug in mock salute.

Her mouth firmed and she said, "Tell me what you love about this girl."

He sighed as if irritated at the idea of playing a useless twenty questions game but he answered anyway. "She's bright, funny, smart, artistic, talented, genuine... should I go on? And she makes me feel like I'm the only man on this planet. Like she only has eyes for me." He shrugged. "No big deal. I'll find another like her. Oh, wait, and *she's having my babies*."

"Yes," she murmured, deep in thought. "There is that." She patted the bed to get his attention and said, "Listen, we have some work to do. You need to shower and shave, eat breakfast and return to the human race, and then we're going to discuss some strategy. In the meantime, I have an errand to run and will return in one hour. Please be ready to work."

"Work on what?" he asked, scowling. "I'm quitting politics."

"Nonsense. You're close to winning. And we're going to work on saving your political career as well as your relationship." She gave his appearance a critical once-over. "I can tell you right now, this look is not attractive and not likely to win any points."

"She doesn't want to be with me."

"Don't be a quitter," she said sternly, reminding him. "One hour."

LILAH WAS DEEP IN HER PAINTING world in the atrium, trying to work out the pain in her heart when a voice surprised her.

"Ms. Bell? A word if you wouldn't mind?"

She turned and saw Justin's mother standing there in a wide-brimmed, floppy hat and looking like a rich tourist inquiring about directions to the nearest shopping hot spots.

"Justin's not here. We…broke up," she said, stumbling on the words because they'd never actually been dating.

"I know that, Ms. Bell. May I call you, Lilah?"

"I suppose," she said. The Caleses were going to be the babies' grandparents; they might as well try acting civil with one another, although a part of her was intensely bitter deep down.

"You're an artist?" Virginia observed, breaking into a smile that nearly qualified as genuine. Lilah stiffened and moved in front of her easel. "Ah, not ready to share your work? I understand. However, I admit, I am curious. Justin said you were quite talented."

"I prefer to keep my work private," she said.

"You can't make any money that way," Virginia remarked in a reasonable tone. "You do hope to make a living from your art, do you not?"

Yes, Damn it. She nodded reluctantly.

Virginia smiled again. "Then, you ought to become accustomed to people wanting to see your work. May I?"

No. "It's not finished," Lilah answered stubbornly, but a perverse part of her wanted Virginia to see her talent and dare to find her wanting. Justin had believed in her. She had to start believing in herself, as well. She lifted her chin and backed up to return to the canvas. "I don't care if you take a look."

Virginia walked around the easel and gazed at the work in progress. Her stare roamed the piece, stopping to study the variations of color and technique, then regarded Lilah with sharp eyes. "Do you have anything else? Perhaps a finished piece?"

"Yes," she answered a bit defensively before reaching into the secret closet and pulling one of the rolled canvases. She unfurled one and secured it to an easel. Virginia gave this one the same studious attention. When she stepped away, she looked to Lilah and smiled. This time, her smile was genuine and warm.

"You are incredibly, *exquisitely* talented. This will be easier than I imagined. Tell me, darling, have you ever shown your work in a gallery?"

Lilah stammered, "N-no."

"Well then, it should be quite an experience for you. I suspect these paintings will go for five to ten thousand with the right buyer. I have quite an eye for these things. It's a hobby, if you will. Keeps me out of mischief," she said, shocking Lilah with a conspiratorial wink.

"Wait a minute…what is happening? A few days ago I was the worst thing to ever happen to your son. Now you're endorsing my work?"

"My first reaction was in poor taste. I apologize. But I've come to realize that my son is madly, deeply in love with you. And since I love my son as madly and deeply in a motherly way, I am willing to take a second look at what I, obviously, misjudged."

"I appreciate your apology, but your husband—"

"Can be an arrogant jerk," Virginia finished for her with an understanding smile. "But he can also be very generous and loyal. Once he gets to know you, I'm sure he will forget his previous opinion. Besides, what he doesn't realize is that once those babies are here, his world will revolve around them. You see, he carries a lot of guilt about the way he missed so much of

Justin's life, a fact I'm sure he will gladly amend with his grandchildren. I know my husband, better than he knows himself. I don't believe that he will reject you or the babies with a little time to adjust to the idea. He has never dealt well with change, I fear, and tends to over-react," she added with a long-suffering sigh. "When I told him I was pregnant with Justin, he'd gone on about the bad timing and whatnot but the minute Justin was born... Well, it changes a man. Everything he has done has been for Justin's benefit. That's how Vernon shows his love."

Tears pricked Lilah's eyes at Virginia's candid sharing. She appreciated her forthright information but it didn't change the fact that she would be political poison to Justin's career. "My past...could be damaging to Justin's career," she admitted in a low voice. "I suffered a bout of major depression and...tried to kill myself. I was committed and I see a therapist regularly. Don't you think that will hurt his chances of being elected?"

"Nonsense," Virginia said airily with a wave of her hand, shocking Lilah with her easy dismissal of Lilah's secret shame. Virginia saw Lilah stiffen and she gentled her voice as she explained with a smile. "You're an *artist*. Artists with your talent are prone to emotional instability. Van Gogh, Michelangelo, Gauguin," Virginia blithely rattled off famous painters as if Lilah had earned the right to share shelf space with them. "They all suffered from some level of mental illness and their work is beyond reproach. Once your paintings start showing up in all the right houses, your past will only increase their value, which in turn, can only help Justin's career. My darling...as I said, this is going to be easier than I imagined."

She stood before Lilah, her eyes warm but sharp. Lilah sensed this was a woman whom she could grow to care about with time and vice versa. The realization gave Lilah cause to hope.

"Are you going to let my son waste away of a broken heart or are you going to help mend this terrible rift in my family so that we can start planning for those beautiful babies in your belly?"

At the mention of the babies, Lilah's hand instinctively went to her stomach. Virginia had systematically destroyed all the reasons she'd believed were justified for leaving Justin. Now all that was left was for Lilah to ignore the fear and take the leap.

"I just wanted what was best for Justin," Lilah said, tears filling her eyes.

Virginia smiled. "I know, dear. Which is why I know you truly love my son. Anyone who would walk away at their own expense to help someone else is doing it for noble—if not misguided—reasons. And you've earned my respect and friendship from this moment forward. Together we'll work on that husband of mine and soon-to-be husband of yours." At the mention of potential marriage, Lilah's breath hitched. "Are you ready to be Mrs. Justin Cales, my dear?" Virginia inquired with a smile.

Lilah let out a shaky exhale and slowly nodded. "Yes. Yes, I am."

"Well, then, let's get on with it. I believe an island wedding is most romantic."

This time it was Lilah's turn to sink into the nearest chair.

She was getting married.

CHAPTER THIRTY-FOUR

WHEN HIS MOTHER LEFT, he'd thought of simply ignoring her instructions and finding another bottle of rum to drown his sorrows into but the ingrained respect he had for his mother overrode his self-destructive intentions. He dragged his half-sauced ass into the shower and scrubbed away days' worth of misery and self-pity, and when he emerged he felt better on the outside at least.

The irony was that Lilah was letting him go to save his career—and yes, he saw right through her reasons because at her core, Lilah was a kind and gentle person who would sacrifice her own happiness to secure another's—but now that he didn't have Lilah, he couldn't give a rat's flaming behind about his career. At this point, he could happily disappear and let the world wonder whatever had happened to that bright, young promising senatorial candidate.

When the hour had passed, and his mother hadn't returned—odd for a woman who prided herself on punctuality—he thought *screw it* and reached for the fresh rum bottle he hadn't managed to polish off last night.

But before he could crack the seal, his door opened and his mother walked in, followed by Lilah.

Did he dare to hope? He couldn't bring himself to take the chance. His heart couldn't take another hit. "Are you lost?" he asked sourly.

"Justin, that was rude," his mother admonished with a disappointed frown. "Now put down that bottle. We three need to take a meeting."

He did a double take. "A meeting? What kind of meeting?"

"Why, planning your wedding, of course. And we have to hurry. We need you two married before you return to New York to continue campaigning. But it's going to take some coordination. Luckily for you, I'm an expert planner of any social event. Including destination weddings. Because of the circumstances, I would suggest family only. No need to set tongues wagging—"

"What the hell is going on?" he interrupted, his head splitting and his vision swimming. Either he was still drunk and hallucinating or he'd died of alcohol poisoning sometime during the night. He looked to Lilah for answers, almost challenging her to explain when they both knew she'd kicked him to the curb a few short days ago. "I don't find this amusing," he said coldly.

Lilah came forward, her expression a combination of bewilderment and happiness—two expressions Justin found out of place given the situation. She shocked him by curling her arm around his neck and kissing him soundly. He wanted to push her away—he was still angry and raw from her rejection, and now he was confused on top of that—but desperate desire and delirious hope spiraled through him and caused him to clutch her to him. He loved the press of her hard belly against his, knowing his children grew safely in her womb, and he slowly softened under the onslaught of her kiss. This was one thing they did well together, no matter what.

His mother made a delicate sound, reminding them that they were not alone and they reluctantly parted.

"What's going on?" he asked softly, the anger leaching from his tone, leaving behind pure perplexity.

"I'm sorry," Lilah said, resting her head against his. "I let my fear get the best of me but your mom and I had a talk and she made me realize that I was being foolish and selfish. I will stand by you, no matter the storm. Together, we'll face anything and be stronger for it." She pulled away, her eyes sparkling. "I guess I'd forgotten that the best love stories are the ones you have to fight for. My Grams used to tell me that nothing worth having came easily and I want you, Justin Cales. I want us. And I want to be your wife."

"Do you mean it?" he whispered, barely able to form the words, his joy was strangling his throat. "Please… don't get my hopes up if you don't."

She nodded. "I mean it. Your mother thinks we can salvage everything. She has a pretty good plan, actually." She glanced at his mother with a grin. "She's a smart lady."

He looked to his mother and sent a silent look of gratitude from his heart for fixing what he'd thought for sure he'd broken beyond repair. "If my mother thinks she can make everything work…I believe her. What do you need me to do?"

"Yours is the easy part. Go find a ring, silly boy," his mother said, moving forward to gently pull Lilah with her. "While we find a dress."

A ring. This was happening. A giddiness fit for a young boy on Christmas Day made him smile like a fool until one thought dimmed his happiness. "What about Dad?" he asked.

"Darling, I've been managing your father for years. I think I can handle this. Go on, find your ring."

Justin grinned, all fear washing away. His mother was right; she'd always managed to get his father to see reason—eventually. He had no doubt she'd do it again.

LILAH STOOD IN AN IVORY GOWN of the softest silk as Lora fussed over her bouquet and Lindy—who'd flown in on a red-eye and had already downed enough caffeine to jolt a racehorse—was fiddling with the hem to ensure it didn't trip Lilah as she walked down the aisle.

"I can't believe you're beating both of us to the altar," Lindy said, pins clenched between her teeth. "I thought for sure I was going to be the one to get married first."

"And divorced first," Lora quipped, causing Lindy to glare. Lora laughed, adding, "I'm kidding, of course. That was before Gabe. Now you're almost normal."

"Yeah? What about you?" Lindy challenged. "How long are you going to keep Heath on the hook without letting him make an honest woman of you? At least Gabe and I have a date now."

"You do?" both Lilah and Lora asked.

Lindy took the pins from her mouth and smiled smugly. "Yep. The big date is April 15 of next year. I wanted a spring wedding so I could wear an off-the-shoulder dress."

"And I'm going to be the flower girl, of course," Carys chimed in, carrying corsages for everyone. "Justin said he got these for all the ladies. Even me," Carys added with a grin.

Lilah smiled with all the serenity that she felt inside. She'd always imagined that on her wedding day she'd be a bundle of nerves and her stomach would no doubt keep her from enjoying the day, but that wasn't the case at all.

Her sisters were with her. Pops and Celly were waiting on the private beach where the ceremony was going to be held. And Justin was out there, waiting impatiently to slip his ring on her finger, proclaiming to the world that Lilah Bell had said yes.

"Are you sure about this?" Lora asked when Lilah was all ready.

More sure than anything in my life. She nodded. "I think I've spent a long time being afraid of commitment and responsibility because I was afraid of failing. I've learned that I'm stronger than I ever gave myself credit and I'm ready to stop being afraid. Justin is everything I never knew I wanted in a man and he's helped me to see who I can be without fear."

"Well, that's the winning combination it would seem. I think it takes a special man to see past all those defenses we seem to like to wall ourselves up with." Lora smiled but added ruefully, "But politics? What about that?"

Lilah shrugged. "It's going to be an adventure. Whatever we do, we'll do as partners."

"And…you're going to move to New York?" Lindy asked, surprised but smiling with approval. "I never thought I'd see the day where you'd leave the island."

Lilah chuckled, seeing herself through her sister's eyes. It was no wonder everyone had gone out of their way to protect her—she'd been too afraid to leave her comfort zone. Now she was excited at the prospect of starting fresh and seeing new places. "Well, we're going to split our time. So I'm not exactly giving up my island time. An artist needs her inspiration, you know."

Outside the music began to play softly and her sisters squealed with excitement, herding Carys out and ushering Heath and Pops in to walk her down the aisle.

With both men flanking her, she smiled and nodded. She was ready.

For it all.

"You're as beautiful as your Grams, sugar bird," Pops said in a rare moment of lucidity. Lilah's heart contracted with pure love and she blinked back tears. Pops patted her hand as he folded it onto his arm. "Shall we?"

"Yes," she answered. Then she looked to Heath and said, "Don't wait for my sister to pick a date because she never will. Her head is always stuck on business but she wants to marry you. Just kidnap her and put a ring on her finger. Soon. She's ready, too."

Heath grinned, the corners of his eyes crinkling. "Lilah, I never knew you had the soul of a pirate. Kidnapping, indeed."

"Trust me." Lilah winked and then focused on her own future with eyes trained on the man of her dreams. "Let's do this. I'm done putting my life on hold."

With that first step onto the shifting white sand, Lilah tossed aside the fear she'd been hiding behind for too long and readied herself for the greatest adventure of her life as a wife, mother and best of all... as herself—a beautifully flawed and complex woman.

EPILOGUE

POPS DIED ON A HAZY September day, mere days before the twins arrived squalling their heads off at the indignant shock of entering the world with nothing but their skin.

The family's sadness at losing Pops was tempered by the arrival of the babies, which could only be described as a joyous event.

Lilah and Justin decided to grace the babies with names that meant something so they named their daughter, Lana Marie—Lana after Lilah's Grams and Marie, which was Virginia's middle name as well—and their son, Jack Vernon, after Pops and Justin's father.

Lilah held Lana, while Justin cradled their son, both staring reverently at the fraternal twins as they enjoyed the first bit of quiet since they'd arrived early that morning. Celly, Lora, Heath, Carys and Lindy had returned to Lindy and Gabe's New York apartment, exhausted after staying at the hospital for eighteen hours awaiting the babies, which gave Justin and Lilah a moment to themselves.

Lilah marveled at the incredible softness of their skin, the intoxicating scent of their crowns as tufts of wild dark hair sprang in every direction.

"Celly said the dark hair will go away," Lilah said,

gazing at her daughter's perfect little face. "She said they will be blond because their eyebrows are light."

"They're perfect," Justin said, overcome with emotion. "I've never felt so… I can't explain it. Instant love."

She smiled with understanding. She felt the same. But then tears filled her eyes as she thought of Pops. He had died peacefully in his sleep. Celly had been the one to find him, said she'd just known that something was wrong when he didn't meet her for breakfast that day out on the patio as they had been doing as part of their routine. The doctor had said a massive heart attack had taken him. Likely, it'd been quick and he hadn't suffered. Still, it was hard not to cry.

Justin came over to her. "What's wrong?" he asked, immediately concerned.

"Nothing," she said, wiping her eyes with her free hand. "I was just thinking of Pops and wishing he'd been able to see the babies. He would've been tickled by the fact that we'd named the babies after him and Grams."

"It felt right," he said solemnly. "Your Pops was a good man. I wish I could've known your Grams, too."

"She would've loved you," Lilah stated with conviction. "She loved a man with a bit of a mischievous spark."

They continued to bond quietly with their newfound joys bundled tightly in swaddling blankets and when Lilah found herself sliding into a sad place, all she had to do was look at her life and take stock.

Larimar was no longer in danger. The combined efforts of everyone had succeeded in putting the resort on more than firm footing. Once again, the resort had a healthy savings account, enough money to pay for the employees it needed, and Lora was in her element running the show with her husband, Heath. Heath had taken Lilah's advice to heart and had simply put Lora on a boat to St. Thomas where he promptly married her and then they sailed around the British Virgin Islands for a quick honeymoon. Lora had returned with a giddy smile and a sparkler on her finger. Lindy was in the throes of planning a giant wedding and loving every minute of being the star. Not to mention, her theatrical work had landed her a top agent and several auditions for top directors in movies that did not require her to be naked. And Celly had sold her small house and moved into the main house at Larimar at Lora's urging. She was as much a family member as anyone related by blood.

Lilah closed her eyes and pictured Grams and Pops smiling down at their little brood, happy as clams that everything had worked out in the end—with only a few bumps in the road along the way.

As for her, Lilah felt she was living the most incredible dream possible.

True to her word, Virginia had worked magic turning Vernon around and creating a mystique about Lilah that shot interest in her work through the roof.

For the first time in her life, Lilah was actually outearning her sisters. Her paintings went for ungodly sums of money that continued to blow Lilah's mind.

And by the looks of it, Justin was going to win the race against his competitor by a landslide. His supporters believed in his vision for New York, his passion for making a difference. Justin made her proud every day and at night, they kept each other breathless.

Yes, anytime she felt a hint of sadness creeping up on her, she simply did as she was doing now.

Being thankful for everything and everyone in her life.

To say she lived a blessed life…well, it was damn accurate.

And she made no apologies.

She deserved it.

* * * * *

#1830 WILD FOR THE SHERIFF
The Sisters of Bell River Ranch • by Kathleen O'Brien

Rowena Wright has finally come home to the Bell River Ranch. Most townspeople thought this wild child would never be back, but Sheriff Dallas Garwood always knew it. She *belongs* to this land. He's doing his best to steer clear of her. The last time they tangled, he almost didn't walk away. And now there's too much at stake for him to risk a second round with her.

#1831 IN FROM THE COLD
by Mary Sullivan

Callie MacKintosh is good at her job. That's why she's been sent to this Colorado town—to persuade her boss's brother Gabe Jordan to relinquish his share of the family land. But she soon learns there's more to this situation than she knows. And her skills are no match for a family feud that runs deep...or for her growing attraction to Gabe!

#1832 BENDING THE RULES
by Margaret Watson

Nathan Devereux has big dreams—and they don't include family. After years of raising his siblings, he's ready for some time to himself. But what is he supposed to do when faced with an orphaned thirteen-year-old daughter he didn't know about? He can't turn his back on her—or ignore her very appealing guardian, Emma Sloane. But when Emma announces that she wants to adopt the girl herself, all Nathan's personal rules about family suddenly seem to change.

HSRCNM0113ENHA

#1833 THE CLOSER YOU GET
by Kristi Gold

As a country music superstar, Brett Taylor seems to have it all. But appearances are deceiving. He's learned the hard way that relationships and family don't mix with a life on the road. Then Cammie Carson joins his tour group, and the pull between them is intense. Suddenly he sees an entirely new perspective...with her by his side.

#1834 RESERVATIONS FOR TWO
by Jennifer Lohmann

Opening her own restaurant has been Tilly Milek's lifelong dream—and she's finally done it. And all it takes is one bad review to derail everything. Of course The Eater, the anonymous blogger all of Chicago reads, was there on the worst possible night! But when Tilly meets Dan Meier and discovers that he's the reviewer, she's determined to make him change his mind—no matter what it takes.

#1835 FINDING JUSTICE
by Rachel Brimble

For Sergeant Cat Forrester, there is only right and wrong. But when former lover Jay Garrett calls to say their friend has been murdered, those boundaries blur. Especially when he admits he's a suspect in the case. She needs to think like a detective and find the truth. But can she balance these instincts with her feelings for Jay?

Wild for the Sheriff

by Kathleen O'Brien

On sale February 5

Dallas Garwood has always been the good guy, the one who does the right thing...except whenever he crosses paths with Rowena Wright. Now that she's back, things could get interesting for this small-town sheriff! Read on for an exciting excerpt from *Wild for the Sheriff* by Kathleen O'Brien.

Dallas Garwood had always known that sooner or later he'd open a door, turn a corner or look up from his desk and see Rowena Wright standing there.

It wasn't logical. It was simply an unshakable certainty that she wasn't gone for good, that one day she would return.

Not to see him, of course. He didn't kid himself that their brief interlude had been important to her. But she'd be back for Bell River—the ranch that was part of her.

Still, he hadn't thought today would be the day he'd face her across the threshold of her former home.

Or that she would look so gaunt. Her beauty was still there, but buried beneath some kind of haggard exhaustion. Her wild green eyes were circled with shadows, and her white shirt and jeans hung on her.

HSREXP0113

Something twisted in his chest, stealing his words. He'd never expected to feel pity for Rowena Wright.

She still knew how to look sardonic. She took him in, and he saw himself as she did, from the white-lightning scar dividing his right eyebrow to the shiny gold star pinned at his breast.

Three-tenths of a second. That was all it took to make him feel boring and overdressed, as if his uniform were as much a costume as his son Alec's cowboy hat.

"*Sheriff* Dallas Garwood." The crooked smile on her red lips was cryptic. "I should have known. Truly, I should have known."

"I didn't realize you'd come home," he said, wishing he didn't sound so stiff.

"Come *back*," she corrected him. "After all these years, it might be a bit of a stretch to call Bell River *home*."

"I see." He didn't really, but so what? He'd been her lover once, but never her friend.

The funny thing was, right now he'd give almost anything to change that and resurrect that long-ago connection.

Will Dallas and Rowena reconnect? Or will she skip town again with everything left unsaid? Find out in *Wild for the Sheriff* **by Kathleen O'Brien, available February 2013 from Harlequin® Superromance®.**

REQUEST YOUR FREE BOOKS!
2 FREE NOVELS PLUS 2 *FREE GIFTS!*

HARLEQUIN®

super romance®

Exciting, emotional, unexpected!

YES! Please send me 2 FREE Harlequin® Superromance® novels and my 2 FREE gifts (gifts are worth about $10). After receiving them, if I don't wish to receive any more books, I can return the shipping statement marked "cancel." If I don't cancel, I will receive 6 brand-new novels every month and be billed just $4.69 per book in the U.S. or $5.24 per book in Canada. That's a savings of at least 15% off the cover price! It's quite a bargain! Shipping and handling is just 50¢ per book in the U.S. and 75¢ per book in Canada.* I understand that accepting the 2 free books and gifts places me under no obligation to buy anything. I can always return a shipment and cancel at any time. Even if I never buy another book, the two free books and gifts are mine to keep forever.

135/336 HDN FVS7

Name _____
(PLEASE PRINT)

Address _____ Apt. #

City _____ State/Prov. _____ Zip/Postal Code

Signature (if under 18, a parent or guardian must sign)

Mail to the Harlequin® Reader Service:
IN U.S.A.: P.O. Box 1867, Buffalo, NY 14240-1867
IN CANADA: P.O. Box 609, Fort Erie, Ontario L2A 5X3

Are you a current subscriber to Harlequin Superromance books and want to receive the larger-print edition?
Call 1-800-873-8635 or visit www.ReaderService.com.

* Terms and prices subject to change without notice. Prices do not include applicable taxes. Sales tax applicable in N.Y. Canadian residents will be charged applicable taxes. Offer not valid in Quebec. This offer is limited to one order per household. Not valid for current subscribers to Harlequin Superromance books. All orders subject to credit approval. Credit or debit balances in a customer's account(s) may be offset by any other outstanding balance owed by or to the customer. Please allow 4 to 6 weeks for delivery. Offer available while quantities last.

Your Privacy—The Harlequin® Reader Service is committed to protecting your privacy. Our Privacy Policy is available online at www.ReaderService.com or upon request from the Harlequin Reader Service.

We make a portion of our mailing list available to reputable third parties that offer products we believe may interest you. If you prefer that we not exchange your name with third parties, or if you wish to clarify or modify your communication preferences, please visit us at www.ReaderService.com/consumerchoice or write to us at Harlequin Reader Service Preference Service, P.O. Box 9062, Buffalo, NY 14269. Include your complete name and address.

HSR13

Rediscover the Harlequin series section starting December 18!